The
Lonely
And
The
Dead

Published by Long Midnight Publishing, 2023

copyright © 2023 Douglas Lindsay

ISBN: 979-8378039944

By Douglas Lindsay

The DI Buchan Series:

Buchan
Painted In Blood
The Lonely And The Dead
A Long Day's Journey Into Death

The DS Hutton Series

The Barney Thomson Series

DCI Jericho

The DI Westphall Trilogy

Pereira & Bain

Others:

Lost in Juarez
Being For The Benefit Of Mr Kite!
A Room With No Natural Light
Ballad In Blue
These Are The Stories We Tell

THE LONELY AND THE DEAD

DOUGLAS LINDSAY

LMP

prologue

It begins on a cold, November morning in Saskatchewan, five years previously. Somewhere in the woods, outside the city of Regina, a body swinging in the chill breeze of an early winter's day. A curious crow in a branch beside the corpse, head dipped, watching the sway of the body.

For a short while the police will think it suicide. Soon enough, however, there will be another body, and this time no one will be mistaking the cause of death.

1

Buchan stood outside the doors of the Winter Moon on a cold January early evening. Work had been slow, and so he'd done an eleven-hour day instead of a fifteen-hour day, and now it was just after seven p.m. and the evening stretched before him with nothing to do.

Still, it was too early to go into the Winter Moon. Even the regulars who haunted this place like forgotten memories had yet to arrive. Duncan the priest, and Leanne, and Herschel and the other guy, none of them were there. It was even too early for Janey to have put the old Sinatra break-up LPs on the record player. Sure, he hated those records, but they were the soundtrack of his evenings, as sure as the clink of ice in the glass and the sound of the slow slide of his life slipping away.

Janey and Tom were behind the bar, talking to two customers at the counter. They were laughing. Buchan watched Janey's face for a few moments. The broad smile he'd always loved. When was the last time he'd been able to make her smile like that?

Having the self-awareness to know he shouldn't go in there now, not with Janey looking that happy, he turned away before she'd spotted him at the door. He paused for a second, unsure whether to walk into town to get something to eat, and then he accepted there was nothing to be done, nothing to be gained from sitting alone in a quiet restaurant on a lonely Tuesday evening, and he started walking slowly in the direction of the river.

*

Lights off, he stood at his apartment window looking out on the Clyde, the river an unmoving flat calm, the still water picked out by the reflections of the lights of the buildings on the opposite

---

bank. Glass of Monkey 47 in his hand, Edelman asleep on the sofa behind him, Buck Clayton playing quietly to the backdrop of the white noise of the microwave spinning out a supermarket meal for one.

Work had been steady and unspectacular over the holiday period, and had yet to pick up. Christmas and New Year might well have presented the police with a raft of cases of domestic and drunken violence, but little of it came the way of Buchan's side of the Serious Crime Unit. Their last big case had been the strange affair of the antiques dealer, found murdered in a locked room in her West end townhouse. A missing Assyrian dagger and a pet capuchin monkey had given that case, as Constable Roth had observed, the feel of an episode of Sherlock Holmes.

Buchan, not one for frivolity, had just been glad they'd been able to get the matter sorted and off the front pages, the monkey found and tagged and handed over to Edinburgh Zoo.

What did you hope for as a bored, underemployed police officer? More crime? More interesting criminals? He'd had that discussion with DS Kane that afternoon. There was no answer, of course.

He put the glass to his lips and took his first sip of ice cold gin.

*

Later. Much later. In those wee small hours, that Sinatra sang about. Down the river, way down the river from where Buchan lived in the centre of the city, round the slow bends and beneath the Erskine Bridge, way beyond, to the opening out of the firth, round past Greenock and Gourock, to somewhere in the short stretch between Inverkip and Wemyss Bay, there was an old, abandoned pier. A burned-out wreck, which had been scheduled for demolition for years. One of those things that was on a to-do list for a next week that never came.

The tide was coming in, the quiet waves washing on the pebbly shore. Dark down here by the river, the blackened frame of the pier lost against the dark black of the firth. Somewhere there was music playing, a haunting choral piece, the voices coming from within the pier, the sound blending with the roll of the sea.

From one of the few solid beams on the Kip side, a body was hanging by the neck. It hung lifeless where it had been left,

—

3

the neck bruised, the face washed of colour, pale death on a starless night, but now the waves were beginning to cover its feet, and soon enough the legs would go, and then the torso, then the entire body, and any evidence the killer might have inadvertently left behind would be washed away in the night.

2

Wednesday afternoon, Buchan summoned to the mortuary by Dr Donoghue. On the way out of the door he'd looked for DS Kane, but she'd been out, working on the Rimbaud Electrical embezzlement case, and he'd been about to head off on his own when Constable Roth had passed, and on a whim he'd asked her to accompany him, and the two of them had taken the short drive to the hospital in Buchan's 1958 Facel Vega.

They had little to say in the car. Donoghue had told Buchan he likely had a murder to investigate, and so far that was all they had. No point in starting a discussion on something when they had so little information, and the possibility of a new murder inquiry gifted a layer of tension to the car that precluded small talk.

Once they knew what they were up against, then they'd be able to relax into the investigation. For the moment, the stress of the unknown.

Donoghue was waiting for them in her familiar spot, standing over the corpse of a man in his early forties. As was usually the case in her workplace, she had the Beatles playing through a couple of ceiling-mounted speakers. Today, something from the early years, *Soldier of Love*, a song Buchan would never have known they'd recorded. He knew far more about the Beatles than he'd ever cared to, thanks to Donoghue. It was about time he got his own back, he sometimes thought, and filled her in on Art Pepper and Hoagy Carmichael. He never played music at work, however, and he wasn't about to invite the doctor round for dinner.

Nearly six years since Janey had left, and he'd eaten alone every night since. Aside from the regular nights when he hadn't eaten at all.

'Doc,' he said, approaching the corpse.

Donoghue glanced up, nodded at them, and turned back to

the body of Daniel Harptree.

Forty-three-years-old, pale, naked and dead. This was the end of the line for Daniel Harptree.

They were all drawn to look at the bruising around his neck, and then Donoghue made a small gesture towards it.

'Died by hanging, as you can see,' she began.

'I saw the report first thing,' said Buchan.

The report had been issued by the station in Gourock. A body found hanging from an old pier on Inverkip Bay. Assumed suicide. Updates when known. He had read it, he had read between the lines and decided, based on very little knowledge, that it was indeed suicide. Another day or two and he'd have forgotten all about it.

'When he died,' she said, and again she indicated specific marks on the neck, 'when this happened, it's very likely he was unconscious. High level of midazolam in his system.'

'Injected?' asked Buchan.

'Nasal spray.'

'Is it possible he took it himself and then…?' asked Roth, finishing the question with a diving gesture, to indicate the victim stepping off the pier.

'Hmm,' said Donoghue. 'Not entirely out of the question. But then, you'd have to ask yourself why. If you're compos mentis enough to even step off a pier, you're going to be compos mentis enough to feel the pain of your neck snapping with the force of the rope. The pain would be brief, but unpleasant enough.'

'It would dull it, surely?' asked Buchan.

Again Donoghue took a moment to think about it, then she nodded. 'Yes. There will be tests. We should be able to establish how long prior to death the drug was administered. However, this says faked suicide to me. Perhaps you'll find Mr Harptree here was depressive by nature. The killer hopes the police are too busy to spend too much time investigating his death, happy to settle for the easy win. Suicide.'

Buchan stared along the length of the body, his eyes ending back, once again, at the bruising of the neck. The course of the rest of the afternoon started running through his head. They would need to drive down to the coast. The M8, then down past Langbank and Port Glasgow. Forty-five minutes to an hour, depending on the traffic. That would give them a good couple of hours of daylight, which would be plenty of time to get a look at

—

the area, and if they put the call in before they left, time for Sgt Meyers' Scenes of Crime team to get down there.

'What else can you tell us?' asked Roth.

'Died around two o'clock in the morning. The rope tightened round his neck with some force. So, of course, you could be right that he jumped off the pier, but obviously you wouldn't be here if I didn't think he'd been thrown off. That he hit the bottom of his fall with such force indicates the tide was out, otherwise the water would obviously have broken his fall. The body was then covered by water. I believe it was half-uncovered again when it was first spotted this morning.'

'Any hint what he was doing last night?' asked Buchan.

The Beatles had moved on to another song from the early days. He didn't know this one. Unusually, he began to find it intrusive. He would, nevertheless, keep his mouth shut. Not for him to tell the doctor how she ought to best spend her days with the dead.

'He ate chicken and rice and drank too much alcohol. The latter was something he did on a regular basis. Liver is shot. Not unrecoverable, but the liver of a drinker all the same. Silly man.'

'Doesn't matter now,' said Buchan. As ever, given the opportunity, his brain would lead him off into dark thoughts about the state of his own liver, so he quickly shut the door on it.

'It certainly does not,' said Donoghue. 'Fingers are calloused, so I take it he's a guitar player. I know nothing about him other than the name, so obviously have no idea if this was a profession. Certainly something he'd done regularly for a long time. And that's where we stand. A guitar-playing drinker. And last night, at least, white wine was his medicine of choice.'

'Would that have been of a level to interact with the midazolam?' asked Roth.

'There was a lot of both, so I think the main way in which it would have interacted, would've been the administering of the drug would've been easier as the man was possibly paralytically drunk.'

'Paralytically?' asked Buchan, eyebrows raised.

'I think so.'

'Why bother with the drugs, then?'

'A lot of paralytically drunk people can suddenly affect a quality of clear-headedness when their life is threatened. Enough, at least, to mean that someone else might not entirely have their way with them without a fight. This removes that

—

7

possibility.'

'A safe murder,' said Roth.

'Yes.'

'Carefully planned. Dumped so the body would freefall, timed so that it would then be covered by the tide, coinciding with the hours of darkness when there would be no one around.'

'Not sure exactly how much planning that would take, other than a basic knowledge of the tides,' said Donoghue, drily, 'but yes, insomuch as that's careful planning, that's what we see here.'

Silence as the song finished, and then a moment, and the next one started up. Again, Buchan found himself momentarily distracted, and this time he allowed himself a comment.

'These tunes didn't last long, did they?'

'They did what they had to do in just the right amount of time,' said Donoghue, and then quickly, 'I take it you have everything you need?'

Buchan smiled and nodded, immediately turning away.

'Thanks, doc,' he said, as Roth turned away with him.

'I'll let you know if anything else comes up,' said Donoghue. 'Report in your inbox by close of business.'

Buchan thanked her with a small wave, and then they were at the door and they were gone.

3

'OK,' said Roth, 'looks like the doc was not wrong. Harptree was a musician.'

They'd called ahead to the local station, and had arranged to be met at the pier where the body had been found. The SOCO team were on their way, ten minutes behind. Harptree was English, divorced, no children, his parents living in London already informed. They'd been given the information, believed correct at the time, that their son had committed suicide.

'Guitar then?' asked Buchan.

'Says on his website he played piano, harpsichord, guitar, French horn and clarinet.'

'In an orchestra?'

'Hmm… nope. He did for a while. LSO, but not for over ten years. He composes soundtracks for film and TV.'

'What's his most recent project?'

'Give me a moment.'

The traffic was busy, but all four lanes of the motorway were moving, and Buchan didn't feel the need to put the blue light on and start flying down the outside. They would get there in plenty of time. The Facel had been recently serviced, the engine tuned, its tone perfect.

'He did a movie last year called *Touch Of The Spider*. Looks like a pretty small affair. You heard of it?'

'No,' said Buchan.

If pushed, he would likely have struggled to name any film that had been released last year.

'Me neither. The next thing on his list is a TV crime drama, *Beware The Watcher*, that's not due out until the autumn. Oh, I read a book with that name, maybe it's the same thing. So, perhaps he's working on it at the moment. Not sure where the music comes in the process. I presume after they've filmed?'

'I guess so,' said Buchan.

'Yeah, you see people in documentaries when they're scoring a film, and they have the action on the screen, and they're doing the music to accompany it.'

'I've never seen one of those documentaries.'

'Yeah, Disney has a terrific one on Abbey Road and there's some of that,' said Roth. 'One day, sir, you'll catch up with the nineteen-fifties and get yourself a television.'

'Funny.'

They drove in silence. The traffic began to thin out once they were beyond the airport. An easyJet flight broke through thin cloud to their right.

'Would be ironic if we end up having to investigate a TV crime drama,' said Roth at some point as they headed off the motorway.

'Ironic would be one word for it,' said Buchan, grimly.

'We can let Alanis know,' said Roth.

Buchan let that sit there for a while before finally tossing, 'I have no idea who that is,' into the silence, and Roth smiled.

*

Police Constable Butterfield was waiting for them by the old pier as they parked the Facel beside the BMW 530 and stepped out into the cold of a January day down the Clyde.

'Constable,' said Buchan, approaching. 'DI Buchan, DC Roth.'

Butterfield was a young man. Far too young, thought Buchan, as he regularly did these days, but he was self-aware enough to know that that was about him rather than the officers he always found himself judging.

'Sir,' said Butterfield.

The end of the pier had been fenced off, but the fencing was an erection that pre-dated the murder. The pier had been officially closed for some time, with large *Danger* signs to the left and right of the barrier, the permanent fencing augmented by the yellow tape, closing off the area anew. Nevertheless, it was apparent from the dilapidated appearance of the original fencing that the previous evening had not been the first time the line had been crossed.

'How long's the pier been shut down?' asked Buchan, indicating the old barriers.

'Twenty, thirty years or so,' said Butterfield. 'Maybe more.

Long before my time.'

'Who uses it? People fish off it, or what?'

'Instagrammers mostly, I think.'

Buchan glanced at him, a familiar raised eyebrow.

'People take photos of this?'

'At some point someone must've taken a great shot of the derelict pier. You know, with the hills in the background. And then all the other Instagrammers are like, oh, that's amazing, I'll go and get that shot.'

They all turned and looked. Low cloud, a grey day, the far side of the firth about two miles away and barely visible.

'Aye, fair enough,' said Butterfield. 'But on a good day you can see the snow on the mountains behind. So maybe you stand on the shoreline and get the full pier in the picture, or maybe you come out here, get a shot of a rotted chunk of wood in the foreground, your snow-capped mountains beyond.' Pause. 'Sea in between.'

'Sometimes life passes you by,' said Buchan to no one in particular.

'And I guess people fish off of here too.'

'How safe is it to walk out there?'

'Oh, it's fine, to be fair,' said Butterfield. 'Despite appearances, the structure itself is reasonably intact. Just got to watch your footing. I'll show you where the body was dropped.'

He lifted the tape for Buchan and Roth to stoop beneath, and then followed them out onto the old wooden structure.

Buchan walked ahead, looking down as he placed his feet, the surface not too uneven, small gaps in the planks here and there. The old fence that had surrounded the edge of the pier was in worse repair, however. Splintered and gnarled wood, broken-off poles, jagged spears. To the left, up ahead, a large hole in the structure, which Butterfield indicated with a warning hand as they approached.

He stopped near the end of the pier on the right-hand side, and indicated a thick support beam, broken away at the top, then firmly attached to the pier all the way down, extending into the water beneath. They stood in a row beside it, looking down at the Clyde. The water was currently a couple of feet deep, and they could see the seaweed and barnacle-covered rocks of the shore beneath.

'A very solid stanchion this one. But, as you can see, its connection to the floor of the pier at the top here has been lost, so there's the gap, but the connection at the next level of support down is intact. Rope around someone's neck, put the other end of the rope around the stanchion, throw the body over. The fall is arrested, full weight of the body against the rope, boom.' He paused, and then added, 'To be fair, it's a decent place to commit suicide right enough.'

'Anyone ever done it here before?' asked Roth.

'Not that I know. Not in my time.'

'How long's that?' asked Buchan.

'Seven years.'

Jesus, thought Buchan. The kid looks like he left school at the weekend.

'What makes you think it wasn't suicide?' asked Butterfield.

Roth waited for Buchan, then when he didn't immediately answer she filled the gap.

'He'd been drugged. Always possible, of course, that he drugged himself to lessen the shock, but we need to take a look at it. You know anything about him?'

'Nothing,' said Butterfield.

'How did you identify the body?' asked Buchan.

'He had his wallet on him,' he said, then just as Buchan was about to ask where the wallet was now, he added, 'Got it back at the station, sir.'

'The wallet give up any secrets?'

'Assuming it was a suicide, we didn't really try, sir,' said Butterfield. 'There was a little money, a couple of credit cards, National Trust membership, Musicians' Union, RAC membership. Fairly standard.'

'OK, thanks. We'll pick it up on the way. How about this music that was playing, what was that about?'

'Yeah, that was weird. There was a small Bluetooth speaker, but powerful, attached to the beam just down there. A small MP3 device attached to it. One tune, playing on repeat. Like a choral piece. No idea what it was. We Shazamed it, nothing came up.'

'How long?' asked Roth.

'How long?'

'How long is the piece?'

'Like three minutes. Song length, I guess. And it was set to repeat, over and over. Still quite a lot of charge left in both the MP3 and the speaker.'

They'd been aware of the sound of an approaching vehicle, and then a police van appeared from in amongst the low trees down by the shore, and parked alongside the Facel. Three people, already dressed in white overalls, emerged from the car. They stood for a moment taking in the scene, Sergeant Meyers greeted Buchan and the others with a lifted hand, then they collected the tools of their trade from the van, ushered themselves beneath the police tape, and began walking up the length of the pier.

A grim Wednesday afternoon, rain in the air, wind starting to pick up, white waves beginning to rise, the mountains lost in the mist, a couple of hundred yards away the sound of traffic on the coast road. A perfect location for murder.

4

'You think the TV show he was doing the music for might have been filmed along here?' asked Buchan.

He and Roth were in the victim's small cottage, no more than fifteen minutes along the coast from where his body had been left hanging. The cottage, so far, had given up few secrets. Two bedrooms, the smaller one used as storage space. Kitchen/diner, leading on to the sitting room. Add in the bathroom, and one walk-in cupboard, and that was the house.

The sitting room had also been Harptree's workplace. There were a variety of musical instruments lying around, and there was a keyboard, set against a table, with a MacBook and a bank of three screens around it.

To the right of where he would have sat and worked, a picture window looking out on the firth. From here, the Clyde had really opened up, the view along the far coast towards the Kyles of Bute and the path of the Wemyss Bay ferry towards Rothesay. Standing at the window revealed the full expanse of the view, with the island of Cumbrae and, out beyond Bute, the snow-covered Arran hills.

'Looks like more of an urban thing,' said Roth. 'Though, to be fair, I'm basing that off the IMDb image for the show. So maybe some of it was done along here. But then, why would it need to be anyway?'

'Yeah, true.' Then he turned and waved a hand around the room. 'No guitar, I suppose that might be significant.'

'Yep, I'd noticed. Nowhere else in the house either.'

Buchan, already wearing a pair of Nitrile gloves, lifted a French horn that was sitting on the floor beside the unused fireplace.

'Don't suppose you'd get any finger hardening from this kind of thing,' he said, taking a close look at a French horn for the first time in his life.

'Presume not,' said Roth. 'Might do something to your lips, I guess.'

Buchan gave her a quick glance to see if she was joking, she didn't seem to be, then he placed the instrument back on the carpet where he'd found it.

He turned away, and now walked to the window and looked down over the shoreline to the grey sea, the wind still picking up, the swell growing. How did he like this, compared to his own view of the river in the heart of the city?

Could take either, he thought. Maybe he'd move down here when he retired. Retirement, however, was something he never thought about. He had plenty of years left, and he had absolutely no idea what he'd do when he was no longer a police officer. It was literally all he had in his life. That's what you got when you drove your wife away with your slavish devotion to the job.

'Stop it,' he muttered to himself, as he turned away from the window.

'Sir?' said Roth, and he shook his head in response.

There was a knock at the door, they glanced at each other, then Buchan automatically looked at the time. Meyers and her team were due to come to the house once they'd finished with the pier, but they wouldn't be done yet.

He walked along the short hallway, a solid wooden door at the front so no way to see who was outside, and opened the door. A young woman, no more than twenty-five perhaps, a bag over her shoulder. Short hair, large glasses.

'Oh,' was across her lips before she could stop it, and then she shook her head, and said, 'Sorry, is Mr Harptree home? He should be expecting me.' Something in her accent, but he couldn't place it.

*

She leant forward, her elbows resting on her knees, her hands cupped around the mug of tea Buchan had made for her. Chloe Harmon, peripatetic hairdresser.

'I've never known anyone who got murdered before,' she said, breaking a silence that had begun with Roth asking her how she'd come to be Daniel Harptree's personal barber.

'How long had you known Mr Harptree?' asked Buchan, to try to get the interview back on course.

The day was getting on, the list of things needing to be

15

done at the start of any murder investigation already long. Back at the office, he'd set Kane, Houston and Cherry to the task of tracking down the principal production staff on the show Harptree appeared to have been working on at the time of his murder.

'What?'

'How long had you known Mr Harptree?' repeated Buchan, trying to keep the impatience from his voice.

'About four years now. First met him at the Q Room in Largs.'

'What's the Q Room?'

'Hairdressers. I mean, a barbershop, I guess, but it had much more of a salon vibe, you know. He used to come in there, used to always book in to see me.'

'And now you do house calls?' said Roth.

'Yeah, went freelance about two years ago. Just became easier with all the Covid restrictions.'

'How often did you come here?'

'Once a week. Unless he was travelling, but he mostly worked at home,' and she nodded in the direction of the keyboard and the bank of monitors.

'You cut his hair every week?' said Buchan, unable to keep the doubt from his voice.

A moment, then she said, 'Sure,' although a little uncertainty had crept in.

Buchan pictured the hair of the corpse he and Roth had stood over at the mortuary. A short back and sides in old money. What would they say at a barbershop now? High and tight, perhaps. Either way, it had at least been apparent that his hair had recently been cut.

'That seems a little unnecessary,' said Roth.

'Hmm.'

'And?'

'Well, you know how these things are.'

'We're police officers,' said Buchan. 'We do know things, but we need them explained to us all the same, just in case we've picked up the wrong end of the stick.'

She held his gaze for a moment and then made the familiar gesture of lifting the mug to her face while she took another drink, leaving the mug in position for longer than was necessary.

'The salon offered a head massage as part of their thing,' she said from behind the mug. 'I mean, none of us had actual training, but really, how hard is it to massage some guy's head, right? You men love that shit.'

'And you would massage Daniel's head?'

'Sure. Then when I went freelance and I started visiting homes, I made a general point of withdrawing the head massage. There's just something about it, you know. Doesn't matter which way you look at it, it's pretty intimate. You're basically doing something that your lover might do during sex. Or after or before or whatever.'

She looked at Roth for her agreement, then turned to Buchan when it wasn't immediately forthcoming.

'But you gave Daniel a head massage?'

A pause, the mug of tea held halfway to her mouth, a look that spoke of much that wasn't just a head massage.

'When did you start sleeping with him?' asked Roth.

She took another drink of tea, and then said, 'First time I came to his house.'

'And that was two years ago?'

She nodded. She looked at Roth, she looked at Buchan, she looked away, her eyes lingering on a random spot on the carpet.

Buchan and Roth watched her for a moment and then glanced at each other. They recognised the look; the forced, casual innocence that spoke of anything but.

'Miss Harmon,' said Buchan, and she lifted her eyes and a pair of guiltless eyebrows, 'I imagine your reticence comes from us judging you. And, perhaps, since we're police officers, you worry we might find some illegality, although I'm not sure what that could be under these circumstances. The constable and I work for Serious Crime Unit. On this occasion we're investigating the murder of Daniel Harptree. I don't like getting side-tracked. We don't do crime investigation side hustles. And we never judge people on how they live their lives. So, in short, I don't care how many of your clients you sleep with. All we're interested in is Mr Harptree, and your relationship with him.'

'Oh.'

He finished what had been an unusually long speech for him with a sigh and an open-palmed gesture to ask that she tell them a little more about Harptree.

'What?'

'Did you ever discuss his work or any other aspect of his life?' asked Roth.

'Sure, all the time. I mean, you know he worked in the

movies and TV?'

'Yes,' said Roth. 'D'you know what he was working on at the moment?'

'I mean, who doesn't love all that? He used to tell me these little bits of gossip, right, it was so interesting. Like when he was at the BAFTAs and he went to the bathroom and there were like… oh…'

Buchan was giving her his familiar deadpan expression.

'What?' she said.

'If it's going to be a tale of two famous men having sex,' said Buchan, 'or two famous men snorting drugs or two famous men doing absolutely anything at all, I'll refer you to my previous statement. We don't care. We don't care about the gossip. Do you know what Daniel was working on at the moment?'

'Yeah, didn't I say?'

'No.'

'Right.' Another drink of tea. Buchan could feel the day getting darker by the minute. But then, was there anything else they needed the daylight for? 'I think it was a serial killer TV drama. That was… he cancelled one day because he went on set. It was being filmed in the city centre. Glasgow, I mean.'

'Did he usually visit the set?'

She sort of shrugged.

'I don't think so. Don't think they have to when they're just writing a tune. Usually when he travelled it was like awards shows and meetings and recording with an orchestra, that kind of thing.'

'So, why this particular film set?' asked Roth.

'TV. It was TV. Not film.'

Roth gave her a quick shot of Buchan's deadpan look.

'Just saying.'

'Why did he visit this set?' asked Roth.

'Something about the director asking him to, so he could meet the main guy, you know, the lead actor, and get a feel for the show. Daniel thought it was unnecessary, I mean, the idea that he'd learn anything by going there, but he was happy enough to go up. It was just Glasgow, right?'

'This was *Beware The Watcher*?' said Buchan.

'Yeah, it was. So you know about it?'

'Did he say anything about any of the film crew, the actors, the producers?'

She held his gaze for a moment, and then looked at Roth, then turned back to Buchan, her brow furrowing a little.

'He said it was poisonous. Like, so bad he was never going back to a film set again in his life.'

'Any specifics?' asked Roth.

'You mean, like names and people and incidents and accidents?'

'Yes, names and people and incidents and accidents.'

She looked away for a moment, then shook her head.

'No, didn't go into detail. Just said it had been horrible.'

'Had he mentioned any of them again while he was working on the soundtrack for the show?' asked Buchan. 'I mean, in the last couple of weeks?'

'I see where you're going with this. I say the atmosphere at the place was horrible, and now you're wondering if someone from the show has murdered Daniel. Wow.'

'Well, had he said anything about them? Had he expressed any concerns?'

Another thoughtful look to the side, and then the head shake. She took a drink of tea, she turned back to Buchan, she kind of smiled.

'Not to me, he didn't. But then, I was just his hairdresser, and, em, the other thing. Just not his, you know, confidante.'

'You think he had one of those?'

'A confidante? Not so he told me,' said Harmon. 'But then, why would he tell me anyway?'

'You know if there was usually a guitar around here?' asked Roth.

'Yeah, there's always a guitar. It's over there…'

Her words trailed away, as she turned and pointed into the corner.

'Oh,' she said.

'It's usually there?'

'Yeah, resting against that bookcase. He played it for me once. Oh my God, that was amazing. Wow.'

'Wow?'

'Sexy as fuck. I mean, he played it after sex, and oh my God…'

19

5

An hour and a half later, Buchan and Roth back at the office with the team, assembling the case. Facts on the board, setting up interviews for the following day, laying out everything they'd learned about Harptree, and in particular, about his work on the forthcoming six-part crime drama, *Beware The Watcher*.

'Basically it's just a serial killer show,' said Constable Roth.

'Not based on a true story, though?' said Buchan.

'No, based on a novel. I was right, it was the one I read a couple of years ago. One of these ones that comes out of nowhere, written by some woman no one's ever heard of, and there's a buzz around it, and the TV rights get sold, then even more people are talking about it.'

'Is she local? The writer, I mean.'

'Lives in Vancouver,' said Cherry. 'I spoke to her an hour ago, double-checked with one of the producers. She has nothing to do with the production. I said, so you washed your hands of it, and she said that's not how it works. *They* washed her hands of it. Basically they buy the thing, then it's theirs and they can do what they like. She said she didn't care as long as she got the money.'

'And when does she get the money?'

'Already got it. Anything else is gravy.' A pause, he noticed the look on Buchan's face at the phrase and added, 'Her words,' with a smile.

'Is the book any good?' said Buchan to Roth, the question sounding frivolous even as he said it.

'Wasn't bad,' said Roth, 'but you know, serial killer books. Ten-a-penny. Not sure this one stood out any more than any other.'

Kane and Cherry nodded. Houston, like Buchan, hadn't read a book since the forced reading of the high school years.

'Ten-a-penny? How come?' asked Buchan. 'I mean, there aren't that many serial killers in real life, are there?'

Roth kind of shrugged, looked as though she had something to say, then she went through with the shrug.

'What?'

'Doesn't seem relevant,' said Roth.

'We've got all night,' said Buchan, drily. 'I mean, no one's aiming to leave before eleven-thirty, right?'

'There are a million crime novels every year,' said Roth. 'People love that stuff, that's just how it is. I mean, I read a tonne of them and I can't explain it. But largely they don't deal with real life. What is real life murder after all? What is it we have to deal with here? Domestic violence, drug gangs, drunk guys outside the pub, guys smacked out of their heads, guys fighting over the last gram of coke. The kind of thing folk write crime novels about, complicated plots, and long-held quests for vengeance and whatever, they're as common as city centre car chases and shoot-outs and explosions. Happens all the time in movies, literally never happens in real life.'

She left it at that, and Buchan, feeling that she'd said a lot of words and not really answered the question, kept looking at her.

'So,' she said, 'I went to a festival once. You know, a crime writing festival. Listened to a couple of writers.'

'Why would you do that?' said Houston with a smile.

'Well, it seemed like something to do,' said Roth, laughing. 'We all make mistakes. Anyway, one of the writers said that basically you get so many serial killers because writers are lazy. The hardest part when coming up with a crime plot is motive. I mean, why does anyone actually kill anyone else? Apart from the domestic asshole, alcohol, gangs and drugs deaths, which don't feature in most crime novels, who actually commits murder? When faced with a problem, or someone getting in someone's way, most people don't think, I know, I'll kill them, that'll sort it. Then I'll kill a few more people to cover my tracks.

'Generally doesn't happen in real life. But the fictional serial killer? Easy-peasy. They don't *need* a motive. A serial killer just kills. It's what they do. They're nuts. And sure, there have been so few serial killers in the UK most people can actually name them, but that doesn't matter. The existence of even one of them means that it can happen. It does happen. And here's a fictional one, and I, the writer, haven't had to bother my backside with tricky things like motive, because this is just my guy's brand.'

She looked at the ceiling for a moment pondering if she'd omitted anything, then looked back at Buchan with a shrug.

'Thanks, Agnes,' said Buchan. 'Well, good to know. Does it help us here? I mean, is there anything different about *Beware The Watcher*? Or anything that might connect it to the manner of Harptree's death, or the piece of music?'

'Just had another quick scan through the book,' she said. 'Got it on my phone. You know, there really was nothing remarkable about it. Not sure why it got to be a thing, or why anyone decided it, over anything else, would make a show. There's a creepy guy, he watches people's houses, he lets them know he's watching them, he stalks them, then he kills them. Does this a few times, then he gets caught.'

'None of these people think of calling the police?'

'Turns out the killer is also the local policeman.'

'Plot twist,' said Buchan, with absolutely no enthusiasm for the expression.

'You know, it kind of works.'

'Didn't see it coming?'

She thought about it, then shrugged. 'Always feels a little bit like cheating when it turns out the authority figures are actually the bad guys, you know? The reader just, like, doesn't even think about them as a potential suspect, so the writer doesn't have to construct alibis and whatever around them. They're their own alibi.'

'Just like a serial killer is his own motive.'

'Exactly.'

'Basically the woman in Vancouver was the poster child of lazy writers,' said Cherry, and the others laughed.

'Anyway, I don't see how it's connected to this crime here,' said Roth. 'No one gets hung, there's no music playing next to a corpse. Music doesn't feature at all in the story. If Harptree's murder is connected to the production, then I feel we're looking at the internal dynamics of the people involved, rather than what they were working on.'

'You've got the piece of music on your phone, sir?' asked Kane.

Buchan had been staring at the desk as Roth spoke, and he nodded distractedly. Tapped his finger, thinking through

---

22

everything she'd said, wondering if he could fit it narratively into what they knew so far.

'But this is where we are?' he asked. 'In crime novel territory? As far as we know, despite being a drinker, Harptree's death is neither drug, alcohol nor domestic violence related, so the killer's motive, whatever that might be, is going to be straight out of crime fiction.'

Roth had no answer, one or two of the others replied with a small movement of the shoulders.

'Yeah, I know, too early to say,' said Buchan. 'I'll play the song.'

He took the phone from his pocket, laid it on the table, brought up the piece of music and pressed play.

Nothing for a moment, and then strings. A minor chord. Something off balance. An undercurrent of menace. Then the chorus of voices.

6

Sinatra was singing and the Winter Moon was ticking all the boxes. Buchan at the bar with his Monkey 47; Duncan the Priest two seats along with his bottle of Budweiser and his Killer Sudoku puzzles; Herschel and the other guy sitting at a table, talking in low voices; Leanne, the Butcher's wife, on her own, reading a book, drinking white wine; Janey behind the bar, always busy, never with anything much to do. Something timeless about the scene, like they'd all been in the same positions for the last five years. Or perhaps, forever. This is who they were, and where they would be, for eternity.

'I don't know that bit of the coast,' said Janey.

'There's the marina,' said Buchan, 'then a stretch of nothingness.'

'And in the nothingness there was a derelict pier.'

'Erected sometime in the nineteenth century. It was closed in the seventies, slowly rotting ever since.'

'Hmm,' said Janey. She was leaning on the bar, somewhere in between Buchan and Duncan the Priest. 'Someone somewhere in the bowels of the council always has a plan to demolish it, but it never gets done.'

'Waiting for some kid to die on it,' said Buchan, 'then there can be an inquiry, and people can blame-shift, and depending how much of a fuss the kid's parents make about it, then the pier gets removed.'

'Didn't someone just die on it?'

'There's no cause and effect,' said Buchan.

'Maybe what it needs is someone deciding that bit of coastline is ripe for an upgrade. A new marina, a hotel, and a development of four- and five-bedroomed executive homes.'

Buchan looked along the bar at Janey, couldn't help the grim smile that came to his face.

'As you say,' said Buchan, 'you don't know that bit of

coast.'

'Ha,' said Duncan quietly. He'd been listening, they'd been including him in the conversation, though he'd yet to contribute.

'You know it?' asked Janey. She could feel the end of the conversation between her and Buchan coming, and it was always the same. The end of every conversation between them felt like an event in itself, that there were always things left unsaid. Sure, they'd talked enough when their marriage had ended, and there was nothing to be done, no compromise to be had. Buchan had made his choice. Me or the job, she'd said, and he'd chosen the job. As she'd known he would.

And yet, the melancholy hung over them, as though the decision had been the wrong one. As though there was some other option. As though there was an option where Buchan had more than twenty-four hours in the day, and would be able to work endlessly, and still be there for his wife when she needed him.

For Janey, the Winter Moon had been Buchan's replacement. *Easier to manage, and always there when I want it*, she'd said.

'Nope,' said Duncan, 'no more than anyone else. Bit bleak on a day like this, I would've thought, Inspector.'

'Apparently people go there to take pictures for Instagram,' said Buchan. As he spoke he felt like he was trying to be someone he wasn't. He was trying to be normal, trying to force regular conversation with Janey, and the words sounded strange from his lips.

'Did you meet such people when you were down there?' asked Duncan.

Janey had started to move away. Still part of the conversation, but in the process of detaching herself. Buchan had a little less than half his drink to go. He thought he ought to down it in one and leave.

'We were told by the local constable. Agnes looked it up, and sure enough, there are a lot of pictures on Instagram.'

And that was that for normal conversation. A glance between the three of them, nothing else of note to be said on the matter. Janey turned away, Duncan took a drink of beer and looked back at his number puzzle, Sinatra was singing *It's A Lonesome Old Town*, and Buchan put the glass to his lips, hesitated for a second, then downed the rest of his gin.

25

He worked when he got back to the apartment, although since he was sitting at his dinner table with a microwaved meal and a bottle of Chablis, with his phone open in front of him, he didn't really consider it work.

There wasn't a huge amount to read about the career of Daniel Harptree, but at least he could see everything he'd worked on, and he could listen to some of his music. There was even an album on Spotify, though with fewer than a thousand streams, he thought that perhaps Harptree had just uploaded it himself as a way of showcasing his work.

And so he turned on the speaker, linked the phone and started Harptree's album playing, and then read about the films and shows in which he'd been involved. And at some point he got a notebook and pen and started making a list of names, looking for people who had possibly worked with Harptree more than once. Presumably it was a word-of-mouth business, and a nepotistic business, and help would be given and jobs for the boys handed out, and it needn't just be the people he was working with at the moment who might have something to say about his death.

He looked at his phone for two hours, by which time he was halfway through his third playing of the album, then finally tiredness and boredom got the better of him, his threshold for the working day had been reached, and he pushed the phone away.

He had a list of seven names of people with whom Harptree had possibly worked more than once. Working on the music meant nothing in relation to anyone else of course, as it would be such a solitary job. But it was the same at the start of every investigation. Throw a wide net, speak to as many people as possible, throw as many darts at the wall as you could, hope that some of them stuck, or, even better, hit the mark.

He tapped the screen again to check the time, then sighed heavily, and even more heavily got to his feet. Edelman walked into the room as he moved, and the two of them regarded each other as Buchan carried the plate and glass to the sink.

'There you are, furball,' he said. 'Where've you been all night?'

Edelman ignored him, walked to the water bowl, took a drink, and then lay down in the middle of the kitchen floor and stretched.

7

'It represents such an elemental fear,' said Adrian Goddard. 'That's the beauty of it. The all-encompassing majesty and strength of it.'

'So it's nothing to do with the writer just being lazy, then?' asked Buchan.

Goddard turned away from the screen, glancing sharply at him.

They were in a small editing suite in the Stillwood film complex out at Linwood. Buchan had been here before, not long after it opened. There still didn't seem to be too much life about the place, but it hadn't gone under yet, and he imagined it would take time to get going.

'Why would you say that?'

Goddard was a serious man. Mid-fifties, mostly bald, the hair above his ears grey and too long. He had the hair of an eighty-year-old, thought Buchan. He hadn't had cause to smile, of course, not given why Buchan was there, but Buchan couldn't imagine him smiling anyway. His teeth were terrible. None missing, but most at strange angles, stained and chipped.

He was the director of *Beware The Watcher*, and Roth had said he'd sounded angry when told over the phone that the composer of his show's music had been murdered. Buchan wished he'd been able to break the news to him in person, but that wasn't how it had worked out. Now Goddard had had over twelve hours to adjust to it. Or possibly longer, Buchan inevitably found himself thinking, if Goddard himself had been involved in the murder.

They had met in the studio café, and now they'd come to the editing suite where Goddard and Stanley Crow, the film's editor, were putting the show together. Kane had taken Crow to the café to interview him there, while Buchan and Goddard were looking at footage of *Beware The Watcher*. They'd just sat through a scene of terror; a woman alone in a dark house, a noise in the night, lights that don't work, the creak of a floorboard, a shadow, a hint of movement, the closing in for the kill, the jump scare that everyone knows is coming but which the director still knows will catch the audience, and then the hand with the glove over the mouth, the terror in her eyes, the knife in the dark.

And throughout, the scene soundtracked by the piece of music that had been left playing to accompany Daniel Harptree's death.

'I read somewhere that the hardest thing for a writer to come up with is motive, and that a serial killer removes that as an issue.'

Goddard's innate look of annoyance slowly faded, and then he made a small movement of his lips to suggest general agreement.

'The serial killer is a psychopath, his motive is implicit,' he said, nodding. 'Yes, I understand. Nevertheless, that thing which you say removes one tricky part of the writing process, is also its strength. When something just is, that it exists within itself without reason, it becomes impossible to understand. And when you don't understand something, you're more likely to fear it. Certainly when it is out to do you harm. Much harder to combat the killer whose motives you cannot comprehend.'

'We understand there were a lot of disagreements on set,' said Buchan, using a familiar tactic of subject change out of nowhere.

Goddard, whose face had relaxed slightly while they'd discussed serial killers and their place in the fears of an audience, tensed again. Shoulders straightened, eyes narrowed slightly, defences up.

'Where did you hear that?'

'Daniel spoke to someone not involved in the production after he'd visited.'

'Who?'

'He said it was poisonous. So bad he was never going back to a film set again in his life.'

Goddard looked at him, an intense stare, a loud swallow. Presumably, thought Buchan, he was thinking about the day Harptree had visited the set, trying to recall it. Or maybe every day was the same.

'Well he certainly won't now,' said Goddard, when he finally found his voice.

—

'Very glib, Mr Goddard,' said Buchan. 'I need you to tell me about Daniel. Everything, start to finish. How did you come to work with him, how much interaction did you have, why did you ask him to the set, what happened the day he was there that so irked him, when was the last time you spoke to him, was there anyone else on the set with whom he worked?'

He ran through all the questions, Goddard staring blankly at him throughout, and then when he didn't immediately answer, Buchan added, 'And where were you two evenings ago, and can anyone testify to your whereabouts in the middle of the night?'

'I've been wanting to work with him since I heard his work on *These Are The Stories We Tell*,' he began, the words delivered in a quick monotone. 'We met at the Nationals a year ago, we talked about *Watcher*. A couple of months later we signed a deal. Since I live in Glasgow and he lives just down the coast we met a few times, it was easy enough. We discussed the direction the soundtrack would take. We decided, as you have heard from the small piece you brought to me here, on a heavy, ethereal choral feel. It is one of Daniel's areas of expertise, after all. I asked him to the set so that he could get a feel for the production. Of course, in general it's not something that's necessary or indeed often happens, but given it was little more than half an hour's drive for Daniel I thought it a worthwhile exercise. Sadly, when he came, things had not been going well. Unusually the problem was not the actors, who were all fine on this occasion. There were two principal producers on the shoot. Benjamin, an independent, who owns the rights to the work, and who took the property to the production company, and Sara, from Searchcraft Pictures. Somewhere along the way, it transpired that Sara and Benjamin did not like each other. I don't know the instigation of the falling out, but fall out they did. The set then became a battleground, each of them briefing against the other, hoping to entice other crew members into their camp. It was, as Daniel observed to your informant, poisonous and quite detrimental to the production. Sadly, it continues to this day. Daniel was not, as far as I'm aware, roped into this fight, but I wouldn't be surprised if at least one, if not both of them, made an attempt to do so. I last spoke to Daniel last week. He'd almost finished, and was due to come to Glasgow shortly for final recording. Fortunately, I will say, though you may think me cold-hearted, he has delivered most of his work, and if we are now not to receive his final submission, we will nevertheless be fine.'

He paused for a moment while he considered what else needed to be said, then he continued, 'And two nights ago I ate dinner at Kha Gai with Benjamin, Sara and two executives from a new streaming service, aiming to secure original product, called MoviePlay. It was a speculative meeting. Then I went home to my wife. My wife's name is Carolina, and while I understand you may not be happy just taking my word for it, I would rather you didn't speak to her as she is very highly strung and easily stressed. If you require proof of my whereabouts, Carolina and I make love every night, and I record it on my phone. I have, as they say, the receipts. If you insist on speaking to Carolina, I will request that you allow me at least to lay some groundwork to prepare her for the interview.'

'By lay some groundwork, do you mean instruct her in what to say?' asked Buchan, who couldn't help but be amused at the tone, though he made sure not to show it.

'Of course not,' said Goddard.

'That's good,' said Buchan. 'Nevertheless, it doesn't matter. We'll speak to Carolina. Who else would have had access to the soundtrack?'

Another pause, while Goddard took in the blunt rejection and the follow-up question.

'What do you mean?' he asked, when he found his voice again.

'You knew this question was coming, Mr Goddard, you've had plenty of time to think about it. I let you hear the piece of music that was playing when Daniel was left hanging. You confirmed it was from the soundtrack to your show, and you've just shown me the scene in which the music was used. You called it the killer's theme.'

'I didn't call it the killer's theme. The piece is officially entitled *Corran's Theme*. Corran is the killer.'

'And it plays every time he commits murder?'

'Yes.' A beat, and then, 'Obviously sometimes murder is planned, and the plan is foiled. We tease the audience in this way.'

'Let's get back to the original question. Who else would have access to it?'

Goddard swallowed again, another obvious sound, an ugly movement of his large Adam's apple.

'You, obviously,' said Buchan, with the nudge.

'Daniel himself, Stanley, who is currently engaged with your sergeant, and the engineer and producer in the studio where the soundtrack was recorded.'

'That was done here?' asked Buchan.

'Of course not. We used Lost World, a studio on the other side of Paisley. I can give you the details, obviously. I cannot attest to whether the crew at the studio will have passed the recordings on to anyone else, but naturally they ought not to have done.'

'What about Benjamin and Sara?'

'Not that I know, but they are in charge of the production, so I cannot speak for either of them. But at this stage, they have not, to my knowledge, been given copies of the soundtrack.'

'They're not in the business of trying to fix up an accompanying soundtrack album, or anything like that?'

'It is too early. *Watcher* will not be released until the late autumn.'

'What about the singers and the musicians?'

'What about them?'

'They wouldn't have copies of the music?'

'Not a chance. They would've been paid for their work, and that's the end of it.'

The back and forth came to a sudden halt, the quickfire question and answer, the rapid deadpan conversation, almost as though the sound had just been turned off. A snap of the fingers, and silence, Buchan having asked almost everything he came to ask, the speed of it all meaning he was liable to get ahead of himself, leaving questions unposed.

'Are we done?' said Goddard. 'I'm very busy.'

'Have you any idea why Daniel might have been murdered?' asked Buchan, regardless of Goddard's impatience.

Another long stare, contempt, Buchan felt, deep within it. Everything about Goddard suggested the artist's annoyance at being interrupted. How would Buchan like it if he turned up at the offices of Serious Crime and insisted on Buchan answering questions related to policing? Goddard had no time for the police and their sense of entitlement.

'I am an artist,' said Goddard, 'and I work with artists. There is, without wishing to sound pompous, something special about us. We are separate from society. We are creators, we see the world in different shades and different colours from you, from the man in the street. And consequently, many of us are troubled, many of us carry demons unknown to normal men. I don't doubt Daniel felt the same way, and had the same kind of demons. He certainly seemed to try to counter them with alcohol. In short, I am more inclined to think that your initial impression, that he committed suicide, is more accurate.'

Without wishing to sound pompous, thought Buchan. *Some chance of that.*

'Did he give any hint of that?' asked Buchan. 'Would you be surprised if he'd committed suicide?'

'I'm never surprised when an artist commits suicide. We live on the edge, Inspector Buchan. We are only ever one wrong footfall from falling over.'

Jesus, thought Buchan.

'Show me the video of you and your wife from two nights ago,' he said. Then he added, 'I just need to see the time.'

8

'Wait, they film themselves having sex *every night*?' said Kane, unable to keep the amusement from her voice.

'Yep.'

'Oh my God, who does that?'

'When they're apart, they masturbate together on FaceTime. If, for some reason, they can't do this, they film themselves and send it to each other.'

Back along the M8, the Facel sitting at eighty in the outside lane.

'Wow,' said Kane. 'I'm not entirely sure I'm the same species as these people.'

'Apparently artists – and he's an artist – often have high sex drives. It's who they are. His wife is more than happy to accommodate him. She has needs. It's why they're so successful as a couple. Although, naturally – his words, you understand – naturally he gets lots of offers to have sex with leading ladies and whoever, he never needs to because his wife satisfies him. She is, nevertheless, prone to jealousy, and so if Adrian is making a movie with an actress who Mrs Goddard thinks he might be tempted by, she comes along and hangs around the set and makes herself available. Four or five times a day.'

'He's making that up,' said Kane, smiling, glancing at the airport as they sped past.

'Possibly. It doesn't really matter. I got a mercifully short view of the video from the other night and at least confirmed that he was in bed with his wife from before midnight until after one in the morning.'

'Wait, what? Really?'

'I saw the start and the end and a brief bit in the middle.'

'The end?' she said, looking at him with ironic concern.

Buchan stared ruefully straight ahead for a few moments.

'They were lying next to each other. They'd finished. I

---

didn't see *the end*, since that's what you're getting at. Anyway, I think we've talked enough about Mr and Mrs Goddard. Whatever his part in the end of Daniel's days, he has an alibi for Tuesday evening and the early hours of Wednesday.'

He slowed behind a Mini doing sixty-five in the outside lane, and then it moved aside, and he sped up again, as ever feeling the thrill of the Facel's acceleration. And, as he always did when he took the car for a longer drive than just around the city centre, he told himself that it was something he had to do more often. Perhaps he really ought to take that couple of weeks off the boss had been telling him to take, and drive through the continent. Really let the car open up on the autobahns, then drive into the Alps. It was the kind of driving the Facel deserved.

'Still,' said Kane, obviously not quite ready to let the sex life of the Goddards go just yet, 'it seems an incredibly perfect excuse. Just right, you know.'

'I know,' said Buchan. 'If it was a one-off, then it might seem odd, but the man has a folder going back years. I mean, you wouldn't believe. So if it's a faked alibi, it's one he's been setting up *forever*. I'm not ruling him out at all, he's obviously the person who was working most closely with Daniel on this, but for now, he's got his alibi and we'll leave it there. If we get any other information to implicate him, then we can start looking more closely at dates and times, we can speak to Mrs Goddard, we can escalate it. For now, we need to get on to these two producers.'

Kane had already filled Buchan in on Stanley Crow. Buchan had known that once he mentioned Goddard's alibi, they were likely to be side-tracked by the discussion on video sex for quite some time, as they would be when they got back to the office, so he'd got Kane to talk first.

Crow, however, had not been of so much use to the investigation. He'd never met Harptree, and had never visited the set. Nor had he had any dealings with either producer. He'd been hired by the director, and Goddard was the only one from the production with whom Crow had had any contact.

He'd been working on the production from the start, receiving daily footage from the shoot, but all his work had been done in the small studio at Stillwood. If he was telling the truth, Kane had established very early on, Crow was likely going to be of little use to them. As ever with police interviews, it was much too early to say how significant the *if* might be.

—

'Funny guy,' she'd said to Buchan. 'Strong Woody Allen vibe. Same glasses and everything. I mean, it's like he's modelled himself on him. Without mentioning this I asked him if he fancied getting into writing and directing, and he said he'd written eight scripts, but hadn't managed to move any of them on beyond early development. Then he started telling me about one, and I had to change the subject or else I'd've been travelling back into town on my own on the one a.m. bus.'

*

Buchan took a few minutes back at the open-plan in familiar position, standing at the window, looking down on the river. Next to them, the old Glasgow bridge. Across the river, the traffic on Clyde Street, before it turned into the Broomielaw, and the monument to La Pasionaria. Beside the small statue with its arms reaching to the sky, there was a woman sitting on a bench, looking at her phone, a cup in her other hand moving metronomically to her lips every half minute or so.

Another bleak January morning, mild and grey and damp, most cars still with their headlights on, little aesthetic beauty in the scene before him. It was not, of course, why he liked to stand here.

He'd just interviewed Harptree's father, who'd arrived from London to make the formal identification of his son's corpse. However he'd reacted to the initial news when he'd received it at his home in London, the walls had now gone up, defences were in place. It seemed shallow to call it the classic British stiff upper lip, but that was exactly what it had been. Son dead, heart ripped out of the family, the worst fear of any parent come true, and here he was, doing what had to be done, discussing his son's life as though it was one of the TV shows he'd written the soundtrack for.

In any event, Harptree Snr had had little to say. Buchan got the feel of it early on, for all the distance and defensiveness. Daniel had gone to Julliard in New York at eighteen, and then to the Berlin Symphony, before a brief tenure as lead French horn with the LSO – during which time he'd barely had time to see his parents, regardless of living in the same city, though he did get them regular tickets to the Barbican – following which he began working freelance as a composer, moving to the Clyde coast having previously visited the area during a week-long LSO residency at the Glasgow Concert Hall. Buchan certainly wondered why you would choose to live there when, as a freelance composer you could live anywhere on earth, but everyone lived somewhere and people always had reasons. Perhaps he wanted coast anywhere, and the Clyde coast was the most cost-effective.

His father had had no idea why anyone would want to kill him. A short WhatsApp conversation about a new recording of Brandenburg aside, they'd had no contact for a fortnight. His son's life, he was afraid to say, had been rather passing them by.

'And now it's gone,' he'd said, determinedly looking Buchan in the eye. The stiff upper lip never threatened to waver.

'Remember crisp winter mornings?'

Buchan turned to his left. Roth was standing beside him, coffee in hand. He wondered how long she'd been standing there.

'I'd be surprised if you did,' he said. 'But I'm pretty sure we had them in the eighties.'

She smiled, took a drink.

'I wonder if there were as many as I remember. Maybe we just recall occasional days, but because they stand out and feature more prominently in our memories, we think there must've been a lot more of them.'

'Even if there were only five a winter,' said Buchan, 'it'd be five more than we've had this year.'

She nodded, taking another drink.

'Where have we got to?' asked Buchan, deciding it was time to get back to work. He'd been standing here long enough.

'Just about to head out to the recording studio,' she said. 'You still want me to take that?'

'Might come with you,' said Buchan. 'It's Paisley?'

'Ralston, but more or less. If you want to take it, I can –'

'We'll go together,' said Buchan. 'It's a decent-sized studio I presume, if they're recording orchestras in there. There'll be a few people to speak to. Sam's talking to one of the TV show's producers shortly, I've got the other in a couple of hours. We good to go now?'

'Yep,' said Roth, and she put the cup to her mouth, tipping it back, and drinking half of it in one go.

9

They were standing in a studio control room, looking through the window into the studio itself, a large area, wooden-floored, soft-covered walls, generally untidy, with music stands and equipment littered around, the floor covered in wires. The studio was easily big enough to host sixty musicians, or perhaps more – Buchan was having trouble picturing it – but instead there were two people sitting in the middle, dwarfed by the size of the room, one at a piano, the other on a stool with an acoustic guitar. They both had microphones set up, but the sound through to the control room was currently cut off.

'You don't have a small studio for this kind of set-up?' said Roth, making a head movement in the direction of the artists at work.

The overweight guy with the beard, leaning back in a very comfortable chair, hands crossed on his enormous belly, barked out a laugh and smiled.

'Sure we do. We got three other rooms. This pair should be in there with one of our apprentice girls doing what I'm doing.'

He was American.

'So how come they're not?'

He made the money gesture.

Roth and Buchan looked back into the studio. Of course, it could have been Taylor Swift and Lady Gaga working together and Buchan wouldn't have recognised them, but Roth was more likely to have some level of awareness.

'They big?' she asked.

The name of the artist – JooJoo Clam – was scrawled on a piece of white tape along the top of the sound board.

'Nope.'

'Where's the money come from?'

'Daddy,' said the fat guy. 'JooJoo has her TikTok account and her Buzzcrap and her FaceFeed and whatever the fuck the kids are all doing now, and she's recording a bunch of shitty tunes at daddy's expense, and she wanted to do it in here so she can get all her shots and videos looking like a *playah*. Amiright? And maybe, just maybe, if she throws enough money at that shit, it sticks. Who the fuck knows?'

Roth wanted to ask to have a listen, but it would've been superfluous. She would've done had Buchan not been there.

'Why'd you take the work?' asked Buchan.

'Nothing else major in this week. We're about to hit a month's long booking with the Scottish National, got Yo-Yo fucking Ma coming in here in the middle of it, it's going to be nuts. This was a down week, we couldn't get in anything major, and along came Miss Moneybags. Might as well. I could've handed it over to one of the kids, but I needed the laugh.'

'Tell us about Daniel Harptree,' said Buchan, and the big guy laughed, head shaking.

'Just like a cop, eh? No time to dick around.'

'There's been a murder,' said Buchan coldly, and the engineer nodded.

'Yeah, fine.'

The fun seemed to leave the interview for him, as though the murder had never been the reason Buchan and Roth were with him in the first place.

'How many times was Daniel here?' asked Buchan, and the guy threw his hands in a small, hopeless gesture.

'That'd be like asking how many times the Beatles were in Abbey Road. Like, a tonne, you know. Yeah, OK, whatever, not as often as the, you know, the fucking Beatles, man, but often enough. A lot. If you really need us to go through the records, I guess we can dig it out. If that's what you really want. I mean, like, is it what you really want?'

'You knew Daniel well then?'

'I worked with him a lot, let's say that. We never hung out.'

'You don't seem upset about his murder.'

The engineer looked away from Buchan while he considered this, and then a short, sudden laugh barked from the back of his throat.

'Wait, does that make me a suspect?'

'You're not currently a suspect,' said Buchan.

'Currently? Like, what the fuck?'

'We have no suspects,' said Buchan, patiently. 'None. Since we're not in a position to say that anyone might have committed the murder, we're equally not in a position to say that any particular person might not have done. You don't seem upset by Daniel's death?'

The engineer finally seemed to accept he was being asked a reasonable question, took another moment to contemplate how to answer, then tossed another pair of dismissive hands.

'Look, man, whatever. Daniel was a bit of a dick, that's all, and often enough a drunken dick, which is way worse. Like, you don't want to see him get murdered, that shit is base, man. But does it affect *my* life? I don't know that it does. I can live without Daniel. Sorry, but that's just the way it is.'

'How was he a bit of a dick?' asked Roth.

'You know, the usual way people are when they come in here. They've done it fifty times before, so they think they know more than the guy who's done it five thousand times. And Daniel acted like, you know, the temperamental genius, the artist who controls everything and people have to accept that maybe he's a dick, but it's worth it because, holy shit, isn't this music amazing? Except, he wasn't really a genius, was he? Not saying he wasn't good, but genius is as genius does, and he wasn't it.'

'The last time he was here was...?'

''Bout a month ago. Working on this TV show you mentioned.'

'How much studio time did he use?'

'A few days. Maybe a week. About half with the singers, you know the Tallis Choral, and the other half with a quintet. There were a couple of pieces he really ought to have been doing with a full orchestra, but we can beef it all up when required,' and he wafted a hand across the mixing desk. 'He was due back in shortly.'

'What about Yo-Yo?'

'Ha! Yeah, nice. The quintet uses Studio B, plenty big enough. Not enough space for the Tallis lot when they're here, there's like fifty of them, but far as I know he was done with the choir.'

'How did the recording go?' asked Buchan. 'Any arguments, any unpleasantness?'

'Smooth as your ass, my friend. Like I said, Daniel could be a dick, and I'm not saying all the musicians and singers would consider it smooth, but from where I was sitting, it went well. Decent music, they were all on top of it, only saw Daniel lose his shit a coupla times, and that really wasn't often for

Danny boy, he was mostly sober, and off they went.'

'Anyone you think might have got to the end of those sessions extremely pissed off at Daniel?'

'So pissed off they murdered him?' he asked with a smile. 'I don't think so.'

'Can I just confirm the recording we have here is from the recordings you did in the studio?' asked Buchan, taking his phone from his pocket.

'Sure, bud, on you go.' He leant over and pressed a button on the console. 'You're good for it to play through here.'

Buchan clicked onto Bluetooth, made the connection, then set the song playing.

Slow start, and then the voices. Listening to it like this, in the control room of a recording studio, the speakers loud, the sound all-consuming and magnificent, Buchan could feel the hairs start to stand on the back of his neck.

He didn't like that feeling, not when he was working, and he shook it off.

'The sound's amazing,' he said quietly, the words just appearing from nowhere.

'Yeah,' said Roth. She was staring into the studio, staring at nothing, taken by the music. 'Wow,' she said, quietly.

This is a sound system, thought Buchan. That small Bluetooth of his that sat in the kitchen/diner, through which he listened to all the old Hoagy and Ella and Buck records, would sound pretty empty when he got home tonight.

Buchan glanced at the fat guy, who was watching them both, smiling.

'You guys are funny,' he said. 'The looks on your faces. Like you never heard music before.'

Buchan felt seen-through, straightened his shoulders, took the wonder and kicked it into the long grass.

'This is the piece that was recorded here?'

The fat guy laughed.

'Nope.'

'What?'

'This ain't it.'

He leant forward, stopping the music with a quick tap of his finger, then he turned to a laptop on the desk to his right, his fingers flew across the keyboard, the same piece of music started up again, and he fast-forwarded through the track to a spot similar to where he'd just stopped it.

It was a different recording, and the contrast was massive. Feeling stupid, Buchan realised it was the same when he'd watched the show footage with the music as the soundtrack. It had sounded different, fuller, with much more depth, but he'd assumed it had been the same recording and that the sound had been augmented in some way through the editing process. And he had failed to ask Goddard about it.

Now, in the studio, the two back-to-back, it was obviously a different recording.

'You get that?' asked the engineer.

Buchan nodded, and the engineer tapped the keyboard, the tune ending abruptly.

'Your one, whatever you've got there, same song, obviously, same arrangement even, but it wasn't recorded here. That's a shitty recording, and with fewer voices. The depth's not there. They've double tracked 'em, sure, but you can tell the difference with what we did here. Where'd you get that?'

'Who's going to have had access to your recording?' said Buchan, asking a question which he'd always been intending to ask. It was no longer as relevant, however, because if there was another recording made elsewhere, the provenance of which they had no idea, then it could have been made by Harptree's killer, or the killer could have got it from absolutely anywhere. The small group of people with access to the track had suddenly become infinite.

'Access? Like, to listen to it or take it away and bootleg it?'

'The latter.'

'Me, Jimbo through in the other room.'

'What about your apprentices?'

They were due to speak to Jimbo next. They hadn't intended speaking to the apprentices, but he knew he couldn't skip.

'Those guys only have access to what we allow them, and we only allow them when it's something they're working on. You know, people are pretty funny about this, right? Like, we had DJ R-Mac in here once, and when you're at that level, that shit is real, man. Those guys are paranoid about their stuff leaking, and who can blame them? I mean, that's their lifeblood, right? When all your publicity is based around the big fucking reveal and how many hits you're getting on YouTube in the first twenty-four hours, you do not want that shit leaking. So we have procedures, and really, they're the same for everyone. Even these two clowns, when no buttfuck on earth would try to steal their stuff, we'll still follow all the usual rules. So, basically, no way that shit leaks, no way someone gets a hold of the recording of your serial killer tune here.'

'So where did this come from?' asked Buchan, indicating his phone.

'That's your million dollar question,' said the engineer.

'And the million dollar answer?' asked Buchan, voice deadpan.

'Ha! Your man, Daniel. He might've made it as a trial run. He could've got someone to do it for him. Or maybe it was someone from the, you know, the Tallis lot, maybe one of them. They shouldn't have been able to take the music, but maybe they did. Maybe they heard the track a few times, and bingo, they knew it by heart. Some people are like that.'

'How many singers were there?' asked Roth.

''Bout fifty. Wait, I said that already, didn't I? So, there's your million dollar answer. You've got about fifty suspects from the singers, you've got the musicians, you've got Daniel, or you've got literally who the fuck knows amount of people that Daniel could have played it to beforehand. Or your director, what about him? And I guess anyone else on the movie. Ha!' again. 'Looks like you've got a lot of interviewing to do.'

'Thanks,' said Buchan. The engineer laughed. 'D'you mind if we take away a copy of the official piece?'

Another barked laugh, followed by, 'Are you fucking kidding?'

Buchan gave him his familiar *does it look like I am* face.

'Can't do it, my friend.'

'This is a murder inquiry,' said Buchan. The words sounded useless as he spoke. They were going to have to go to court, and given they'd be up against a large TV company, if they chose to fight it, there would be lawyers with far more resources than the police could throw at it. And the TV company would love the publicity and make everything of it that they could.

'You'll need to speak to the show. I mean, like the producers. It's their product, it's up to them to let you have it, not me. My hands are tied, my friend.'

'Is there any guitar work on the soundtrack?' asked Buchan, changing tack.

A pause, a vague look of confusion which blended perfectly into amusement, then a shake of the head. 'I don't know why

---

you'd ask, but no.'

'Daniel was a guitarist.'

'A great guitarist. But this wasn't that kind of thing.'

'You've heard him play?'

'Sure. A bit of the John Williams about him. I mean, obviously, the guitarist, not Indiana Jones.'

'You've seen his guitar?'

The engineer stroked his chin, as though contemplating where this line of questioning was taking them, then he smiled and said, 'Yep. You know, that was the thing with Daniel. You know you get these guitarists who have entire rooms full of instruments. Fucking nuts, man. Posturing bullshit. At least Daniel just had the one. Very nice little piece. A pre-war Martin, D45. The phrase *a thing of beauty* is tossed around like an out-of-control kid on a trampoline, but it applies to Daniel's guitar. The sound was *perfect*.'

'How much is it worth?'

A disappointed look crossed the fat guy's face as though the question possessed a vulgarity all its own, and then he answered with a dismissive wave.

'Doesn't matter. No way Daniel was selling it. Still, I guess it'd probably be valued around half a million. And if it ever were to be sold, you know, like at auction and shit, then who knows? Strange things happen at auction.'

Buchan held his gaze for a few moments, then looked away, staring into the studio. The two young girls were singing earnestly, a phone set up, one of them in particular playing to the camera.

'They couldn't hire someone to shoot footage for them?' said Buchan, the signal that he was giving up on the interview.

'Shoot footage? All right, old timer,' said the engineer laughing. 'Kids, they do all this shit themselves. That's what makes it real.'

'Can we hear them?' asked Roth. She hadn't intended to ask, yet there were the words, her tongue loosened by Buchan letting the interrogation end.

The engineer leant forward and pressed a button, and they were listening to the music from next door. Two voices, guitar, piano.

Buchan had no idea what to think. He glanced at Roth.

*

And so, twenty-four hours in, they had a problematic film shoot in which Harptree had not been closely involved, and a missing acoustic guitar. On face value, Buchan would be more inclined to say that perhaps this murder had been about the guitar, because that would mean it had been about money, and people got murdered over money. Roth had not been wrong when listing off the most common causes of murder that crossed their desks, yet she'd missed that one. People got killed for money, and if his guitar had really been worth half a million, then that would be reason enough.

However, the notion of the guitar being the principal cause behind the murder was undermined by the tune that had been left playing beside the hanging corpse. The murder theme from *Beware The Watcher*. A clear statement, an obvious line drawn from the television production to Harptree's death.

The possibility had already occurred to him that Harptree was playing them. The artist staging his own death, having written the theme tune to his own faked murder. Yet nothing other than vague possibility pointed in that direction; it had to be acknowledged, but every instinct said that Harptree had not chosen the timing of his own end.

'Of its type,' said Roth.

Sitting in the car, Buchan asking about the music they'd heard from the two young women.

'I can't tell if it's any good,' he said.

'Me neither.'

Buchan glanced at her, then turned back to the traffic. Too busy to be going too fast, no requirement for the urgency of the blue light. After the initial rush, he could feel the investigation slowing down. Soon enough, if they didn't get on top of things, they would have reached the dog days.

Dammit, Buchan, he thought, *you're only just getting started*. Plenty of players in the game still to be contacted for the first time.

'You don't listen to that kind of thing?' he asked.

'Do I look like I listen to it?' said Roth. 'I mean, what are you thinking, boss? I'm young, that was young people's music, ergo…'

'Right enough,' said Buchan nodding. 'You nailed it. I was being that shallow. What do you like?' he added, aware he was mostly asking so that he didn't have to dwell on superficiality.

'I like the Foo Fighters, Fall Out Boy, some others. But I

also listen to Brahms and Mahler and the like. Just background, really.'

Buchan drove on, eyes forward, then allowed himself a quick glance at her.

'I don't know Brahms and Mahler,' he said.

'You'd recognise some it, I expect.'

The traffic ahead of them started to free up, Buchan dropped the car into third and accelerated into the outside lane.

10

Kane had spoken to the TV show's producer Benjamin Collins, and while Buchan had intended going straight from the recording studio to speak to the other producer, Sara Albright, when he learned that Kane was off the call, he'd decided to stop off and get her on the way. She'd be well-placed to pick up on discrepancies in what they'd said, and the level of animosity between them.

Roth, meanwhile, had stayed at the station to do follow-up work on the Tallis Choral, and the string quintet who'd been used on the recording. There were a lot of phone calls to make.

Buchan had taken the opportunity presented by the short time back at the office to report in with Chief Inspector Liddell.

'Maybe we need to set up an arts division,' she'd said, as she twirled the unlit cigarette around her fingers, reading the brief summary of where they'd got to thus far.

'What d'you mean?' Buchan had asked.

'You had the murders at the publishing house, you had the case with the paintings that tipped over into film and television, and now you've got television and music. You're becoming a specialist.'

Buchan kept the dismissive look on his face until she looked up.

'Inspector?' she'd said, not smiling but amused at his reaction.

'We're just forgetting the Ardbeg double murder, which could not have been further removed from the arts, and the fraud case in Merchant City. Not to mention that bastard Higgins. Nothing artistic about him, ma'am, was there?'

'Nevertheless, it's something to think about. Maybe if we get a death at the opera, or some poetry murders or something, then it might be time for you to head up a specialist Arts Division.'

'All poetry's murder,' was all he could muster in response, and this time she had smiled.

*

Sara Albright worked in the top floor office of a block overlooking the M8. High enough, and at the top of town, to have a terrific view all around the city, from the river and beyond, to back out across the west end to the spire of the university. Floor-to-ceiling windows on two sides, Buchan felt like he could be standing in one of those seventieth-floor apartments overlooking Central Park that you see in movies. It seemed out of place here.

Her desk was a riot of paper. Everything about the way she talked and her mannerisms and the way she was conducting herself, the way she constantly lifted the phone and barked instructions to her assistant, all of it suggested a woman whose life was run at one hundred and fifty per cent capacity.

She was drinking coffee. When Buchan or Kane talked, her right index finger tapped rapidly on the desk, as though trying to dictate the pace of the question.

'I'd never heard of him. I'd been thinking of Gerry, you know, he worked on *Plague of Crows* for us with Marc and Neil. But then Adrian suggested Daniel Harptree, and you know, he sounded decent, and, obviously this is major from our angle, he was cheap. By original music standards, obviously. No music is actually *cheap*. Not as much dead money as what you have to pay the owner of the product, but still, it feels like a burden. You're paying for this thing that, at its best, no one's going to even remember.'

'Is that true?' Kane couldn't stop herself asking. 'There's lots of famous film and TV music.'

'Whistle me a tune from a six-part TV drama.' She paused, but only for about three quick taps of her finger, then added, 'I'll wait,' which people say when they have no intention of waiting, then she said, 'Movies, sure, that's one thing. And the long-running TV show, the *Friends* or the *Morse* or the whatever, where the theme tune has year-upon-year to weave its way into the human psyche... But one-off drama series? The music serves one purpose, and that's to create atmosphere. And when the music really works, you don't even know it's there. That's what we're hoping we get from Daniel. From what Adrian says,

---

47

sounds like he might've nailed it.' A pause, and then, 'Too bad he didn't get to finish the job, but it's a decent epitaph.'

Brutal, thought Buchan.

'How much contact did you have with Daniel?'

'Me? None.'

'He didn't speak to you the day he was on set?'

'OK, almost none.'

'Almost none?'

'We had a quick five minutes at the office, but it was little more than a meet and greet. There was no real need for it, and you know what it's like for the producer on set.'

'Not really.'

'Busy. I mean, you're the go-to guy. Every problem from the lead actor taking too long to take a shit, to make-up running out of wet wipes, to the cameras breaking down, to the permit to film not coming through on time, all of it. It all ends up on my desk.'

'What about Benjamin?'

'He's a fucking idiot.'

'How do you split the work with him?'

'I do it and he doesn't.'

'That's not what Benjamin said,' chipped in Kane.

She looked disparagingly at Kane, the first pause in speech and activity and movement since they'd sat down with her.

'Bennie's an amateur. He plays at being a film producer, but in reality, he has no idea. You ask him about his background? Is it in film? No. Is it in business, or management? No. Is it even in getting things done? No. Made his money on Bitcoin, did a one-day, three-hundred pound course on filmmaking at Raindance, and boom. Thinks he's Jerry-fucking-Bruckheimer. So he comes on set and swans around like he's the boss, he collects his daily stipend... I mean, seriously, if you want to talk about dead money coming out the show's budget, that tops the fucking list. And he does nothing, except get in the way. Thank God the filming's done. We're now into the boring bit for us. Selling the product. A lot of phone calls, a lot of pressing flesh, a lot of boring meetings. Fortunately young Bennie is mostly happy to leave the boring stuff to me, so I don't have to spend half my working day correcting his mistakes, which was what was happening on set.'

'You argued a lot?' asked Buchan.

'Not enough.'

48

'You dragged other people on set into your arguments?'

A brief pause, but nothing lasted very long with Sara Albright, and she crushed the pause with a sharp, 'Too fucking right. Bennie started it, since you ask.'

She looked harshly at Kane, waiting to see if she was going to give Benjamin Collins' side of the story.

'How about Daniel?' asked Buchan.

'Really? Is this why we're here? So you can stretch the piece of chewed gum all the way from Daniel's fifteen-minute on-set visit to his murder? Let me save you some time. You can't.'

'Daniel's dead. His killer left the killer's theme from *Beware The Watcher* playing beside his corpse, unquestionably linking the two. We need to cover every aspect of the production, and we need to start narrowing down suspects.'

'Like I say, Daniel was on set for fifteen minutes. He dealt with Adrian. Will he have talked to any other fucker while there? Sure, he probably did. But how on earth are you going to go from Daniel having some brief chat over a sandwich, or asking the guy wafting the smoke from the smoke machine if he gets job satisfaction, to someone wanting Daniel dead? His involvement with the making of our show was almost zero, and all of it was in post-production, so I suggest you just leave us the fuck alone. Talk to Adrian, though I've got to say, unlikely he murdered anyone.'

'Your very welcome naked aggression aside,' said Buchan, deadpan, 'can you think of any reason why anyone involved in this project, on the music side or otherwise, might have wanted Daniel dead?'

She smirked, shook her head.

'No. I mean, I just can't... there's nothing else to say.'

'Were you aware of Daniel's guitar?'

'His guitar?'

Buchan nodded.

She made a kind of hopeless gesture, looking around as though she might have an audience, then turned back to Buchan with a head shake.

'I didn't even know he played the guitar. I mean, I guess those people, those professionals, they can pick up anything and play it, but no, I don't know about Daniel's guitar.'

'You all right with us getting a copy of *Corran's Theme* from the show?'

—

A pause, and then, 'What?'

'*Corran's Theme*. We'd like you to authorise the studio to send us a copy.'

'I thought you already had it from Daniel dying?'

'It's a different recording. We'd like to have a copy of the official version to get them compared.'

'Why don't you just ask the guys down at Lost World to compare them?'

'Because they're amongst the people who could potentially have leaked the recording to someone else. We need to be able to play it to an independent.'

'And then, Bob's your uncle, it's all over the Internet, right?'

'Thank you for your trust,' said Buchan, drily.

'Prove to me otherwise.'

'How do I do that without you giving me the recording?'

Albright shrugged as an answer.

Buchan sighed, already tired of the negotiation that had barely got under way.

'We'll take a USB stick,' said Kane. 'It may well all be done in-house anyway, but if we take it to an outside recording engineer, we'll play it to them, and we won't allow them to download it.'

'So you say,' said Albright, looking as bored with the negotiation as Buchan.

'Jesus,' muttered Buchan, unable to stop himself. 'Didn't you just say no one cares about six-part drama incidental music? So why would anyone care about it being leaked? Why would anyone even think to leak it?'

Caught in her own logic, she had no answer, eventually a small movement of her head.

'Very well, I'll let Darryl know you can take a copy.'

'Thank you,' said Buchan, then happy to move on, he continued, 'let's remove Daniel from the discussion. Let's imagine that, in some way, Daniel was collateral damage, or Daniel was a warning, or Daniel was picked at random. This wasn't about Daniel. This was about your show. The killer selected Daniel, when in fact they could have selected anyone.'

'I'm not sure that makes sense,' said Albright, 'but please, talk on.'

She glanced at her watch.

'So far no one has suggested any reason why Daniel might

———

have been killed,' said Buchan. 'Maybe the murder wasn't Daniel-specific, and we spend all our time on his life and his relationships with colleagues and whoever, and we're wasting that time.'

Albright made a small gesture. *If that's what you think.*

'In amongst all this arguing on set, which we're beginning to understand spilled over from the starting point of you and Benjamin, was there anything that might have escalated out of hand? Any disagreements over money? Any open hostility on set, beyond you and him? Maybe Daniel didn't even get caught up in it, he just got killed as a warning. *There goes that guy, you're next.*'

Buchan and Kane could always recognise it. The familiar look of the interrogatee when they automatically wanted to say no, but that would be lying, because there were stories to tell.

A moment, then she leant forward, elbow on the desk, glasses off, hand rubbed across her face. She looked at Buchan, face suddenly drawn, and he knew they'd reached the confession part of the interview. Not all confessions were blessed with honesty, however.

'The producer, like all managers in every walk of life everywhere, the woman in charge, the whoever, they set the tone. If they're sloppy, that sloppiness flows down. If they're corrupt, the whole organisation will be corrupt. If they're sharp and efficient, that's what follows. Well the producers on this show were rancorous. Ergo... Sure as eggs is eggs, that rancour funnelled down. There was a lot of stress on set, and when there's stress there are arguments. A lot of them heated. It was an unpleasant environment, and every time Bennie and I tried to reset, well... I'm going to say he fucked it. I'm sure he'd say different, but then he's a moron.'

'Any particularly rancorous people we ought to know about?' asked Kane.

'Speak to Blake. I mean, it's not like I think he'll have killed anyone, and I don't want to go landing him in the shit or anything, but Blake was pretty angry the whole time.'

'Blake?'

'Philips. The cinematographer.'

'Is that important?' asked Buchan.

'Is what important?'

'The position of cinematographer.'

'Principal cameraman. They'll work with the director, of

course, but they'll set the feel for the film, how it looks, camera positions, everything related to the actual filming. So, yes, important.'

'Tell us about Blake,' said Kane.

'Blake is temperamental. Very demanding. He has a reputation. I guess he was let loose on set when he saw what was coming down from the top.'

'Did he fight with anyone in particular?'

'Blake fought with everyone. We got a lot of complaints. At least nine different crew members by the time the shoot was over. I don't want to go into any more detail, and I'm not going to give you any of those names. And, before you ask, I have no idea if there was any interaction between Blake and Daniel. You can ask them.' A pause, and then she corrected herself. 'You can ask Blake. Daniel, not so much.'

Daniel, not so much.

She looked at her watch again.

*

'Now that you've met them both, whose side are you on?' asked Buchan.

Sitting in the car on the way back down through town. Kane stared at the traffic ahead, having not previously thought to compare and contrast.

'Good question,' she said. 'Interesting pair. I can see how they wouldn't get on. I mean, sometimes opposites attract and all that, but obviously not here.'

'Is that you avoiding the question?' he asked, with the hint of a smile in the words.

Having been thinking about the personalities, she had to think back to what the question had been, then she unconsciously rubbed her chin.

'On the face of it, Benjamin's way more likeable. I mean, he's an affable guy, but you can tell he's going to be nuts to work with. Kind of a poundshop Elon Musk. You know, he's going to make a movie, throw some money at it, and why shouldn't it be easy and straightforward and go exactly as he thinks it should? Grab the cameras, and we'll be at the Berlin film festival in time for cocktails. As we can see, Sara is a much harder, more practical nut. Not taking anyone's shit, doesn't think movies are thought magically into existence. Down-to-earth, pragmatic, no time for dreamers. Almost what you expect a film producer to be like, arguing over every last purchase of a roll of toilet paper.

'It could be that two such people get along in a strange kind of way, but when they're thrown together, having never met before, in the way they were here, it's understandable. It was never going to work.'

They were moving again, consecutive green lights, almost at the river.

'And still she doesn't actually answer the question,' said Buchan, and he couldn't keep the laugh from his voice this time.

'Sara!' she said, laughing. 'Definitely Sara. Sara and I would get on just fine. As would you. She's good, she's efficient. Everybody wants to work with good and efficient apart from the wealthy, invariably male, control freak.'

He let the smile go, as they finally stopped at the last set of lights by the Broomielaw. He liked her assessment, but as ever, despite his confidence in Kane, he still felt the need to meet Collins for himself. He'd get to it eventually.

'You OK to write up a report on your chat with him?' he asked.

'I'm on it when we get back,' said Kane.

Cars drove by in front of them, clouds moved slowly across a haunted, grey sky.

11

End of the afternoon wrap-up in the ops room. Buchan, Kane, Houston, Cherry and Roth. *Corran's Theme* was playing, Buchan setting it on a loop, the two different versions on rotation, allowing the music to seep into the fabric of the room. Pictures of the deceased on the wall, names and places and faces linked where appropriate, the roundtable just getting going after they'd all allowed themselves to be swallowed up by the music.

'We got nowhere with the Tallis lot, I'm afraid,' said Roth. 'Complete blank across the board. Quite a lot of them outright laughed.'

'God, aye,' said Cherry, with whom she'd split the calls.

'Did you meet anyone,' began Buchan, 'or was it all...?' and he let the question go as Roth was obviously about to answer.

'I met the conductor straight off,' said Roth. 'Lives in town, so it was easy enough. Had a coffee at the place across the road, you know the one with that weird guy doing jigsaws in the corner.'

Buchan nodded. 'I've seen him.'

'What is *that* about?'

'Living his best life,' said Buchan, with a small shrug. 'What'd the conductor have to say?'

'He was fairly dismissive. I mean, pleasant enough guy 'n all, but just no way anything was getting taken away. No recorded music, and no sheet music gets out of this kind of place.'

'Don't they get to practice?'

'Don't need to, apparently. They get their parts, they sing them. A couple of run-throughs, and that's enough. *We're professionals*, he said. And it wasn't complicated.'

'How about the chances of people remembering what they'd sung, then going off and recording it for themselves?'

'Unfortunately, high.'

'Ah.'

'Yeah. He says everyone there, everyone in the choir and everyone accompanying them in the ensemble, would have been capable of going off and making their own recording. They could make sure they didn't take any music, and they could make sure they didn't have phones on them to record what they were performing, but they can't do a brain scrub at the end of the session. Again, his words. His main answer to that was, however, why would they make their own version? It wasn't like they were recording the soundtrack for *Star Wars X*, or, I don't know, the next *Lord of the Rings*.'

'Well, we have an answer to the why,' said Kane. 'So they could use it to taunt their victim in death.'

'I guess, Sarge, but there's no one giving off a strong hating-the-composer vibe. Although Daniel was known to be quick-tempered, most of them seemed to view him as a kind of grumpy, Alan Arkin type, you know? There was a comedy element to his snarkiness.'

'Yeah, I had *three* people say that if only he'd had a Jewish New York accent, he'd have been hilarious,' said Cherry.

'And you spoke to them all?' asked Buchan looking between the two.

'Every last one,' said Roth, 'including a woman in a bikini on a beach in the Maldives.'

'She hasn't done a runner?' asked Houston.

'Been there for the last week,' said Roth. 'I checked. And she looked way too tanned for having left Scotland yesterday,' she added, smiling.

'All right,' said Buchan, 'for now, at least, we can park that lot. Hopefully, they can stay parked.'

'And I spoke to another guy on the crew, Adam Zelinger,' said Roth. 'Assistant director. He was a little vague. Not too keen to meet up. We definitely need to chase him again.'

'Where is he?'

'He didn't like to say. I mean, he just sounded like he was being obtuse for the sake of it –'

'Classic police wariness,' said Cherry.

'Right? It's like a condition. When we call him again he'll probably say that us calling him is giving him mental health issues,' said Roth, and a couple of the others laughed.

Buchan lifted the coffee, took a drink, set it back down on

the desk. He hadn't needed it, having drunk too many coffees already, and he pushed the almost-full cup away from himself.

It was dark outside, the January day having long since passed, replaced by a night that still refused to grant a winter's chill, being instead bleak and a little damp, the temperature barely beneath ten degrees.

'Ian, you get anywhere?'

Houston glanced at his notes, nodding as he refamiliarized himself with them, then he looked up.

'There's not an awful lot, but I did find a couple of cases of this guy you're seeing in the morning, Philips the cinematographer, having worked with the director. I guess that's quite a close relationship. Nothing involving Harptree, however. I called him, Philips I mean, and he told me he was busy and that I should fuck off and leave him alone.'

'Yeah, said the same thing to me when I called to arrange to see him tomorrow,' said Buchan. 'Nevertheless, we managed to get past that and he acquiesced. Any others?'

Houston shook his head as he glanced down the notes he'd made on an iPad. 'Slim pickings, boss,' he said. 'You'd think Scotland was a small place, the industry would be small, and people would always be working with the same folk, over and over, but it's just not like that.'

'OK, send the report over before you go today, please, then at least I'll know what I'm taking to the interview with Philips in the morning.'

Buchan looked at his own sparse notes before him, then lifted his head to the board. A familiar meeting at this stage of the investigation. Enough information to keep them going, plenty of avenues still to explore, but still so much they didn't know, and still no firm line of inquiry.

'All right, people,' he said, pushing his chair back, 'think we're done for the day. Finish off what you're doing, and don't linger. We've no idea when we might have to suddenly pull a long shift because of this one, so there's no need for you to hang about tonight when you don't have to.'

He looked around the room, eyebrows raised, questioning whether anyone had anything to add, there were a couple of noiseless replies, and then he got to his feet. A moment, while he considered the music that was still playing, then he paused it on his phone, turned off the speaker, a new silence, and the meeting was over.

---

*

Despite what he'd said to the rest of the staff, when they were gone, he found himself staying on at the office. Last man standing. He trawled through film and television sites, reading about the players in their game, he made himself a cup of tea and stood at the window looking out on the city at night. He stayed so late, he wondered if he'd still be there when one of the others thought to sneak back into work, as he knew they sometimes did.

No one came.

It was well after eleven p.m. when he left the office, and he stood out on the street for a few moments, wondering which direction he should go in, and then inevitably he headed for the Winter Moon.

If the place was dead, always possible Janey had shut up shop already. It happened reasonably often. No reason why she should keep it open just for him.

Tonight, however, that was exactly what she'd done.

When he entered, Sinatra was singing *It Gets Lonely Early*, there were no customers, and Janey was standing alone at the bar, opposite his usual spot, elbows on the counter, nursing a slow glass of gin and tonic.

She looked at him as he hesitated in the doorway, and then he closed the door, walked across the bar and eased himself into his usual stool.

She held his gaze for a few moments – *God, she looks sad*, he thought – then she turned away, poured him a glass from the bottle in the freezer, placed the drink in front of him and leant forward again, so that their faces were now less than the width of the bar apart.

'You don't look great,' said Buchan. 'Everything OK.'

'Just get a little lost sometimes.' A pause, and then, 'I was about to close up. Been waiting for you for a while.'

'You should've called.'

'Didn't want to sound needy.'

'I wouldn't have thought you needy.'

She lifted the glass, took a drink, and when she lowered it again her lips were moist.

'Who are you, Buchan?' she said after another few moments.

'What does that mean?'

'I never knew you. You're a police officer, you treat it like it's an achievable goal. It's something with targets, with a prize at the end you can work towards. And yet, it's just another job, and no matter how good a job you do, there will always be more crime. Always more work to do. So what's going on in there?'

She moved slightly closer, lifted her hand, gently touched the side of his head.

'Sometimes it's as though you're a cipher, filling the spaces in between. And yet... I don't know, maybe that's why I always found you so attractive. The mystery. Then maybe it got to the point where I wondered if there was just nothing behind the mask. It wasn't even a mask.'

He lifted his glass, took a drink. He wasn't sure what to say. He'd never liked talking about himself, which would be one reason why no one ever thought they really knew him.

'Brutal,' was all he could say.

She touched his face again.

'I don't mean to be. You just confuse me sometimes.'

Her voice was soft. He could have wondered where this had come from, but he knew human nature at least. Sometimes people don't need a reason. Sometimes things just happen.

He leant forward the few inches they were now apart and their lips met. If he'd thought about it, he might have wondered how she'd react, but this was one of those moments when their history was forgotten. She gave in to the kiss, and they stood like that, kissing across the bar, for some time.

His hand touched her face, and he could feel her shudder.

*

He walked back into his apartment at some time after three a.m. Jacket on the hook in the hallway beside the map of old Rotterdam, keys tossed onto the small table, into the open-plan. Curtains open, the room illuminated as ever by the lights of the Science Centre across the river.

Edelman was asleep on the sofa and did not stir. Buchan paused for a moment, and then walked to the window and looked down on the river. He had no idea how he was feeling. Maybe he should have stayed, but the chances were that Janey would wake up in the morning, and the memory of this evening, whatever it was that had led her to wait for him, to kiss him across the bar, and to invite him back to her apartment, would've been long gone. Discomfort and confusion would have followed. They had such a callous way of hurting each other.

In any event, he was tired, and he was due to meet Blake Philips, the cinematographer, at his house the following morning. Eight a.m. He had a reason to go to bed, because he had reason enough to get up early. Less than five hours away.

He turned, Edelman finally lifted his head as he walked past, he leant over the back of the sofa and scratched his head, said, 'Sorry, furball, I'll feed you in the morning before I go out,' and then he headed into the bedroom, tossed his phone on the bed, remembering to set an alarm, got undressed, and walked naked into the bathroom to brush his teeth.

12

Don't think about Janey.

Philips lived out beyond Rutherglen, up the East Kilbride Road, down to the top of the hill above Cambuslang. Buchan parked the Facel by the pavement, got out, and stood looking around the quiet, suburban street in the grey light of a January morning. A little more of a chill than they'd had all winter.

Large Victorian houses on either side, and Buchan briefly wondered how much something like this cost now, then he swung open the low, black, wrought-iron gate, and walked up the path to the front door. The garden on either side was unkempt, featuring the wasted dull weeds of winter, but the house itself was in good condition.

Buchan stopped at the door, thought about rapping it loudly, then went for the more prosaic pressing of the bell, and took a step back. Aware of music playing somewhere inside, though it was quiet enough to sound distant and vague, then it was drowned by a passing car.

He had primed himself to deal with aggression, his limited interaction with Philips so far leading him to think it likely. Some people did not take to police interest in their lives, regardless of the circumstances, the police being expected to take care of crime in a vacuum, leaving the witnesses and bystanders of the world untroubled.

More than likely, him being in the police had nothing to do with it. Philips sounded like he was liable to object to anyone who attempted to insert themselves into his life, regardless of the circumstances.

He rang the bell again, taking another small step away. A quiet road, now the only sound of traffic was a low rumble, far in the distance. The music came into focus again, and then for the first time, for reasons that he couldn't understand, he felt the hairs stand on the back of his neck.

He waited, couldn't help himself glancing over his shoulder, then he stepped forward and listened more closely at the door, allowing the tune playing quietly inside to become clearer.

The hairs on his neck did not settle. He recognised what he was listening to, although he had obviously subconsciously already known.

He rarely said the work fuck, but now it came softly from his lips.

He took the small lockpick from his pocket, worked the lock, and let himself into the house. Closed the door, and stood for a moment in the quiet.

A regulation hallway, stairs leading up to the left, rooms off to both the left and the right. The music, *Corran's Theme*, was playing upstairs.

He knew Philips did not live alone, and this was also giving him an ill feeling. If someone had come for Philips, then what had happened to Philips' wife?

'Bugger it,' he said quietly to the house, then he walked down the long hallway, deciding to start the search in the kitchen. Things happened in kitchens, partly because they contained so many means to commit murder. Ultimately, though, this search would end upstairs, where the music was playing.

The kitchen was large and modern, with a door leading out to a conservatory. By the sink an unwashed coffee cup, and an empty bowl. There was a coffee percolator still switched on, the room infused with the smell of it. There remained plenty of coffee in the container.

He turned quickly, walked back through a different doorway into a small dining room, then through to the sitting room at the front of the house. Nothing untoward, no sign of upset or distress, then back out into the hallway. Nothing in the room opposite, and then he walked quickly up the stairs, two at a time.

The music louder now, coming from an open door at the end of the hallway. The haunting voices that he'd already listened to so much in the last two days, the sound beginning to plague him.

He pushed the door open, then stopped just inside, looking at the floor.

He'd only seen a small photograph of Philips when he'd

---

looked at his career on the Internet, but he had no doubt this was him.

The music was coming from a small speaker placed on a white wooden chest of drawers. The same version of *Corran's Theme* that had been left playing to accompany Harptree's death.

The room had been given a washed-out, nautical theme, at odds with the décor he'd seen so far, and with the house's location, forty miles from the sea. White furniture, white wooden floorboards, one large pale rug, two maps and one nautical chart on the wall, plus a painting of an old packet ship. The curtains and bedspread were matching, elegant, pale, cream and blue that could have been a Rothko painting.

Everything about the room served to emphasise the splay of blood. Philips had been stabbed in the face and twice in the chest. In the mass of blood, it was possible there were other wounds. The body had been left by the foot of the bed, lying flat on his back, arms and legs laid out neatly to the side.

Buchan stood for a moment, taking as much of the scene in as possible. There was plenty of blood on the floor, and he made sure not to step in it as he walked to the chest of drawers to turn off the music. Having done that, the corpse now no more than a couple of yards away, he stood in silence listening to the house. No sign nor sound of Mrs Philips.

The door to the ensuite was open, he finally dragged his eyes away from the victim, walked into the bathroom, confirmed there was no one there, then came back through to the bedroom. Stepping carefully between the spatters he approached Philips, laying his fingers gently against his neck.

As he did so he got a flashback to when he'd had to do the same thing on discovering the corpse of the famous writer. Then, as now, it felt like failure. Arriving at the scene of the crime too late. Another murder occurring during an investigation, another murder that would not have happened if they'd been able to quickly find an answer.

Unlike Malcolm Ritter, however, who'd been dead for a couple of hours by the time they found him, Philips had not been dead long, his corpse still with the residue of some warmth.

He stepped back, took his phone from his pocket, turning his head away from the corpse. The wound in the forehead, the two brutal wounds in the chest. Worst of all, the open eyes, staring blankly at the world. Face at peace, piercing green eyes having lost the lustre they would have had only an hour earlier.

'Boss,' said Kane, answering the call.

'I'm at Philips' place,' said Buchan, his voice dull, so that Kane knew from the first word he was calling with bad news. 'Dead. No sign of the wife. Can you ramp it up?'

'No faked suicide this time?'

'Definitely not a faked suicide,' said Buchan grimly.

'Boss,' said Kane.

'Thanks, Sam,' said Buchan.

He hung up. Hesitated for a moment, but then ultimately chose to leave the room without looking back over his shoulder. It wasn't as though Philips was going anywhere.

13

She was on the sofa, curled almost into a foetal position, clutching a cushion between her chest and her knees. There had been no words, no gasps, no tears. She had returned to her house from a regular early morning run. The police presence had already been in place. She had gone immediately into semi-power save mode, shutting down all emotion until she knew what it was about, and how the other side of it was going to look. She'd been ushered into her own house, having persuaded the duty constable she belonged there, she'd been shown into her own sitting room, and Buchan had given her the grim news. He had not yet allowed her to see her husband's corpse. Not that she'd asked. As he was reporting the minimum amount of detail about the murder, she'd lifted the cushion next to her, and then, almost in slow motion, she had curled herself around it.

'You're out every morning at this time?' asked Buchan.

She showed no signs of having heard him. Her expression had been set before entering the room, and now she was staring straight ahead, her eyes resting on nothing.

He gave her some more time. They were alone in the room, although the hubbub of noise continued around them, in the corridor, in the kitchen and up the stairs.

'You're out every morning at this time?'

Her lips parted slightly. A precursor to words that were not ready to come. Buchan waited.

'*Sure, Frank*,' cut through the sounds from upstairs.

Her lips moved, her eyes did not change focus.

'No.'

Her voice sounded stronger than he'd been expecting. Strong enough to allow him to hope she would continue talking, but that was all she said.

'What time did you leave the house?'

Another pause. Nothing would come quickly. Eventually,

'Just after seven.'

'There was no one else here when you left?'

A step into another vacuum. There was a clock ticking loudly somewhere in the room, but Buchan didn't scan the shelves to see.

Finally, for the first time since he'd sat down, she seemed to notice he was there, that the questions had been coming from another living person in the room, and her head shifted a little, her eyes moved, and she looked at him.

'Sorry?'

'There was no one else here when you left?' asked Buchan.

Another pause, and then, 'Adam. Adam was here. He's not... Adam's not dead, is he?'

'Adam?'

'Yes.'

'Who's Adam?'

'He was here,' she said, without really answering the question.

'Adam was here at seven a.m.?'

'He stayed over. He was with us for a couple of days. He and Blake were discussing a project.' She seemed to finally focus on Buchan, as though only just realising the implications of her husband being dead while there was a guest in the house.

'Sorry, where is Adam?' she asked. 'Have you spoken to Adam?'

She lifted her head to look over her shoulder, and then slowly sat up, beginning the process of detaching herself from the cushion.

'Wait, where is he?'

'Adam's not here,' said Buchan. 'There's no sign of him.'

There had been evidence of someone sleeping in the spare room, but none of whom it might have been. They'd been assuming that possibly the couple had slept in different rooms.

'That...'

The words ran out.

'Adam was here when you left?' asked Buchan.

'Of course.'

'You saw him?'

'Yes,' she said, her voice now with the annoyance of confusion. 'He was already up, making coffee in the kitchen when I came downstairs. We talked... we just talked for a few minutes. Not even that. Then I went out. Are you sure he's not

65

here? Something must have happened to him.'

'There's no sign of him,' said Buchan.

The confusion on her face grew stronger. She looked questioningly at Buchan.

'What?' she said.

*

Buchan and Kane were back at HQ, having stopped off to brief Liddell, on their way to the mortuary. Liddell was sitting back, arms folded, tapping an unlit cigarette, held between two fingers, against the maroon wool of her warm, winter sweater.

'And this Adam Zelinger had worked on *Beware The Watcher*?'

'He was the assistant director,' said Buchan, and then at the look on her face, he continued, 'The man who –'

'Or woman,' chipped in Kane.

'The AD,' said Buchan, 'is the person who runs the show on the ground. The director says they want whatever set up, and the AD's the one who makes sure it actually happens. And they might be in charge of filming filler scene shots, that kind of thing.'

An hour earlier Buchan had learned what the tasks of an assistant director entailed, and now he was explaining it to someone, not a situation that was ever likely to make him feel very comfortable. At least it was not, as far as they were aware at this stage, of particular importance.

'Agnes spoke to him yesterday. Said he was a little cagey. Could have been because he's who we're looking for, or it could have been he just didn't like talking to the police. Or didn't want people to know he was discussing some project they considered top secret.'

'When, of course, we couldn't care less,' tossed in Kane.

'So, Zelinger was looking to take a step up to being a director,' he continued. 'He'd identified a project he wanted to work on. We've looked into it already, and it checks out. A feature film based on a novel called *Alice On The Shore*, and he'd asked Blake Philips to be cinematographer.'

'Were they filming already or…?'

'That prospect remains some way in the future,' said Buchan, drily, 'and not just because Philips is dead and Zelinger's disappeared. So, Zelinger turned up two days ago.

They had dinner the first night, Mrs Philips said the two men stayed up late talking about their thing. Same thing yesterday during the day, same thing last night. She'd said she was going to go running this morning, something she does every few days. Husband never went with her. Zelinger was in the kitchen making coffee when she got downstairs, they spoke briefly, they said they'd all eat breakfast together around nine.'

'Any sign of disagreement between them? Between the men, I mean.'

'She said it'd all been amicable. I guess if it hadn't, why would Zelinger wait around?'

'Were they old friends?'

'They'd only just met while working on *Watcher*. She said her husband had invited Zelinger down for a couple of days so he could get to know him, decide if he liked the cut of his jib. Things seemed to be going OK, although Philips had so far been non-committal on whether he was actually going to do the job, or just suggest some apprentice of his take it.'

'You believe her?'

Buchan took a moment to answer, glancing at Kane as he did so.

'Impossible to tell yet, ma'am,' said Buchan, deciding not to leave the reply to Kane. Her impressions of the new widow were largely second-hand, after all. 'Something's happened to Zelinger. If he and Philips fell out, he could have killed him and done a runner. Or perhaps the wife is lying about their level of amicability. Or maybe she's lying to set Zelinger up, either because she doesn't like him, or to distance herself from the whole affair, when in fact she's bang smack in the middle of it.'

'In short, still too many options,' said Liddell, nodding along in agreement. 'That's reasonable. Try and narrow it down a little further by the time we get to COB, please, inspector.'

'Will do,' said Buchan.

'And when Constable Roth spoke to him yesterday, that was about Daniel Harptree's involvement with *Watcher*?'

'That's correct. She reported that Zelinger remembered Harptree being on set, but claimed not to have talked to him beyond a brief introduction. His exact quote was, when you're the AD you don't have time to take a piss, never mind get into idle chitchat.'

'Good to know,' said Liddell. 'That aside, did Agnes take anything away from the conversation?'

'Nothing, ma'am,' said Kane. 'There are so many calls at this stage, and she said his was not one that stood out.'

'OK, thanks, Samantha.'

Liddell took a look at the window, a brief glance at what there was of a January day outside, and then she turned back to Buchan.

'Well, that's a composer and a cinematographer on the list,' said Liddell, her tone dry, 'one step nearer setting up the Arts Crime Division, Inspector. I'll leave you to it,' and she nodded in the direction of the door.

Buchan gave her a rueful look, turned to the door, held it open for Kane to go first, and then followed her out into the short corridor.

'Arts Crime Division?' asked Kane, as they headed for the stairs.

'Don't ask.'

'She wants a specialist division for all those times people glue themselves to the walls beside the Dali in Kelvingrove?'

'Don't encourage her,' said Buchan. 'Or them.'

*

'Work colleagues talk about your husband as being pugnacious,' Buchan had said to Mrs Philips. He'd had plenty of time during their interview, her on the sofa with her loosening grip on the cushion, to think of how to diplomatically put that question to the widow. He'd settled on pugnacious, rather than obnoxious, angry, repugnant or *such a total asshole*, all of which had been said about him by others who'd worked on the set of *Watcher*.

'Is that the word they used?' she'd said.

Acceptance was creeping across her, insinuating into her, making conversation slightly easier, questions answered more readily.

'Something like that,' said Buchan.

'If I had one word to describe Blake it would be *argument*. Everything about him was an argument. Everything he did, everything he thought, everything that happened to him. Blake disagreed with everyone else's opinion. And it was abstruse, he wasn't arguing for the sake of it. It wasn't that he'd argue white or black, depending on what you said. If you said something was black, and it obviously was black, he'd be annoyed that you pointed out the obvious, and he'd take you to task, likely arguing along the way that it wasn't black anyway, and nor was it white, but in fact it was two-point-three, or it was a tetrahedron, or it was Michelle Yeoh in *Crouching Tiger*.' She'd stopped for a moment, aware that she wasn't particularly making sense, then she'd added, 'Like I say, abstruse.'

'Must have been tough to live with.'

She'd stared at him for a while, then slowly her eyes had drifted away to the carpet. An air of defeat and sadness had fallen across her face.

'Sometimes I enjoyed it,' she'd said eventually.

14

'This is your cause of death,' said Donoghue, just the hint of glibness in her tone. She was indicating the stab in the face. Neither Buchan nor Kane responded. The wound was just below the cheek. 'Upwards motion with a long-bladed knife.'

'How long?'

'Eight inches,' said Donoghue and Kane was nodding.

'Ties in with the missing knife from the set in the kitchen.'

'So, a stab in the face here isn't necessarily going to be fatal,' said Donoghue, 'but like I said, upwards motion, long blade thrust into the hilt, the knife deeply penetrated the brain then exited the skull.'

Buchan hadn't noticed the exit wound when he'd stood next to the corpse, but then he hadn't examined it too closely, and hadn't spent any further time in the bedroom once he'd called in the incident.

'These two were post-mortem?' asked Buchan, indicating the stabs to the chest.

'Yes,' said Donoghue, 'by a few minutes. You know how the murder played out?'

'Not yet.'

'Too early for me to add to your lack of knowledge, I'm afraid. The killer achieved their aims with the first blow, so why they then stabbed him twice in the chest shortly afterwards, I don't yet know. Hatred maybe. Another couple of stabs for good measure, the pleasure of it. I don't think there's any attempt at a hoodwink, because I'm not sure what difference it makes to our thinking. In any case, presumably these people watch shows. They *know* we're going to know the two chest wounds are post-mortem, so why bother?'

Buchan and Kane stood staring at the wounds in the chest.

'I like hatred,' said Kane. A brief pause, and then a slightly rueful, 'It's what I'd do.'

'Good to know, Sergeant,' said Donoghue.

Nothing ever changed about Donoghue's workplace. Everything where it always was, and where it was meant to be. Everything tidy. The only things on the walls were instructions, aimed at anyone other than Donoghue who might be working in here. And playing from the PA system, the Beatles. Always the Beatles.

For some reason Bob Dylan was singing. Had been since they got in. Buchan asked the question with a small movement of his head in the direction of the ceiling.

'The Traveling Wilburys,' said Donoghue.

'What does that mean?'

'Do you live on earth, Inspector?' asked Donoghue. 'I mean, if you were twenty, then I'd understand. I wouldn't expect Constable Roth to necessarily know, but you must be sixty by now, right?'

Buchan was forty-eight. He answered with an eyebrow.

'They were a band,' said Donoghue. 'George started them. Dylan was in the band.'

'Good to know,' said Buchan. 'How about this? The murder takes place in the ensuite, or elsewhere upstairs. The killer leaves the body, goes and does whatever. Searches through drawers, I don't know, something. He comes back, he decides for whatever reason to drag the body through to the bedroom, and he thinks, I don't want to touch it. Maybe he doesn't have gloves. Stands behind the corpse, leans over, two knives into the chest, then he drags the corpse through to the bedroom.'

Donoghue was staring at the two wounds.

'You would have noticed that,' said Buchan, his tone and words giving her the obvious out.

'I had,' she said. 'I was just about to examine those two wounds properly. I'd thought, at first glance, that the killer had stabbed the corpse from behind, dragging the knife out harshly towards himself thus causing the extra damage, but I wasn't sure if the damage, on first inspection, fit that narrative. I'll look into it further, and get back to you. If it is as you suggest, then we'll have two different knives, and that should be quite evident.'

'But then,' said Kane, 'didn't the splay of blood in the bedroom indicate that was where the murder took place?'

Buchan nodded, the words *you're right* on his lips.

They all stood for a moment, staring at the chest wounds. Around them *Tweeter And The Monkey Man* finally came to an end, with *Hey Jude* kicking off in its place after a brief silence.

'Would it be wrong to observe,' said Kane, 'that this man was prodigiously well endowed?'

Buchan couldn't help but make the glance down the length of the naked body, although it was not something he'd failed to notice already.

'Good spot, Sergeant,' he said. 'That's the sharp eye for detail that keeps you in a job.'

Buchan and Donoghue shared a glance, the doctor ending it with a small movement of her head in the direction of the door.

'I'll keep you posted,' she said, and then Buchan and Kane turned away.

As they passed through the door, Kane shook her head and let out a low whistle.

'Wow,' she said. 'That is not something you see every day, boss.'

'We've moved on, Sam, we've moved on.'

15

Buchan was on a video call with a member of the Serious Crime Unit team through in Edinburgh. It was possible Zelinger had just turned into their prime suspect, but at the moment there wasn't nearly enough information. Nevertheless, the other options – that Zelinger had also been killed, and his corpse removed, or that Mrs Philips was involved, or that Zelinger just happened to have lied to her about eating breakfast together, and had in fact left the house to go home, just before the killer arrived – all had the air of the unlikely, or possibly even the fantastical.

'Nothing here, sir,' said Sgt Rogan.

She was standing in the lounge in Zelinger's apartment, an open-plan layout through to the kitchen, not unlike Buchan's own place. As she swept the camera around the room, in the distance Buchan caught the blur of Arthur's Seat in the drizzle through a large window. The apartment was orderly to the point of not really looking like anyone lived there. Again, not so different from Buchan's own place, he thought.

'When was the last time he was there, d'you think?'

'Impossible to say.'

She turned the camera back on herself. She was Buchan's age, and from this distance, she looked far more engaged, far less tired than Buchan ever looked when he was on the job.

'Bethan has just spoken to one of the neighbours, and she said he's not around much. They never hear anything from the apartment. I guess his is the kind of job that involves a lot of travel.'

'Could she remember the last time she'd seen him or heard him?'

'A few days ago. Met him in the lift. They didn't speak other than hello.'

'OK. Don't suppose he has anything so old fashioned as an

answer machine?'

She answered with a smile, and a small head shake. 'And no computer lying around either. I guess he'll work on a laptop, and take it around with him.'

'No home movie editing equipment, anything like that?'

'Nope.'

Buchan let out a long sigh. Sitting in the car, Kane having returned to the office, about to head off to his next port of call.

'We've got the paperwork in place to get a camera installed outside the apartment door, so we'll know if he comes back,' said Rogan. 'We'll keep an eye on the building until we get that set up.'

'OK, thanks, Ro, appreciate it.'

She nodded, he returned the small gesture, then ended the call.

He laid the phone on the passenger seat, took a moment to consider where they were in relation to looking for Zelinger – Kane had taken charge of that angle of the operation, and had initiated the countrywide search for Zelinger and his white Tesla Model S – and then he pulled on his seatbelt, started the engine, and moved slowly out onto the road.

*

He was heading back down the M8 to the film studio to speak to Adrian Goddard, the director of *Beware The Watcher*. When Buchan had called him to establish his whereabouts, Goddard had cursed. Buchan could picture his ill-kempt teeth, his lips in a snarl.

'Blake Philips is dead,' Buchan had said sharply, before Goddard could progress to objecting about Buchan once again interrupting his work. After the necessary *What?* and the equally frequently used, *I don't understand*, Goddard had finally accepted the news with the words, 'Dear Blake...' spoken wistfully, as though Philips had finally succumbed to consumption while attempting to recuperate beside a Swiss lake.

'Not another suicide?' Goddard had said.

'One hundred per cent not a suicide,' Buchan had replied, stopping himself saying anything blunter.

Goddard had relented, albeit it wasn't as though Buchan had been giving him any choice.

He had a team, and there were lots of different ways to

communicate, and so he didn't need to go driving all around the city, one side to the other, north to south, east to west, but there were two advantages to it. He could never get enough of driving the Facel; and he got to think. Thinking was underestimated, thought Buchan, only to be discouraged when it had actively replaced doing. No matter how much thinking you did, at some point you had to do something as a result of it.

As he ran the current status of the investigation through the internal computer, Oscar Peterson was playing. *Night Train*, an album he'd first discovered twenty-five years earlier through the instrumental version of Hoagy's *Georgia On My Mind* that he thought the finest recorded.

Two murders, undeniably linked to the TV series, *Beware The Watcher*. A show about a serial killer. They had no idea where or when the killings would stop, but these weren't likely to be the random acts of a psychopath. This was a killer with intent. Currently, however, there were so many leads, so many characters in play, that it was as yet impossible to discern what the intent might have been.

Was the repeated use of the music a clue to the motive, or nothing more than an embellishment? Someone from within the film and television business attempting flamboyance? After Harptree's murder, it had seemed it might be related. The composer killed, listening to his own music. Now, however, Buchan feared they were just dealing with someone showing, in their own estimation at least, artistic flair.

For all they could attempt to pin down everyone who might reasonably have been able to recreate the music, it was clearly a long list. And since they had no idea with whom Harptree might have shared the piece, quite possibly an incomplete one.

Buchan parked in the familiarly empty carpark at the Stillwood Film Studios, checked his phone to make sure nothing needed his attention, then he walked quickly across the carpark.

There were two men standing outside the building, one of them smoking, looking back at the entrance. An air about them that suggested they were more important than what they were looking at, thought Buchan. As he walked quickly by, he caught a snippet of a line, '… test case, but this is it around here, so we take it or leave it…' and then he was at the door, and the men were behind him, and Buchan was standing at reception, a quick conversation, and then he was walking along short corridors, and soon enough he was being shown back into the same editing room in which he'd been the day before.

Goddard, the director, and the editor Stanley Crow, turned to look at him as he entered. Above the editing room there'd been a red light showing, indicating work was taking place and that the room shouldn't be disturbed, so they were quick to anger at the interruption, and then backed down when they saw Buchan.

Crow leant over the console and pressed pause, the music that'd been playing stopped instantly, the pictures on the three side-by-side screens froze mid-frame. A sweeping vista of a Scottish glen. It might have been the Highlands, but since the show was set in Glasgow, quite possibly somewhere closer. Enjoy the Highlands though he did, the hills and glens all pretty much looked the same to Buchan.

'Inspector,' said Goddard. He looked as though he was about to offer Buchan a seat, but the quick glance around the room revealed none spare. 'Shall we go elsewhere?'

'This is fine,' said Buchan. 'I've just got a few questions about Blake Philips, and about how his murder might relate to that of Daniel Harptree.'

'You're absolutely sure Blake was murdered?' said Crow.

'Knife to the face,' said Buchan, mimicking the stabbing movement, 'entering through the cheek and piercing the brain from below, then two knife wounds in the chest.'

Goddard closed his eyes, his hand drifting somewhere near his mouth. Crow was a different matter, however. There was something in the eyes, and Buchan could tell he was one of those who found the description of brutal murder at least a little exhilarating.

'Dear God,' said Goddard.

'Any hint to the killer's identity?' asked Crow.

'Not as yet,' said Buchan, 'but we are interested in speaking to Adam Zelinger.'

Goddard's shoulders straightened a little, and again Buchan noted the zeal with which Crow heard this news. Crow was a man who enjoyed true crime and, even more than that, seemed to be quite happy to be in the middle of it.

'What does Adam have to do with this?' asked Goddard.

'You know Mr Zelinger well, I presume, since you've worked together a few times?'

'Yes, of course. Any director would be happy to work with Adam. From day one, every shoot with which he's involved runs like absolute clockwork. Really, what does Adam have to do with any of this?'

'He's missing.'

Goddard looked disbelieving, then inevitably said, 'What?'

'Adam Zelinger is missing.'

'That's ridiculous.'

Goddard took a phone from his pocket, quickly dialled a number and held the phone to his ear, looking at Buchan with disdain. A moment, and then he lowered the phone, looked at it in the same way he'd been regarding Buchan, said, 'He's probably working on something,' then returned the phone to his pocket.

'Did Adam have any working relationship with Daniel Harptree?' asked Buchan, having watched the small performance play out.

Goddard employed a familiar confused look, then shook his head. 'No. I mean, why would they have, they're involved in two completely separate parts of the process?'

'They'd never worked on the same project before?'

Goddard looked non-plussed to be even asked the question, glanced at Crow to include him in his bewilderment, then turned back to Buchan, confusion intact.

'I don't know. I just don't, but I can hardly think... Why would they even? And I have no idea why you would expect me to know. You do realise that we're not one giant company, one big family of happy artists who all know what the other is up to? This isn't the nineteen-thirties Hollywood studio system.'

Buchan switched his look to Crow without comment.

'You have anything?' he asked. 'You know of any connection between Zelinger and either Harptree or Philips?'

He was shaking his head before Buchan had finished asking the question. In response, Buchan nodded away his own impatience, aware that he hadn't made any kind of breakthrough yet. Nothing gained, nothing to even set them on a path. People getting murdered, the police directionless.

'Let's talk about the relationship between Daniel Harptree and Blake Philips,' he said.

The two men stared blankly back.

'They've been murdered,' said Buchan. 'These two men, who worked on the same television production, are dead. The killer, for reasons we're not yet aware of, left the killer's theme from the show playing beside the corpses.'

'Really?' said Crow, again his face lighting up with some strange enthusiasm. 'They also did that with Blake?'

Buchan held his gaze long enough that the look on Crow's face faded, although the light was clearly still in the eyes. The thrill of it. The work of the killer, the game he was playing.

There was absolute quiet in the room. It was an editing suite, after all, perfectly soundproofed. Nothing from outside, complete stillness inside.

Goddard held Buchan's gaze for a moment, and then turned to take a quick glance at Crow.

'That's…,' he began, then his eyes widened slightly in the way Crow's had done.

'That's?' said Buchan.

'I don't think I should say it.'

'Jesus, Mr Goddard, we need to get on here, so please. No one's judging anyone else.'

That wasn't true, but it hardly mattered.

'Artistic,' said Goddard.

'What?'

'That's artistic.'

'What is?'

'The music playing beside both corpses.'

'Yes,' said Crow, nodding along.

'Almost as though the killer is planning their true crime drama. They're creating the piece.'

'An *Only Murders in The Building* type of thing.'

'What?' said Buchan. 'What are you talking about?'

'The Hulu show, *Only Murders in The Building*,' said Crow. 'It's a show about true crime podcasts, where the people making the podcast actually get involved in actual crime.'

'*Actually* get involved in *actual* crime?' said Buchan.

'Look, I'm an editor, not a writer, right?'

'Jesus,' said Buchan, and his eyes dropped for a moment. He wasn't going to bring up what Crow had told Kane about writing scripts.

He knew Liddell was teasing with her line about setting up an Arts Crime Division, but if there ever was such a section at the SCU, Buchan would instantly ask for a transfer. He'd rather deal with benefit fraud, regardless of how dull that might be.

The day-to-day artifice and thuggery of crime he could handle. Artists and their whims were getting tiring. When it came down to it, people were still getting murdered. There was still blood, and there were still bodies.

'So, if we can think about the original question,' he said, little expectation in his voice, 'Philips and Harptree have both been murdered. The cinematographer and the composer. The playing of the music directly links both these murders to this show. So, in what way might those two men have been involved with one another workwise?'

'They weren't!' said Goddard. 'I keep saying.'

'Wouldn't you have scenes,' said Buchan, 'where camera angle, camera placement, or whatever, is perfectly aligned with the music?' He wasn't really sure what he was talking about as he asked the question, how the editing of a scene fitted into the process.

'Hello,' said Goddard.

'Like, yeah, hello,' said Crow.

'You do realise filmmaking is a team effort,' said Goddard.

'So, the camera guy and the music guy could work together?'

'Except they usually don't,' said Goddard, 'and in this instance, I can confirm, they definitely didn't. Yes, of course we have alignment between sound and film, which is more or less what you're talking about, but that,' and he waved at the screens beside them, 'that's what you've blundered into here. That idea, where you have the perfect moment, the perfect camera angle juxtaposed against the perfect piece of music, that could have come from the writer, or from me, or from Stanley, or Daniel or even Blake, but ultimately, Blake had his job on set, and once it's done, it's done. He's here,' he said, holding his left hand out to the side, 'while Daniel is here,' his right hand held away to the other side.

Buchan glanced at Crow to see if he had anything to add, and the editor sort of shrugged in response. Still enjoying it, thought Buchan.

'Mr Philips seemed to be a particular type of person,' said Buchan. 'Very argumentative.'

'Yes, of course,' said Goddard. 'Fierce. And look, I know what you're going to say. The difference between a bully and someone who demands high standards is often, well, not even paper-thin, it can be entirely dependent on perspective. And there will be plenty who thought Blake a bully. And if not, very difficult. But he was one of the best, he really was. People might not have enjoyed the process, but they were always happy with the result. I liked to equate it with a ketogenic diet, or going running every morning at five a.m. Not enjoyable in any way whatsoever, but one feels the benefits.'

'Taking Daniel Harptree out of the equation, did Philips get into any arguments on the set of *The Watcher* that might have spilled over? Anything that got out of hand?'

'They never got out of hand,' said Goddard. 'I mean, in the moment they could be dreadfully heated, but that was just Blake. A firebrand.'

'What about these constant arguments between the producers?'

'No, that wasn't for Blake. He was completely separate. He was like the Franco-Thai war during World War Two. Yes it happened, yes it was brutal, but it wasn't actually anything to do with this other bigger, even more brutal thing that was happening here.'

Another line of questioning going nowhere. A glance at Crow brought a similar look as before. Nothing to say on the matter.

'So, neither of you have any idea why these two men have been murdered?'

'I wish I did, inspector,' said Goddard, 'I truly do.'

Crow with the same gesture as before.

'Well, you know what this means then,' said Buchan, deciding to stick a knife in the balloon of Goddard's fascination and Crow's delight in the whole thing. 'If someone is randomly picking off senior crew members from the production of *The Watcher*, that puts you two in the firing line. You might want to watch your backs.'

In response, he got the looks he might have expected, had he thought about it. Goddard swallowed, and instantly paled. Crow straightened a little, but the light did not leave his eyes. That he might be on a hitlist seemed as exciting to him as the murders so far. Perhaps he felt impregnable. He was certainly young enough for that kind of hubristic invincibility. Perhaps he had some other reason for knowing he wasn't in any danger, albeit Buchan currently had zero reason to suspect him.

'Why would somebody…,' began Goddard, but the words trailed away, as though he suddenly couldn't bring himself to refer to the murders.

'That's why we're here, Mr Goddard.'

Another gaze across a short distance, then Goddard's eyes

80

fell away. He noticed Crow glance to the side, looking at nothing, and Buchan wondered if he was speaking internally to an invisible camera.

16

Driving around in the Facel had been enjoyable in itself, but it was time to be back at the office, to make a reassessment of where they were, a meeting with the team in the ops room set for twenty minutes. Standing at the window, his familiar spot, looking out on the river. Trying not to think about Janey. Trying not to think about last night. Trying not to think about what came next, because previous experience suggested that what came next was regret and an even greater distancing than before.

It was a nothing day, the kind of nothing day you get in Scotland at any time of the year. The January nothing days just seemed worse here than anywhere else.

'What do I know of nothing days in Hawaii and Wengen?' he muttered to himself, before putting the cup of coffee to his lips.

'Talking to yourself again, sir?'

He glanced to his left, smiled, shook his head.

Constable Roth had joined him at his spot, as she often did, coffee in hand. Pink hair spiked more prominently today, oversized white T-shirt protruding from beneath a black sweatshirt with the Boston Red Sox logo. Since it was just the logo, with no team name, Buchan didn't know what it represented.

'Beautiful day,' said Buchan, indicating the grey January day outside.

'Isn't it?'

'You getting anywhere?' he asked.

He wasn't sure that he had finished thinking. The internal monologue maybe hadn't been going anywhere, but he'd been enjoying the space. But then, he'd come to the office, and made himself available for conversation. If he'd wanted to drink coffee in solitude while looking at the river, he could've sat in the jigsaw man's café.

'Kicking myself about Zelinger,' she said. 'Should have made more of it.'

'You highlighted him, he was on the list,' said Buchan, not wanting to linger on it. 'It's unavoidably been a long list. What else?'

'Been calling around the crew of the show,' she said. 'Any connection between Philips and Harptree. No one has anything specific, I'm afraid. No one can put them in the same room at the same time. Not even in the same e-mail chain. A couple of people did draw the one obvious comparison, however.'

'They were both quick to temper,' said Buchan, nodding.

'Exactly. Even then, though, they still drew a distinct line between Harptree's occasionally comic or drunken cantankerousness, and what a few observed as Philips' frequent downright nastiness.'

'A mean streak'

Roth nodded, took another drink of coffee, and said, 'Yep, I heard that a few times.'

Buchan took another drink, let his eyes drift along the queue of traffic on Clyde Street on the other side of the river.

'You suppose someone fell out badly enough with both men that they decided to take revenge upon them?'

'No,' said Roth. 'I mean, obviously, it wouldn't be the most ridiculous thing, but as we've previously discussed, in real life, people don't usually murder for trivial reasons, and killing someone because they were mean to you is pretty trivial. And, especially in the case of Daniel Harptree, his mean streak appears to have been not that far removed from the level of an American sitcom.'

'What about this novel,' asked Buchan, 'the *Watcher* novel? Now that there's been another murder, are there any similarities we could be looking at?'

'Well, actually, and sorry if I sound like a try-hard here, sir, but I read it last night.'

'Didn't you read it the day before?'

He glanced at her. He never ceased to be surprised by Roth's capacity to read fiction, because he himself could never see the point in it.

'I skimmed it then just to remind myself about the basics. I thought I should read the whole thing, you know, to get into the detail.'

'And?'

'I'd forgotten, it's a women's skin type of plot. I mean, like low-key the most generic serial killer thing on earth, but, like I said, perhaps that was part of its appeal. Every cliché in the book.'

'Women's skin?'

'The killer …'

'The police officer?'

'The police officer, yes, he likes to flay his victims, then he drapes their skin around mannequins in his garage. He has a kind of museum of them in there.'

Buchan took a drink of coffee, his eyes back on the cold water of the Clyde.

'In short,' said Roth, 'beyond the presence of a killer, it really couldn't be further from what we're looking at here.'

'Nothing in the fine detail?'

'Not so that I could draw any worthwhile correlation.'

'It's not set in Glasgow, is it?' said Buchan. 'I mean, that doesn't really sound like a Glasgow type of crime?'

'Oh no, it's in Philadelphia. This won't be the first time Glasgow's doubled for Philadelphia in movies. Don't know if they've done any exteriors in the suburbs out there. But looking at the cast, they obviously got a lot of American actors across for it. Not really sure how that all worked out, like, how it comes to be a British production.'

Buchan took another drink of coffee, annoyed at himself for not knowing more about the show itself.

'But really,' said Roth, as though she could read his mind, 'I don't think the plot of the story is impacting at all on whatever storyline our killer here is intending to create.'

'How about the actual TV show?' asked Buchan. 'They can be quite different to the book, right?' He paused, and then added, 'Look at *Moonraker*.'

He remembered reading *Moonraker* when he was twelve, and hating it for its lack of exotic locations and worse, the absence of space travel.

'Sure, *Moonraker*,' said Roth. 'Terrific book. The best Bond novel, I always thought.'

'You've read the Bond novels?'

Buchan had stopped after *Moonraker*. When he'd been young he'd joke and say he couldn't bear the thought of finding out Bond didn't actually go to the Caribbean in *Thunderball*, or that Goldfinger didn't actually like gold, but in truth he just couldn't be bothered.

'Yeah, they're great. A little racist sometimes, and,' and she whistled, 'they have misogyny coming out of every orifice, but I guess they were of their time.'

They stared at the river for a few moments, silence starting to fall, a lift of the coffee cups in unison, then Roth found she wanted to talk about those old Bond books.

'There's something about action sequences,' she said. 'You know, a sameness, a repetition. No different in books than it is in movies. The real interest comes in character. I always preferred the bits at the start of a Bond novel when he's stuck in London, and we learn about the minutiae of his life. The clubs, the drinking, the cigarettes, the women, the days at work when he's bored, looking through endless reports on some new Russian handgun, or a Chinese coding machine. The trips to the firing range with Tanner, Mrs Maxwell making him breakfast in the morning. I love all that stuff, it was fabulous. And occasionally when you begin with Bond already on location, the action already under way... tragic. I could've read an entire book on Bond being bored in London. *Moonraker* did the best job of that. Never leaves the UK, and at least the first third is in the city. Love it.'

Her enthusiasm sounded so heartfelt, that Buchan suddenly felt the weight of his inadequate twelve-year-old self, who'd been unable to enjoy anything about the story. Maybe it would be different now. Not that he was about to find out.

'Anyway, sorry,' said Roth, and she sort of laughed at herself. 'I'm getting carried away. Doesn't answer the question. I don't know, sir. I have asked a few people and everyone is very cagey about the storyline. Like, very cagey, but I don't think it's related to our murder case. It's got more of an NDA vibe.'

He glanced at her, his blank face asking the question.

'Non-disclosure agreement.'

'Right. Yes, that'd make sense.'

Buchan held her look for a moment, and then turned and looked back over the open-plan. The old familiar scene, a few empty desks, a couple of people talking quietly on the phone, Cherry and Houston chatting across the desk divider, everyone else with their heads down.

'Who was the writer for the TV show?' asked Buchan, the name escaping him. He hadn't spoken to the writer so far.

'Louise,' said Roth. 'Em… Hathaway. Louise Hathaway. I think Sergeant Houston spoke to her, yesterday or today. Maybe both.'

Buchan nodded, looked along the office at Houston, who turned instinctively, although perhaps he'd just heard his name mentioned.

'You've spoken to Louise Hathaway?' asked Buchan.

'Yep, a couple of times. Yesterday afternoon, and this morning after the second murder. She hadn't heard about that one when I called her.'

'She local?'

'Largs,' said Houston. 'Lives in an apartment overlooking the sea. Nice view over to Cumbrae. She showed me on FaceTime.'

'You didn't mention that before,' said Buchan.

'The view?'

'Largs. Same as Daniel Harptree. Seems like that might be a thing.'

'Only found out this morning,' said Houston. 'I met her yesterday in town. She didn't say where she lived, and I didn't ask. It didn't seem relevant at the time. Sorry, sir.'

'No, that's OK, she's hardly a person of interest or anything. Just curious. Did she have anything useful to tell us?'

'Nothing. The conversations were bland enough that they were barely worth reporting.' A pause, and then he felt the need to add, 'Always the possibility she has a good poker face, but so far I don't know of anything to elevate her above the pack.'

'She have anything to say about Harptree, once you learned she lived in the same place?'

'She seemed surprised he lived there. She'd had no idea.'

Buchan turned away, staring blankly out at the river, trying to decide if that sounded contrived. Roth answered it for him.

'Not unreasonable, sir,' she said. 'The writer's part in the process comes before the show's made, the composer's afterwards. No reason why they would have anything to do with each other, and while Largs ain't Shanghai or Delhi, it also ain't a one-street town with four houses.'

'Was she ever on set?' asked Buchan, turning back to Houston.

'Five or six times, she said, but since it was spread over two and a half months, it wasn't so often. She said the script was worked to death, down to the merest detail, before filming started. There was no requirement for her to be there, though she committed to being available for call-ups as and when.'

'And that happened five or six times.'

'Yes.'

'OK, thanks, Ian.'

He took another drink of coffee, he looked at his watch, he turned back to the window. Felt like he'd been all round the houses today, but really he hadn't been travelling too far. Nevertheless, would it be a good use of his time to get back in the car and head down to Largs?

He could ask Houston to do it, to make the point of interviewing face-to-face. He was more likely to pick up any contradictions in what she'd said to him earlier.

'Bugger it,' he muttered, bringing the interaction with Roth back to where it had started, talking to himself.

17

It was already dark by the time he parked opposite the building where Louise Hathaway lived. He should have been here earlier, but he hadn't called ahead in any case, so the time he arrived was of no great importance.

'She virtually never leaves her house,' Houston had said.

'But she visited the set, right? And you spoke to her yesterday in Glasgow?'

'Her words, not mine. I said the same thing. She said she leaves when someone begs her to, and only ever for work purposes. She had a meeting yesterday with some guy about a thing. That's her for the year, she said. Couldn't tell if she was joking.'

Taking her at face value, and presuming he'd find her at home whenever he turned up, Buchan had not only not called ahead, he'd also taken the opportunity to stop off again at the site of Daniel Harptree's murder.

The pier had been desolate and haunting in the half-light of dusk. He could see why it appealed to photographers. The police tape remained across the end of the pier, yet there was a member of the public out there, standing at the edge, looking down into the dark waters of the Clyde.

The young guy had glanced over his shoulder at the sound of the car stopping, but had quickly turned away again, disinterested. Another glance at the sound of the Facel door, again little concern shown.

Buchan had bent beneath the tape and walked the length of the pier.

'What are you doing?' he'd asked.

The young guy had turned. His phone was in his hands, turned on, in camera mode.

'What?'

'You just magically walked through the police tape without

noticing it?'

The kid had smirked, kind of shrugging.

'Big Alan said there was like a thing across there, but, I'm like, when are the police ever actually going to check something like that, right?' A pause, then he'd said, 'Wait, you're not the police though, right?' and he'd laughed.

Buchan had shown him his ID card.

'Fuck.'

'Yeah,' said Buchan, 'fuck. You know there was a murder here two days ago?'

Although the murder had obviously been reported, the police had made sure the exact site had not yet been mentioned. They hadn't wanted even more Instagrammers turning up. Nevertheless, the police guard that had been in place at the site hadn't lasted very long, ending at lunch on the second day. 'Like a test match on a green wicket in September,' Cherry had said.

'A what?'

Buchan didn't reply. He'd obviously heard the question, and he let it stew for a few moments.

'Someone got murdered?'

'Someone got murdered,' repeated Buchan.

'That's nothing to do with me.'

Trying to distance himself so quickly, Buchan wouldn't have been surprised if he'd stepped back off the pier.

'Why are you here?'

'Look at it man. Everyone comes here to take photos. Like, everyone. Like, every Instagrammer I know, it's like their most liked photos come from this spot. Course, in Nelly's case that was 'cause she more or less got her tits out, but even so. Folk love this stuff, they love this, you know, the pier and the sea and the mountains and that.'

'What's your name?'

'Ryan.'

'Ryan?'

'Ryan Jack. Like the footballer.'

Buchan didn't know the footballer.

'Right, Ryan, you can go.'

'You're not arresting me?'

'Why would I arrest you?'

Ryan Jack had stared at him, then pointed over his shoulder.

'I crossed police lines. I don't know, interfering with a

crime scene, something like that.'

'Would you like me to arrest you?'

He'd stopped himself smiling as he'd said it. He never usually had too much trouble stopping himself smiling.

'What? No!'

'You can go,' said Buchan.

The fact that the police guard on the pier had been allowed to leave said it all. There was nothing here that hadn't been examined, everything gleaned from it that there possibly could.

'I can go?'

Buchan had nodded over his shoulder, and the kid had legged it. A brief hesitation during which Buchan could see him pondering what to do with the phone in his hand, then he'd thrust it into his pocket and quickly left the scene. Buchan had turned and watched him, until he was on his bike and cycling away, enough of a look to make sure the kid wouldn't stop and film him.

Then he'd turned back, expelled the short meeting from his thoughts, and relaxed into the quiet of the scene. The wind had barely been blowing, the sea was calm, the wash upon the shore gentle.

Buchan had tried to recapture the moment of the murder. He'd stayed awhile. It had been dark by the time he'd left.

Someone was holding the door open for him, as he surveyed the intercom panel, looking for Hathaway's button.

'Thanks,' he said, as the woman left the building, and Buchan entered. He stood briefly in the foyer, glanced over his shoulder at the woman as she walked through the carpark, unconsciously judged her for having so unquestioningly let him in, and then he walked to the stairs and headed on up, quick now, as he usually was on stairs, taking two at a time.

A short landing on the top floor, only three well-spaced doors, one at either end, one in the middle. He rang the bell and stood back, feeling that vague, familiar sense of discomfort. The cold call. Sure, he was a detective, this was one of the things he did almost every day, but he'd never quite got past the inherent discomfort of being the unexpected and unwanted visitor, turning up to add a little stress or disquiet to someone's life.

As Kane had observed to him on more than one occasion, plenty of people deserved the stress and disquiet.

Buchan got the sense of someone on the other side of the door, of the eye at the peephole, and then the door opened and there was a large woman in her forties framed in the doorway, wearing a long, turquoise floaty dress that seemed to contain all the material in the world. Her hair, dyed blonde and shorn short, did not match the dress in its flamboyance.

'Police?' she said.

Buchan held forward his ID.

'Inspector? Sending the big guns. Did your sergeant register me as a person of interest?'

'I'd just like a word,' said Buchan.

She regarded him with amusement for a moment, and then stood back, ushering him into her apartment.

*

They were sitting at a table by the window. The curtains were open, but darkness and the lights in the room obscured the view. In daylight it would be better, more expansive, than Buchan's view of the Clyde that he enjoyed so much. The firth no more than seventy yards away, stretching across to the Isle of Cumbrae. Sure, this was Scotland, and there were a thousand more spectacular views on offer up the west coast, but this was still a nice place to have an apartment.

There was music playing. Norah Jones. Buchan hadn't listened to Norah Jones since Janey had left. They'd never been so foolishly romantic as to have a song, or an anything really, but they'd listened to Norah together a lot, so many times had she been the soundtrack to a long, flirtatious evening that had ended in the bedroom. Now it was too painful to listen to. He'd tried once, thinking he might enjoy the melancholic nostalgia of it, but he'd barely got three songs in.

Janey never played Norah Jones at the Winter Moon.

'I didn't think Daniel Harptree would commit suicide,' she said. 'It didn't seem right.'

'You knew him well?'

'Didn't know him at all,' said Hathaway. 'Just heard about him, the things people said. Sounded like a bit of an egotistical ass. That kind don't kill themselves, at least not without a moment of self-realisation beforehand.'

'How d'you know he hadn't self-realised?'

'I don't.' A pause, and then, 'Doesn't look like he had now, does it?'

Buchan took a drink of tea. She'd also placed a plate of

91

biscuits on the small table, but he hadn't touched them. They were speaking to him though.

'Tell me about your part in the show,' he said. 'Start to finish.'

'I had this conversation with your sergeant.'

'I know.'

'You're a micro-manager.'

'Maybe. Tell me the thing,' and he made a small gesture to back up his not particularly apt use of the word thing.

'Miriam wrote her book,' said Hathaway, already sounding tired of the explanation, but then, she'd possibly told this story a hundred times to a variety of people, long before anyone had ever been murdered. 'Seems it was quite popular.'

'You read it at the time?'

'Never read that kind of thing. I prefer the likes of Sayaka Murata. You familiar with Murata? Really fucked up.'

'Not so much. Tell me about *The Watcher*.'

'Sure. Miriam's book made a splash, the TV people started getting interested. Way I understand it, she was about to sell the rights to like Prime or something, and then Bennie came along. Collins, Benjamin Collins, you've spoken to him?'

'My sergeant has.'

'Your sergeant talks to a lot of people. What is it you do?'

He answered with a rather tired, can-we-just-get-on gesture.

'Bennie came in with all his Bitcoin ill-gotten gains. I mean, the lad must've made more from crypto than virtually anyone else on earth. He loves *Beware The Watcher*, he fancies it getting made in Scotland. He's a bit rogue, he's off-centre, outside the usual field of players in the business. Something guerrilla about him, you know, and Miriam obviously fell for that crap. Or maybe it was just the money. Anyway, he buys the option, and goes about making his show in Glasgow.'

'Except it's set in Philadelphia.'

She laughed, the laugh gave way to a smile, that eventually died given that she was getting nothing from across the table.

'Sure. Bennie, inevitably, hit the wall of practicality. Money can get you a seat at the table, but if you want anyone to fund your production, if you want anyone to air your show, you have to get buy-in. And when it came to it, the buy-in was only going to come when he agreed that this was an all-American, skin-flaying, serial killer tale. It just plain wasn't going to work in Scotland.'

92

'I thought he had tonnes of money?'

'Sure, but buying into a project is one thing, funding the entire thing on a whim? Production costs, post-production, talent, marketing, the whole shebang? That would've been everything he had. He's naïve, and he's all sorts of things, but he's just not plain stupid. Everything washes down, and we are where we are. He gets to film in Scotland, and use the locations and the new studio up the river, and whatever. He gets to play his part in the great Scottish renaissance. You know he's big on independence, flying the flag and all that. Nice volte-face he made there, you know, in his own head, when he told himself it'd be just as great to have the show set in the US as it was in Scotland. Needs must, et cetera.'

'How did you get the job of adapting the book?'

'Circumstance. I know Bennie from way back.' She paused, the sly smile, Buchan knew what was coming. 'I was his first, you know. I was like ten years older than him... still am, ha... just the one night, you know. But we knew each other through uni, and we kept in touch. Basically, I was the only screenwriter he knew. I thought I might get the boot when the decision was taken to shift focus from Glasgow to Philly, but the Yanks they brought on board liked the script, liked my initial draft when I rewrote it as a US-based drama. They liked the dialogue. Said I'd nailed it. Good thing I'd watched *It's Always Sunny In Philadelphia*, right?'

'How does the show compare?'

'To the book?'

'Yes.'

'You mean, is the story the same?'

'Yes.'

'Can't say.'

'You wrote it.'

'Not allowed to say. Obviously there are differences, that kind of thing always, always, arises from page to screen.'

'But you signed an NDA and you're not allowed to talk about it,' said Buchan.

'Correctamundo.'

She looked embarrassed to have said the word. Lifted her tea, then a biscuit, as something to hide behind. Buchan cracked, reached out, took a biscuit. Chocolate-coated, orange-flavoured, crunchy.

'Nice biscuit,' he said mundanely.

———

'From a packet.'

'Two people have been murdered,' said Buchan, getting back on track. 'We're going to get to see the script one way or another. Paperwork's already in the works. There's clearly no relation between the book and the two murders so far. Can you at least tell me if there's any correlation between what you know of the murders, and the changes you made to the storyline?'

'I don't know anything of the murders.'

Buchan had already thought this through on the way here. How much to tell, gauged against how likely it was to make her talk.

'Daniel Harptree left hanging from a pier. That's it. Dropped from the pier, neck snapping with the force of the rope.' He reflexively snapped his fingers. 'Blake Philips, stabbed in the face, another couple of wounds in the chest, left lying on his bedroom floor. Music playing beside both corpses.'

'Music playing? Really? That's a nice touch.'

'Beautiful,' said Buchan, drily. 'Any of that strike a chord with your rewrite?'

She smiled, and shook her head.

'Sadly, no. I wish I'd thought of the music thing, though, that's really nice. Very haunting. Wait, it is haunting music, right, it's not, you know, BTS or Lil Nas?'

'What are these differences, then?' asked Buchan. Asking the question with a sense of hopelessness, that occasionally people bit on. It worked.

'Jesus,' she said, head shaking. 'You know, I wouldn't spend *too* much effort trying to see the screenplay, it's really not that different. Like, I can't say for, you know, *reasons*, but there's nothing to say anyway.'

'You told my sergeant you didn't know Daniel Harptree lived in Largs?' he said, deciding to move on.

She took a moment to adjust, took a drink of tea, nodding as she placed the mug back on the table. The tea was cooling. Neither of them would be finishing it.

'That's correct. You have a tone of disbelief, inspector.'

'You both worked on a show from a few years ago. *A Room With No Natural Light*.'

'Ha! Well, look at you. That, I'm afraid, was no different to this. I did my bit over here, Daniel did his thing over here. Never the twain shall meet.'

This time Buchan got the sense of a lie, but said nothing for the moment.

'Look, inspector, I never meet anyone,' she said, 'not if I can help it. You can't see it properly,' and she indicated the window, 'but I live in an apartment with a wonderful view of the sea. I could sit at this window all day, and indeed, some days I do. I can go on the balcony, I get fresh air. I get my shopping delivered from Waitrose.' She paused, then smiled and said, 'I don't exercise, so there's that. You can probably tell.'

'I wouldn't like to judge,' said Buchan.

'Nice. Well, there you have it, I didn't know Daniel.'

'How about Blake Philips?'

'Met him on set. He called me fat.'

Buchan washed down the last of his biscuit, gave her another of his familiar eyebrows.

'He literally used that word, or he implied it?'

'He said, and I quote, *didn't expect you to be such a fat bird.* Thereafter we did not speak. Adrian apologised for him, for what that was worth. I do think the poor man was quite embarrassed by it.'

'How about the relationship between Benjamin and Sara Albright.'

Another laugh, this one accompanied, somewhat theatrically, by a backwards movement of her head.

'She is such a bitch. I mean, sure, Bennie might be a little naïve 'n all, but she came on board, or she was sent on board, to make sure he had as little to do with the whole thing as possible. From day one she was undermining him. The way she treated him made that prick Philips calling me fat look like the most flirtatious come-on in history.'

She laughed again.

'Do you see any correlation between the fight between the producers and the two murders?' asked Buchan. The interview, the useful part of it at least, was ending. He could tell. If she was hiding something, and she may well have been, he didn't have enough intelligence about the case to know where exactly to probe, and she had toughed it out. If she wasn't hiding anything? Then the interview would likely prove to barely matter.

'Nah,' she said. 'The two of them did their best to, you know, create alliances, that kind of thing, but while some people might have sworn allegiance or whatever, really when their backs were turned, everyone was like, yikes, keep me the fuck away from that.'

'How do you know if you only visited the set five or six times?'

She lifted the mug again, this time taking a drink with a slurp.

'I talk to people,' she said. 'I mean, don't get me wrong, I can go five years without talking to anyone, but once there, you know, in company, I talk to people. And what d'you think there is for a writer to do on set anyway? The director or one of the so-called stars says, can we rewrite this line? And you're thinking, you know, you're fucking kidding me. That line, every damned line, was discussed and scrutinised and developed and tested and agonized over for the past two years by me, the director, the script editors, the producers, every damned clown in the clown car put in their tuppence ha'penny's worth to hone the script to perfection, and then you want to change it on the hoof on the afternoon of the shoot? What are you even on? You know, when I get called to the set, for me it's not about rewriting, it's about defending what's already there. Because, of course, everyone there has already read the script a hundred and fifty times. They're probably bored with it, we all are. But it doesn't mean it's not terrific. Like, let's say, you ever seen *The Sting* for example?'

Buchan nodded. She was just talking now, but he didn't get the sense that it was question avoidance. More likely it was as a result of loneliness, if she really did leave this place as little as she said.

'The script is… oh my God, it could not *be* more perfect. Every fucking word. But's let's say you watched that movie a hundred and fifty times, then someone comes along and says, how about we make this little change? Might make it more interesting. Yeah, sure, numbnuts, it might for the people that have seen it a hundred and fifty times because it's different, but can we focus on the fact that it will, for literally everyone else, make the film *worse*?'

'So when you visited the set for the day,' said Buchan, deciding he'd had enough of the screenwriter's shoulder chip, 'you spent five or ten minutes defending your previous work, and the rest of the time hanging out, chatting amiably with the crew about all the arguments happening on set?'

She smiled, the smile became a small laugh, she shook her head, she took a drink of tea, the laugh died with the taste of the tea which was now definitely too cold, and she laid the mug

---

back on the table.

'Very good, Inspector,' she said. 'Look, people talk to me. Confide in me sometimes. Look at me. I'm no threat to anyone. I'm everyone's overweight aunt who's there with a cup of tea and a slice of pie in times of trouble. I mean, they don't know me, no one does, but they think they do. So they talk. And that set... there was a lot of bitchiness, a lot of squabbling, a lot of petty backstabbing. But... you know, it all seemed so inconsequential. I mean, I'm a writer, right? I know people. That's what I do. That's my job. All stories, regardless, doesn't matter whether it's *Casablanca* or some dumb-fuck *Terminator* reboot, they all boil down to people. And the best ones are convincing because they get people right. So people are my job. Like I say, I don't go out much, but when I do, I like to talk. That's how I learn things, that's how I pick up new ideas. And I can recognise evil and I can recognise narrow-minded resentment, and this was definitely the latter.'

'Except two people have been murdered.'

'Coincidence out of the question?'

'They both worked on the show, and there are other aspects of their murders that link the deaths to the show.'

She held his gaze now. He could see her wondering whether it was worth her time asking, and then she decided not to.

'Nevertheless,' she said, 'I don't think you'll find your answers in the on-set friction.'

'In your estimation as a people expert?' said Buchan drily.

She didn't answer, regarding Buchan with a certain disdain instead.

18

Sinatra was singing *Stormy Weather*, the usual characters in the Hopper painting entitled 'the Winter Moon' were in place. Janey behind the bar, Duncan in his spot. Herschel and the other guy talking in low voices. Leanne, the Butcher's wife, sitting on her own, reading the *Aosawa Murders* by Riku Onda, the cover of the book on display so that anyone who was interested could see. Perhaps she was literary virtue signalling. Perhaps it was just the way she was sitting and holding the book.

Janey had barely spoken to him. Just as he'd feared. Like she was annoyed at herself for going too far.

He knew not to push it. Or maybe it was because he had his own doubts. Maybe there was something different after the previous night. Maybe there'd been something about it that hadn't been there before, or maybe there'd been something missing.

As a result, he was talking to the priest, something to occupy his mind.

'We're standing in the middle of the forest. A dense forest. There are fifteen paths. Paths all over the place. And we're not even in a clearing with a few paths leading off, we're just there in the middle of the trees, and through the trees there might be paths.' He paused, took another drink, winced slightly as it passed across his tongue, then he laid the glass back on the counter. 'Usually by this point, a few days in, a couple of murders in, we've got some idea of how the forest is laid out. Where the certainties are, which paths we need to follow.' Another stare forward, another head shake. 'Not this time, though.'

He lifted the glass again, and finally turned to look along the bar. Duncan had been watching him as he spoke, elbows on the bar, all the while gently tapping the bottle of Heineken against his forehead. He was wearing his dog collar today, as ever the brilliant white of it a sharp contrast to the colour of his skin. Sleeves rolled up, a familiar benevolent look on his face as he listened to Buchan explain where they were. He thought, in fact, the metaphor rather clumsy and obvious, but was not going to say. Buchan must have had the need to talk. It didn't really matter what he said.

'How many people have you interviewed so far?' asked Duncan.

Buchan looked away, staring straight ahead at the familiar bottle of Edradour, the level of which never seemed to drop. The words *too many* were on his lips, but that sounded cheap, and so he considered more carefully and said, 'Between the team and I, in the region of a hundred and twenty.'

'And no one stands out?'

'There are people with things to say, and some disagreements amongst the various players in the drama, but nothing that says murder. Because murder…'

The sentence drifted away. It wasn't, however, because he'd been distracted by a sudden, insightful thought, it being more as though he'd decided he'd said enough now. He'd reached his quota of words for the evening. What was he doing talking anyway? It wasn't as though it was going to do anyone any good. It wasn't as though it was bringing Janey to the conversation table.

'Murder?' said Duncan.

Buchan stared into the glass, took another sip – this one passing without impacting his facial expression – and then he placed the glass back on the bar.

'Murder is exceptional. It doesn't just *happen*. Lots of people fall out in life, it takes a very particular set of circumstances, or a very particular person, for it to lead to murder. Trivial arguments at work are not usually enough.'

'Nevertheless,' said Duncan, 'it would appear that someone thought the arguments were not so trivial after all.'

Buchan thought about it for a moment, looking as tired and deflated as he felt.

'And that's where we are.'

'Maybe you could just chop down all the trees,' said Duncan, with a small smile he could not keep from his face.

'Thanks, father, I'll keep that in mind.'

He glanced along the bar. Janey was leaning back against the opposite counter. As if she could feel his stare, she looked up. Their eyes met, and for a moment that lingered, they could not break the stare.

Duncan the priest glanced at them in turn, could not fathom what was going on, and then, as he looked back at his number puzzle, the bottle still held in his hand, he said a silent prayer.

*

Buchan's phone rang when he was walking up the stairs to his apartment. Dinner awaited. A couple of hours trying to detach himself from this case, before falling into bed. He stopped, the ring of the phone loud in the stairwell, even though the phone itself was still in his coat pocket. The thought immediately came to him that this would be Kane calling with news of another murder. What else were late evening phone calls in his world other than bad news?

Unusually, this call was from Roth, and he tried to remember if she was on duty. It could still be murder.

'Agnes?'

'Sorry to trouble you, sir,' she said. 'Just…'

She went quiet, he got the impression of her holding the phone away from herself, and he could hear music, quickly recognising it, despite its distant quality. *Corran's Theme*.

'Where are you?' asked Buchan.

'Just got home.'

'What's with the music?'

'It was playing when I got here, sir.'

Buchan turned and was already running down the stairs.

'Tell me,' he said.

'There's a small speaker in the kitchen, an MP3 physically attached to it,' she began. She did not sound at all stressed or worried, as though being greeted at home by murder music was a common enough occurrence. 'I already checked, and it's the same as the others. Just the one track, on repeat.'

'Any sign of the intruder?'

Out the door at the bottom of his building, running along the river pathway. Just over a mile, then across the river on the old Glasgow Bridge, to his car, parked at the office.

'Nothing. Checked everywhere, locked all the doors, think I'm all right. You know, I think… well, I don't know what it is. A warning? Seems a bit weird, that's all.'

'I'm hanging up,' said Buchan. 'Call it in, and I mean, call

999, get a …'

'I'm fine, sir.'

'Call it in, Agnes, dammit,' he shouted. 'Now!'

'Sir,' she said. She'd known he'd insist on it anyway when she'd called, any argument was futile.

He hung up, leaving her to it. A few hundred yards, his pace gradually, inevitably slowing.

'Dammit,' he spat at the night.

*

Seven minutes later, as he breathlessly got in behind the wheel of the Facel, he called Roth. There was no answer. Engine started, tyres screeching out of the carpark, out onto the road, blue light on top of the car.

He redialled.

The phone rang out.

19

There were three SOCOs, as well as several members of
Buchan's team in Roth's apartment. This place was smaller and
in a less attractive area, but had a not dissimilar layout to
Buchan's flat, with the open-plan kitchen/diner/sitting room.
Although, as Buchan noted, it seemed most apartments were
now designed to this configuration.

The music was still playing. It hadn't been turned off by the
time Buchan arrived, and he'd instructed that it be left on. It did
nothing for the investigation, but he felt it an integral part of the
scene. While the hardware used would again be worthwhile
following up, the music itself was all about atmosphere and
setting.

More than that, Buchan felt it the perfect accompaniment to
the awful, haunted twisting of his stomach. It seemed like a long
time since he'd felt fear.

He stood in the middle of the room, watching the silent,
slow-moving drama of the crime scene investigation, trying to
decide what he should do now. What he even could do now.
There were CCTV cameras to check, there were people in the
building to interview, but it was already all in hand. What he
himself was going to do was the question, and he didn't know.
Just after eleven p.m. and he was standing in the middle of an
apartment, feeling impotent and useless. And worse, in charge,
everyone here looking to him for direction.

'Boss,' said Kane, coming back into the room, having been
doing the rounds of the building.

'What have we got?' asked Buchan, Kane's arrival having
sparked some life in him.

When he'd arrived half an hour earlier, there had been a
police car parked up at the entrance, one of the officers inside
making a call. Buchan had flashed his card, the officer had said,
'There's no one there, sir,' and Buchan had broken into a run

again, not waiting for the lift, quickly up the four floors to Roth's apartment.

He'd never been there before, but it was one of the things he knew about his staff. Where they all lived, who they lived with. Given that he did nothing with the information, it did not feel intrusive. Useful, he'd always thought, although this kind of situation aside, he probably could never have thought what would be useful about it. And yet, here he was, taking steps two and three at a time, and dashing into Roth's place.

The music had been playing, there was a lone female officer on her radio, making a hopeless gesture to him as he entered, and from there the calls had flown, the team had been assembled, one of their own missing.

'Guy downstairs says he heard a thump about, he wasn't sure, maybe forty minutes ago, something like that. One-off sound, nothing thereafter. Says he didn't think anything of it at the time. Just one of those things you get in blocks of flats. Could be Agnes was attacked from behind, then her body dragged out to the lift.'

'Alive or dead,' said Buchan, grimly.

'Yes. The building has basement parking, so if her abductor took her body down there on the lift, then they wouldn't have had to risk taking her out the front door.'

Buchan nodded at the thought process on how it all might have played out, finishing with a low, 'Dammit,' cursed at the room.

'We have to be positive, sir,' said Kane. 'Our guy, whoever this is, has left two people dead so far, music playing. If Agnes was dead, there's a fair shout we'd currently be standing over her body. That she's not here means she's not dead. Look, the guy killed two men. Maybe he's just thinking, I'm not killing a young woman. It's not about that. It's about this other thing over here, whatever that is.'

'I know,' said Buchan. 'It's hard to cling to it, but I agree, she's likely not dead. For whatever reason.'

'And she's pretty fierce, by the way,' said Kane, 'you wouldn't want to cross her,' eliciting a cold smile from Buchan. 'She can take care of herself,' said Kane, wrapping up her attempt to convince them both.

Buchan looked around the room, glancing at the window as he did so. There was little to be done right now, right at this moment, but thinking. Thinking through motive and possibility, and it seemed natural to stand at a window. His usual position.

'You're right,' he said, 'we need to be positive. If there's no body, then it's a kidnap, which means there will be contact made. And if there's no contact made, it means he's sending us a message. It's specifically aimed at the police, and the music unquestionably ties it to the two murders, which are tied to the TV production.'

He puffed out his cheeks, folded his arms. His jacket hunched around his shoulders, he rubbed his mouth and chin.

'A hanging, a stabbing, an abduction. What's the message?'

He looked at Kane, and got nothing in reply. There was nothing to give at this moment, there being no way for them to know what the message could possibly be.

Movement at the door, and the chief inspector arrived, collar of her coat drawn up, a maroon beanie on her head that Buchan had never seen before. She removed it as she walked into the room, stopped for a second to consider the scene, and then approached Buchan and Kane.

'Anything?'

'Nothing so far,' said Buchan.

'Phone, laptop…?'

'Nothing stolen, as far as we can see,' said Kane. 'Agnes's phone was on the counter, there's a laptop in the bedroom.'

'Any blood?'

'Nope. Downstairs heard a single thump, and that's all. No one else in the building reports hearing or seeing anything.'

Liddell took a moment to look around the room, and Buchan followed her gaze, really studying the sitting room part of the open-plan for the first time. The only wall decorations were a mirror, and three framed posters. One a Schoenberg concert at the Royal Concert Hall, one for Glastonbury 2019, and one for Ullapool Book Festival 2016. A small TV in the corner. Unusually small for the times, thought Buchan. It was the size of TV you find in the house of an older person, who refuses to catch up with the modern way of the excessively large flatscreen. One sofa, one comfy chair. Next to it, a low table. An iPad, an unfinished mug of coffee, a book turned upside down. Buchan hadn't looked at it, though he'd noticed Kane doing so. He remembered that Roth read three crime novels a week. In the middle of the floor, the centrepiece, was another low table, this one with a large ornamental chess set in the middle. The pieces were all on the board, but had been left mid-game.

'You know Agnes played chess?' asked Liddell.

Buchan and Kane shook their heads, but both in a way that suggested regret at not knowing much about their constable, rather than finding it odd she had an ornamental chess set.

'What are the figures?' asked Liddell.

No one had paid much attention yet to the chess set, and now Kane walked over and lifted a piece, nodding as she did so.

'Holmes, Watson, etc,' she said. 'Guess this is Moriarty on the other side. Baker Street Irregulars as pawns...'

She placed the piece back on the middle of the board, then Buchan approached, shaking his head.

'Put it back in the same spot,' he said, an absent-mindedness to the comment, his brain already whirring. How much did he know about chess beyond the basics?

'Either of you play?' he asked Kane and Liddell.

'Never,' said Kane.

'Not in forty years,' said Liddell. 'What are you thinking?'

Buchan didn't answer, then looked around the room at the SOCOs and the couple of other officers in attendance.

'Anyone play chess?' he asked, his voice raised so they all knew it was aimed at the room. 'And I mean, really know the game. Know about openings and gambits and whatever.'

A couple of blank faces. One of the SOCOs said, 'I think the boss is a player. Sarge?'

They glanced at the door through to the bedroom, and Sgt Meyers appeared, eyebrows raised, looking at Buchan, even though it was one of her staff who'd called her in.

'You play chess, Ruth?' asked Buchan.

'Sure.'

'Like, you know it? You know moves and sequences and –'

'Play tournaments every second weekend.'

'You know what's happening here?' he asked, indicating the chess set, and she walked over and looked down at the board.

The game that had been started had not got very far. She studied it for a few moments, followed the course of the moves, then shook her head, emitting a low curse as she did so.

'Crap, I should've paid attention to this already. Has anyone touched this?'

Kane lifted her hand, but also indicating she was wearing nitrile.

'Lifted the white king, put it back in its place,' she said.

Meyers nodded, then indicated for one of the others to

come over.

'You haven't done this yet, Stuart?'

'Nope.'

'Can you get on it, please? Principally the pieces that have been moved. Thanks.'

'What have we got,' asked Buchan.

Meyers nodded, confirming her thoughts, giving herself another couple of moments.

'I'm not sure this is going to help you, and... I guess it depends if whoever did this knew Constable Roth had the chess set. It might just have been a passing thought, an opportunity taken to leave a message, such as it is.' Another pause, Buchan didn't push her. 'What we have here is White opening with the Smith-Morra Gambit. It's aggressive, but can also be a little perilous. Depends how Black answers, of course. Generally, Black accepts the gambit and things get complicated, or Black declines and gives White a small advantage. Here, though, if this is a message like I believe we're supposed to take it, Black is playing a completely different game. Black has no idea what's happening.' A pause, and then she added, 'Bluntly, Black is an idiot and is about to lose.'

'So, he's mocking us?' said Kane, looking unimpressed.

Buchan stared morosely at the board.

'Yes, he's mocking us,' said Meyers. 'There hasn't been a chess theme to the previous murders, has there?'

'Not unless we missed it,' said Buchan.

'We don't miss things,' said Meyers. 'There's been nothing like this at the scene, and unless there's been anything communicated to you by some other means...'

'There's been no communication.'

'Then, there are two options with this. One is that Sgt Roth was playing a game, or left the pieces in this arrangement for her own reasons. Or, her abductor took the opportunity to play a game with us, just because the chess set was here. The chess set is a cheap metaphor, done on the hoof. The actual moves themselves... I don't think they mean anything. He's taunting us. He's saying, I killed someone, you did nothing. I killed someone else, you did nothing. Now this, getting bolder, moving in for the kill...' She paused, she thought about it some more, as she knew what was likely coming from Buchan. 'I don't think he's then asking, what are you going to do now?'

'He won't be looking for us to find some way to

communicate pawn-to-d6?'

'No. If that was his game, he'd have been doing that from the start. This is just... screw you, I'm on the attack, and you're helpless. This is that thing the Americans say. You're playing chequers, while I play chess.'

The three of them stood and stared hopelessly down at the chess set for a few moments, then Liddell snapped the silence with, 'Let's hope he at least breathed on the set while he was about it,' and then the other member of Meyers' team was kneeling down beside the set, and Buchan and the others backed off.

*

Four-thirteen a.m. Home to get some sleep, but sleep was not to be had this evening.

He was standing at the window, the glass of gin in his hand, feeling lousy for a hundred different reasons, drinking gin at four in the morning being one of them. He was going to be working again in three hours, and the chances of getting any sleep in between were minimal.

Knowing he'd have just the one, he'd poured himself a slightly bigger glass than usual, feeling a familiar self-loathing as he'd done so.

He liked Roth. He would never allow himself the thought, but she was his favourite amongst his staff. The best and most promising detective – certainly with a lot more promise than he himself had ever shown – but he also enjoyed her company more than any of the others. She was more challenging, brought something out of him that no one else did.

If he ever thought anything beyond that, anything about the attractiveness of this woman who was on his staff and who was twenty years his junior, he forcibly expelled the notion as soon as it arrived. Somewhere in his head there was a *not appropriate* compartment, and Buchan could open it quickly, thrust something inside, and leave it there. That's what he told himself, at any rate.

And now she was missing, and the buck stopped at him when it came to finding her. Liddell might take on that mantle for herself, but she wasn't in the office with Roth every day. It wasn't on her now to pull the investigation together. It wasn't her who'd been in charge of an investigation that had already seen two murders.

He took another drink, cursed with the taste of it, then turned away from the window, ignoring Edelman who glanced at him as he walked past the sofa. Then he went into the kitchen, tossed the rest of the drink into the sink, and went through to the bedroom, into the ensuite, and set the tap running.

20

7:07 a.m. Saturday morning. Middle of January, still dark, the day set to be light grey, Sunday promising clear blue skies, laying down frost into Monday. So said the weatherman.

Buchan and Kane were already in the ops room. Cup of coffee and a chocolate croissant each, Buchan picking them up on the way to the office. They were looking through the list of names of crew and staff from the production of *Beware The Watcher* who'd been interviewed by Roth. Her kidnapper could easily have come from outwith the list, but it was a good place to start.

'You get any sleep?' asked Buchan, as though remembering he should try to relate to his staff on a personal level.

'Think I managed about an hour,' said Kane, her eyes not leaving the list she'd printed off. 'You?'

'Yeah, it was fine.'

He'd lain in bed for an hour and a half, and sleep had never been close. She knew he was lying. She'd lied herself, after all.

There were fifty-nine names on the list, and they were weeding out the ones who Roth had spoken to on the phone. They'd certainly need to speak to them again, but those who were in town obviously held greater possibility. They would need Cherry to arrive in order to finalise the list.

'Why Agnes,' said Buchan, 'I think that's the crucial pointer in the first instance. She's one of a team, so why was she chosen?'

'I think we have to be on the right track with this,' said Kane. 'We may be a team, but it's not like anyone, any outsider, has an overview of us. Those people out there, the non-combatants, they only see whoever's standing right in front of them, or they only know whoever's on the other end of the phone. Whoever did this, Agnes must have spoken to them. The alternative is some weird, fiction-level mastermind, with eyes on everything we're doing, and...,' and she let out a long, tired sigh, 'Jesus, let's just not go there.'

'She also spoke to Goddard,' said Buchan, indicating the list.

'When? That was just us, right?'

'She made first contact, though it was on the phone. She set up our original meeting down at Stillwood.' A pause, thinking it through, and then, 'Hmm... we'll need to speak to Danny, see if she spoke to any of them on FaceTime, that feels a little more... well, it is more visually interactive. And, of course, there's Zelinger. She didn't meet him, but he's leaping off the damned page. And there's this guy,' and he tapped the name of Darryl Henderson, the large sound engineer at Lost World Studio. Even as he tapped, however, he was shaking his head. 'But he, while intimately involved in the music, had nothing to do with the filming. Same for all of these, the singers, the orchestra. Why would they have anything to do with the filming?'

'And the crew members had nothing to do with the music,' said Kane.

'All we have then is the possibility there was some coincidental crossover. Perhaps someone who works locally on film crew also happens to be one of the Tallis singers...'

'Which isn't out of the question, because that choir isn't full-time. They're professional, and they're good, but there's not many of them doing this as a living.'

They stared at the list. Unthinkingly they lifted their coffee cups and took a drink. Kane took a bite of pain au chocolat.

'I keep looking at Zelinger,' said Buchan. 'If he has taken Agnes... then God knows where. It obviously wasn't back to his apartment in Edinburgh.'

'I think he's dead,' said Kane. She took another bite of pastry.

Silence returned, not in stages, but sweeping through the room. The sound of their hopelessness.

Quick footsteps along the short corridor, Cherry, arriving at a rush.

'Just heard about Agnes,' he said, agitated accusation in his tone. 'Why didn't you call me?'

'It was late in the evening,' said Buchan, holding up a pair of placatory hands, 'and there was no need for everyone to be there. A positive decision that I made, Danny, not an oversight. We can't all be walking around like zombies today.'

'You told literally everyone else.'

'Danny,' said Kane, sharply, and Cherry took a step back, the physical act of pulling away from the confrontation.

'I did not tell everyone else,' said Buchan. 'Agnes's place is small, and there was no point in the entire SCU staff turning up there at eleven at night. Now, there's a lot of work to do today, a lot of calls to make, everything we had yesterday multiplied by a hundred. So, take a seat, take a look through this list, see who we've missed.'

Cherry looked unconvinced, and Buchan felt he'd made a mistake. How much thought had he given calling Cherry late at night? No more than a few seconds. *Should he call him? No. Next question.* That had been it, no more than an afterthought. But of course he should've called him. The things about Roth that Buchan found so attractive, would also likely be attractive to Cherry, just as much as they were to Kane and the rest of the team.

Cherry sat in the seat opposite, turning the list around and giving it a quick look through.

'Two columns,' said Kane. 'Everyone Agnes either saw in person here, or spoke to on the phone, here,' and she indicated the second column. 'And if you know she spoke on FaceTime rather than the phone, note that down.'

Cherry, imbued with a sense of urgency that perhaps the others had lost to their despair, ran his eyes quickly over the list, and Buchan and Kane felt compelled to watch him, pen in his hand, marking off occasional names.

'I know she FaceTimed these people,' he said. 'Some of the others, I'm not sure.' The agitation had not left him.

It did not take long, and he looked up, his eyes moving between the two of them.

'I think you've got everyone else, that I know about at least. You want me to take some of these?'

'Thanks,' said Buchan. 'Will the two of you split them up? And get Ian on it too. If you can see people, doesn't matter whether Agnes saw them or chatted on the phone, but if you can physically see them, all the better. And if you know where they are and can doorstep them, go for it. If, by chance, one of them is holding Agnes, then calling them and inviting ourselves round there will not work well.'

Buchan pushed his chair back, getting to his feet. 'I'm going to see Goddard again. Hopefully catch him at home. You good?'

'Yep,' said Kane.

'OK, thanks, Sam.'

Another moment, a couple of steps towards the door, and then he stopped, turned back to Cherry.

'Sorry, Danny, you're right, I should've called. I wasn't thinking straight.'

The annoyance, which had lingered on Cherry's face, drained away, more with Buchan's tone than the words. The genuine regret.

'That's OK, sir,' he said.

'We'll find her,' said Buchan, although, for all that he felt it and for all that he could not have been more determined, he did not sound at all convincing.

He turned from the office and was gone.

21

'Doesn't look like my problem,' said Goddard.

Buchan had interrupted him in the middle of breakfast. Goddard, at least, had not seemed to mind, had ushered him to a seat at the table, and had continued to eat throughout. Full Scottish fried breakfast, the plate overflowing. Two slices of toast on a side plate. Large cup of coffee, the percolator bubbling away to the side.

Goddard was stick thin, and Buchan wondered if he took a strange health supplement that he'd learned about from some celebrity actor that allowed him to eat this many thousand calories in one meal and it have no effect.

Radio 3 was playing, the volume lowered upon Buchan's arrival. Mrs Goddard, who Buchan recognised from the start and end of the late night sex video, was in the kitchen, drinking coffee, two other glasses on the go, one of orange juice, the other a yogurt drink. She was running after her husband. In the room, but not sitting at the table with him.

'It's all tied to your production, Mr Goddard,' said Buchan. 'Everything that happens in relation to this case, every time a crime is committed and the music from the show is woven into the fabric of the scene, it's your problem.'

Goddard cut into a sausage, as though carrying out an act both brutal and skilful, put the piece in his mouth, took a bite of toast, then a drink of coffee, then he leant forward on his elbows, and pointed the fork at Buchan, somehow managing to speak as though his mouth wasn't full.

'I have one job, inspector, and one job only, and that's to deliver the finished cut of six episodes of *Beware The Watcher* to Sara by the middle of next month. End of. Blake's dead? Sad, sure, but it doesn't affect me. Adam fucked off somewhere or he's dead or whatever. Ditto. Daniel's hanging is, as we've discussed, a mild inconvenience, but we've already played around with it, and we're solid. We're good...'

He paused while Mrs Goddard placed a cup of coffee on the table beside Buchan. She hadn't offered it first.

'Milk and sugar?'

Buchan shook his head. He didn't want it at all.

Goddard took more food, the act of eating played out extravagantly, as though done for the camera, the man a screen presence himself. This, thought Buchan, is how Orson Welles would have eaten breakfast.

'So, your officer's missing?' Goddard continued. 'Must be tough for you, I get it. I'm not surprised you're here, looking to lash out, or do whatever. But here we are, Inspector. What does your Constable Roth vanishing mean to my production?' A pause, and then the inevitable, 'Nothing. Zero. Zilch. An hour from now Stanley and I are going to be working on the edit of episode five, and you're going to be doing your thing, and the two will be completely unrelated.'

'What were you doing at eleven last night?'

Goddard smiled, shook his head, took another large mouthful of food. Behind him, Buchan noticed Goddard's wife glance quickly over her shoulder.

'Same as every other night, inspector. It is what it is.'

Now the woman turned, looking warily at Buchan, and then drawing her husband in so that he turned towards her.

'You told him about that?'

'Had to show him the video, hun,' and he smiled and shrugged as he said it, obviously enjoying her annoyance. 'Blame this guy,' he said, 'classic pervy police officer, wanting to see everything.'

Jesus, thought Buchan.

'You can vouch for your husband being here yesterday evening?' he asked.

She stared over her husband's shoulder, then she folded her arms and her expression dulled.

'Not sure that I can,' she said. 'You'll just have to ask Adrian for the video. Why don't you show it in court?'

Goddard burst out laughing.

Buchan stared grimly across the table. The conversation was currently out of his control, and proving utterly useless. One of his officers was missing, the only conceivable suspect was also missing, albeit he was only a suspect because they couldn't find him, and he was sitting here being laughed at by a couple of clowns who didn't seem to care that people were dying.

'Mrs Goddard, would you mind leaving us for a few minutes,' said Buchan, all the time with his eyes on the director sitting at the other end of the short kitchen table. He would like to have added that maybe she could get dressed, as she was still wearing her night attire, with a silk dressing gown only loosely fastened at the belt. Another sharp glance from her, and now she walked from the kitchen, closing the door sharply behind.

'She's a livewire,' said Goddard. 'I'm going to get it in the neck for showing you that video. You're going to have to take the fall, I'm afraid, inspector. I don't suppose you'll care.'

'I need you to help me, Mr Goddard,' said Buchan, attempting to reset the conversation. 'You can distance yourself all you like, but there's something happening with your production, and we have no idea where it might stop. Who it might stop with, or who else is going to get taken out of the game along the way. At the moment, I'd say you're going to be bloody lucky getting your edit done by the middle of next decade, never mind next month, so start cooperating.'

This time, toast dipped into the yolk of a fried egg, the crunch of it on his teeth, and then bacon, sausage, mushroom, and some beans layered on a fork and put into his mouth. It should be disgusting to watch, thought Buchan, and yet somehow it felt like a scene from a black and white, art house movie.

Goddard took a drink of coffee, then leant on his elbows, and once more pointed his fork at Buchan.

'I'm not sure what you want from me, inspector. I don't know anything. I don't know anyone who hates this show, or who hates young Bennie and who'd want to ruin his big entrance into TV production.'

'What about someone hating you?'

Goddard shrugged, took another slurp of coffee.

'Maybe someone does, but I can't say. And why would they kill Blake and Daniel? I don't give a shit about those guys.'

'To harm your show.'

'It's not my show. I don't give a shit about the show. Sure, I want to do a good job, but that's just basic job security one-o-one. Don't fuck up, and your next job will present itself. This is Bennie's show. Or maybe it's Searchcraft's show. You need to find someone that hates them, because this doesn't affect me *at all*.'

He waggled the fork to indicate he had something else to say, but made sure to take another mouthful of food first, which this time he chewed for a while, washed down with some more coffee, then he lifted another piece of toast from the rack, even though his current one wasn't finished, seemed to hesitate because this new piece was no longer warm enough, then he decided to butter it anyway, and when he'd done that, he popped the last of the first piece of toast in his mouth.

'If I can give you a piece of advice,' he said, and Buchan managed not to grimace. 'I mean, I've said this before, but I'm not sure you're listening. You're either looking for an artist, or someone who aspires to his art. And, just to be clear, I don't mean artist like Renoir or one of those guys. We're talking a true artist, in film, sound, various visual media. Your killer here, they're creating a story, they're painting a picture, setting a scene. The way you described Daniel hanging... that was a *thing of beauty*. Under, admittedly, different circumstances, Daniel would have loved it. Desolate coastline, the waves, the hills in the distance, the music playing. God, it's perfect. So, yes, whoever's doing this obviously holds a grudge. A deeply held, resentment-filled grudge, but by God, they have a way about them. They have style, panache.'

He lifted his eyebrows at Buchan, the invitation for him to be impressed, and then he cut into the next sausage. For all that he had been eating continuously throughout, there still seemed to be a lot of food on his plate.

'You got that, inspector, because that's pretty much all I've got to give you? You're looking for someone creative, and that person is going to have to be pretty pissed at either Bennie or maybe Sara, maybe the company. They're the people really affected by this.'

'What about Miriam Carr?' asked Buchan.

For all that he was staring blankly across the table at Goddard, and for all that the man could be lying for no end of reasons, he nevertheless sounded convincing. Indeed, it sounded like the most credible thing anyone had said to him since the investigation started.

'Who's that?'

'The writer of the novel.'

'The novel?' More food. 'Ah, right, the novel. Never read it. And nah, not her.'

'Why not?'

'The creators of the original work see the vast bulk of their money up front. The day the show goes into production, boom, they get their cut. Out of nowhere, bang, a hundred thousand dollars or a million dollars or whatever. Maybe, like here where it's a book, their book sells more down the line. Maybe not. Doesn't matter, they're unlikely to get as much as they get in that first hit.'

'What about *Trainspotting*, that kind of thing?'

'How many *Trainspottings* have there been, huh? It's an outlier. Sure, it's not the only one, but there are way more TV shows and movies made from books where people never even realise there's a book, than there are *Trainspottings*, that's for sure. Miriam got her cash, and she won't give a shit what happens now, and anyone in the business looking to seek their revenge is going to know that.'

'And you think this is someone in the business?'

'One hundred per cent.'

The kitchen door opened, Mrs Goddard returned, still in her night attire. She leant against the door and looked at her husband. Buchan might as well not have been there.

'You still eating, hun?' she said. She smiled. Goddard laughed.

'Give me a minute to get rid of this guy, and I'll be right there.'

He laughed again, she winked at him, she left the door open, and retreated silently out of sight.

Goddard took another large mouthful of food, another drink of coffee, and smiled breezily across the table.

'Looks like my presence may be required elsewhere, inspector. You got anything else to say?'

22

Saturday mid-morning, heading to see Benjamin Collins, the Facel sitting in traffic on the way to the far end of Newton Mearns on the south side of the city. Call just finished to Kane, where they'd talked through what needed to happen.

There was no news on Roth. She was gone, that was all, with no contact coming from her abductor. All they had at the moment was the hope that she had been abducted, rather than murdered, the body dumped out of sight.

They discussed the usefulness of Goddard's input, the idea of the killer being someone from the arts community, Buchan presenting it to Kane without comment. She too had liked the sound of it. Of course, they couldn't just take his word for it. They needed other perspectives, other people in the creative business to say that it sounded plausible. And even if it was, they were still back at square one, needing to find someone who resented the production enough that they wanted to completely ruin it, which was where they'd been all along. Even then, if that was the killer's ultimate aim, it was odd they'd chosen to wait until filming was over before making their move.

'Why the change this time?' Buchan had asked, when discussing their hope Roth might still be alive.

'It feels like…,' Kane had begun, before pausing. Buchan had sat at thirty-three miles an hour, the phone on speaker, waiting for her, giving her space. 'I wondered if he's been intentionally particular. Like, specific. He's following a pattern. First victim is hung, the second victim is stabbed in the head, then the body dragged by knives in the chest, the third is kidnapped. In fact, the third is a police officer who's kidnapped. And, well, who knows what comes next?'

'If there's a pattern to be followed, maybe someone does know.'

'Unless the creative is following his own path.'

'Even then, the path must come from somewhere,' said Buchan. 'The more personal it is to the killer, the less chance we can work it out, but what if it is a copycat? Some real life thing, or maybe the plot of some crime novel or TV show playing out.'

'I like the sound of that. That's the world we're in, after all. A melding of fact and fiction.' A pause, and then, 'Crap. You think it's significant that the one of us they've taken is the one who best knows crime fiction? The one who watches the shows and reads the books?'

'Shit,' said Buchan, 'you might have a point. No, no... that has to be a coincidence. What good does it serve someone for them to make Agnes disappear? She might be our resident expert, but it doesn't mean we can't get hold of a hundred others who are liable to read and watch this stuff even more that she does.'

'Yeah, you're right. I was calling her a nerd once for reading three of these things a week, and she said it was nothing. There are people reading two, three *a day*. There are people where it defines what they do, and who they are. Which, of course, makes sense. That applies to everything. There's always someone who does the thing to extreme, and there are a lot of crime fiction geeks.'

'I like the sound of this. Can you speak to some people? Get Danny on it as well. I'm not sure who we're going to find to trust on this, where it won't immediately get all around the crime fiction world that the police in Gla –'

'Maybe that's what we need. We need people talking about it. There are so many of these damned things, so many novels and shows, that even super-geeks can't have read and watched them all. What if our killer is using the plot of some, I don't know, really niche, little Bulgarian novel that only five people in Britain have read?'

'OK, put together a plan. And you don't need to run it by me, just get on it.'

'Right, boss.'

And so the conversation had gone, and now the further Buchan had driven away from it, the less likely it seemed. He was not at all persuaded, yet it was something to chase after. It was a possible, and often enough the possible led to the definite, and for now that was all they had.

*

Benjamin Collins lived in a large house with a long driveway at the far end of Newton Mearns. There was a closed gate across the drive, and a gatehouse, and when you pulled the car up at the gate there was an intercom.

Buchan found himself staring at the intercom and the gate and the driveway and the house, which wasn't so far in the distance that a gatehouse seemed terribly appropriate, but there they all were, and in between the gatehouse and the main building was the most immaculate garden Buchan had ever seen in his life, and on the front of the house were Doric columns either side of the door.

'This is what Bitcoin gets you, I suppose,' he said to the car.

He lowered the window, looked reluctantly at the intercom, noticed the small camera next to it, then reached out and pressed the button. He waited a moment to see if anyone would speak, then he said, 'Detective Inspector Buchan. Mr Collins is expecting me.'

'Can you hold your ID up to the camera, please,' said the disembodied voice. Broad Glasgow accent.

Buchan reached into his pocket, produced the ID, showed it to the camera. A moment, and then the voice said, 'You've been granted access. Park in the designated area adjacent to the front entrance, please. Someone will be there to show you into the house,' and the gate noiselessly swung open.

'You have got to be kidding me,' muttered Buchan, as he drove through. He glanced at the gatehouse as he passed by, but the glass was expensive, dark and mirrored, and there was nothing to see.

Up past perfect winter flowerbeds, a neat lawn, a low, box-leaved honeysuckle hedge, rose bushes cut back for winter. Buchan ignored the three marked spots and parked his car across the front of the house. His back was up, already annoyed.

'New money,' he cursed to himself, not bothering to wonder why he was so irked by this whole set up.

He got out of the car, looked around, back down the length of the garden, noted that you couldn't see any of the neighbouring houses from here, even though this place was not particularly remote, and then he turned to ring the bell just as the door was opened.

A butler. Buchan was not surprised, and this time managed

to keep his contempt to himself.

'Mr Collins is expecting you,' said the butler, and then he stepped back, waited for Buchan to enter, closed the door behind him, and walked past with a, 'This way, please.'

He spoke with the same broad accent as the gatekeeper. Perhaps, in fact, it was the same person, and there had been no one in the gatehouse. Buchan wasn't entirely sure why, after all, there would need to be someone in the gatehouse.

Buchan listened to his shoes as he walked across the tiled flooring, past ornaments and classical art, and for all the money Collins had earned, given the price of original, classical art when it came to market, perhaps there was nothing here of particular value. He, of course, didn't know, and had no intention of finding out.

He paused, hearing a noise upstairs. He looked up to the upper landing, almost expecting to see someone peering at him over a banister.

Silence.

'Sir?'

'Mr Collins is upstairs?' he asked.

'One of the staff,' he said. 'Mr Collins is in the conservatory. This way.'

They ended up in a large, bright conservatory, which looked out over the rear garden, in the middle of which was a swimming pool, which had not been drained for the winter. Steam rose from the heated water. There was a woman swimming, naked as far as Buchan could make out from a quick look, then he was pulling out a seat at the table, and he was once again watching someone eat breakfast.

'Sit down,' said Benjamin Collins, just as Buchan was doing it anyway. 'You want something to eat?'

Buchan looked at Collins' plate, then turned and looked over his shoulder at the butler. Collins and the butler were cut from the same cloth, and Buchan saw it all play out before him. Collins had earned his money, he had his big house with its classical art and columns, he had the beautiful woman swimming naked in the pool, there was a TV show on order, and there had been jobs for the boys, the house full of staff. And why shouldn't there be all of that? Bitcoin may be the absurd tulip fever of its day, but if you were lucky enough and smart enough to benefit from it, then it was hardly for Buchan to sneer at him. If he'd turned up to a family home like this where generations had lived off money originally made from the slave trade, would that have allowed him to be more forgiving?

'What have you got?' he asked.

'This is a blend of kale, arugula and chopped raw Brussel Sprouts, doused with fig vinegar and salt & pepper,' said Collins. 'Grilled sourdough, fried eggs. Totally delish, man. You want some? Fuck man, we got everything though, so if you want a bacon butty or a bowl of cornflakes, you're good.'

The need for food finally got to him in a way it hadn't when sitting with Goddard, and he accepted that he hadn't eaten anything since early the previous evening.

'I'll have what he's having,' he said, turning back to the butler. 'And a coffee with hot milk, please.'

The butler nodded and turned away.

'Epic,' said Collins.

They were drawn by movement out in the garden as the woman emerged from the pool, water running off her naked body. She stood for a moment in the cold, slim and beautiful in the grey morning, as she ran her hand through her hair, squeezing the water from it, then she lifted a white robe, slipped it on, then walked around the pool into the low pool house, which was built in the same style as the building at the gate.

Together they'd watched her, and now, as they turned back, Collins smiled at Buchan, as he took his first mouthful of food since Buchan had arrived at the table.

'They say money can't buy you happiness,' he said. 'Ha. You are pure going to love this, by the way. Tasty af.'

'Tell me about Sara Albright,' said Buchan, getting straight to it, freeing himself from the moment.

Collins shook his head, his face showing disappointment at having come to the mention of the woman so quickly, and then he flicked open his phone, pressed a playlist and set some music playing. Vivaldi, *Four Seasons*, volume on low.

'You don't mind?'

Buchan was non-committal.

'I've got this thing, man. When I'm in here on my own, I love silence, you know? I love to sit in silence. See soon as someone else comes in? I need something going on. I need sounds, man. I need music.'

'Tell me about Mrs Albright.'

Another mouthful of food, the nod of acceptance.

'I know why you're asking, and your people, I presume

they're your people, and you're the boss 'n that, I know why you're all asking. She's such a bitch, and it was so ugly on that stupid set, you know. Fuck me. And she was like, I don't know, Machiavelli multiplied by some wee bitch in *Mean Girls*. If it wasn't for me there wouldn't have been a show. At least, there wouldn't have been this show getting made in Scotland. I'm the only reason she was involved at all. But apparently, I was to be grateful all these artistic geniuses had graced the production with their presence, and I should step aside and let them get on with it. Fuck her, man, what a cow.'

Buchan had quickly realised he'd started on the wrong tack. This wasn't about the producers' argument. They'd been all over it already, it was petty, it was human nature, but Buchan and his team had examined it from all sides, and it screamed distraction. Not a calculated one, not something that had been set up all along with the intention it would cover for murder, yet a distraction, nevertheless.

The butler arrived, another pause while he laid the plate of food and the coffee and a glass of water in front of Buchan. Buchan watched the movements of the man's hands, but he was thinking about where to take this conversation. And he already had an idea, and he didn't have to look too much further than what he'd seen of his own prejudices upon arrival.

The butler retreated, Buchan couldn't stop himself taking a drink of coffee before speaking.

'Nice,' he said, making a small unconscious gesture with the cup.

'Great, in't it? Brazilian.'

'You made many enemies, Benjamin?'

Collins held his gaze for a moment, then gave himself more time, putting greens on his fork, putting it in his mouth. He did not eat with the same cinematic panache as Goddard.

'You'd call Sara an enemy, I expect.'

'Not Sara. I don't think this business is anything to do with Sara,' said Buchan.

'The murders are nothing to do with Sara?'

'I don't think they have anything to do with you and Sara arguing, regardless of who either of you managed to rope into your fight.'

'Don't bring me into it, man, she was the conniving cow.'

'Where d'you go to school?'

'Really?'

'Whatever,' said Buchan. 'Where'd you grow up?'

'Castlemilk.' A pause, and then, knowing where Buchan was coming from he continued, 'Council house. Social housing, as they say now. Poor af, all right?' He tapped the side of his head. 'But I had smarts, knew how to make money on whatever business thing was going. Always legit, didn't want to end up like my old man. I did all right, not that I'd ever managed to get out of the scheme. And then along comes Bitcoin. Not many people knew about blockchain and all that back then. There were opportunities. I bought in. Wasn't a huge amount to be honest, you know, but I fucking nailed it man. I was there, right at the kick-off more or less. Then I sold at fifty-five K a pop. Left a few hundred K on the table when I sold there, but if I'd left it a year, that would've wiped like eight million off, so it panned out pretty fucking decent, by the way.'

'What happened to your old man?'

'In and out of the Bar-L. Last time he was in he got chibbed by some wee sparky from Cumnock. Died on the way to hospital. An inglorious bastard if ever there was one.'

Buchan ran the database, trying to think of someone named Collins, but there was nothing there. Finally the hunger got the better of him, and he took a bite of food. Started with toast and egg as a way of avoiding the greens as long as possible.

'Great for your skin this, by the way,' said Collins, as he took another mouthful.

'How much resentment did you leave behind, going from Castlemilk to this?'

'There's always people going to resent success. And with Bitcoin, people don't understand it. None of us who've really profited from it get any respect. Everyone thinks of it like free money, more or less the same thing as sticking a couple of quid on the National Lottery. But like I said, I knew stuff, man. I did Economics and Computing. I studied. I learned things.'

'How much of your money did you put into *Beware The Watcher*?'

'I told this stuff to your sergeant lassie. And as I says to her, it's on the public record, man.'

'I know how much you paid. I mean, what percentage of your Bitcoin went on that book?'

There we go, thought Buchan. The stare across the table, the crack in the veneer from one question, then the retreat to greens and sourdough and eggs.

'What percentage?' repeated Buchan.

'About sixty.'

'Just to buy the rights to make a book into a TV show? When you had no experience and you didn't have the money to then make the show? That doesn't make a lot of sense.'

'I really wanted that book, man.'

'Aren't there a million crime novels? Most of them can't have been made into shows or films. Why not just buy one of the others for a tenth of that money? A hundredth of that money?'

More food, another drink. He was getting there, and Buchan decided to leave him to it, and took his first bite of kale and arugula. People went to some lengths, he thought, to avoid mention of the fact they were serving cabbage.

'I got into a stupid bidding war. I was… as my mum said, I was a bit of a dick. Overbid by, like, ninety-five per cent maybe. Fuck, I don't know what that other lot were doing, but I guess they could afford it better than me. No wonder yon writer was happy. She must've been peeing in her fucking pants.'

'I thought the writer only got the bulk of the money when you go into production? Why not just let the option lapse if you'd realised you'd made a mistake?'

'I won the bid by giving her a million straight off the bat,' he said. 'You didn't hear that from me, by the way. The guy I go through says not to admit that.'

'So, you have to get the show made as way of getting that back, and in doing so, you had to pay her a tonne more money once filming started.'

'Aye.'

'But at the same time, you needed to get Searchcraft on board to fund the actual production?'

'Aye.'

'How is it you'll make your money back?'

A nod, another drink.

'Decent question. It's complicated. You should see the paperwork, man, fuck me. Basically, the show needs to sell in other countries. Hopefully going out on Sky here, so we should be good, but it has to play elsewhere. Need to sell it to the States. Hasn't happened yet. We're speaking to MoviePlay. So, aye, that Sara might be a right cunt, but she needs to sell it just as much as I do.'

'So, sixty per cent of your money on that book. You bought this house, you had the pool and the pool house and the gate –'

'The pool was here already. Fair play, I added the heating. Who wants to shut a pool in the winter? What's the point of having one in Scotland if you're going to do that?'

'And you've got your staff, and I'm guessing a nice car or two…'

'Aston and a Beemer.'

Buchan took some more food, holding Collins' gaze the entire time. The look that said they both knew where the conversation was going. Collins held the look for a moment, then nodded, staring back at his plate.

'Aye, all right,' he said eventually. 'I've over-reached. You don't need to tell me. I need something to start happening with the show or else… well, Larry's going to have to go in the first instance. I've already had to release Malky from the gatehouse.'

'Larry's the butler?'

'Aye.'

'So that was Larry who answered the intercom at the gate?'

Collins nodded.

'And, there was someone upstairs?'

Collins stared blankly across the table. Buchan got the sense of something amiss.

'Maisy,' he said. 'Forgot she was even in today. She cleans.'

'Right.'

Collins smiled, took another mouthful of food. Buchan suddenly wondered if Albright was up the stairs and that the two of them were in a relationship, the whole fight narrative some strange sleight of hand.

Over-thinking, Buchan.

'So, you're in trouble if the show doesn't come off?'

'Not in trouble, so much, you know. I'm just going to look stupid. I can sell this place, move into a two-bedroom in town, I'll be fine. Set for life, 'n that, you know. But I'll have fucked it, man. Royally fucked it. No cunt wants to look like a clown. My mum'll be like that…'

'Mothers,' said Buchan, and Collins nodded.

'So, is there anyone who'd want to see you fail?'

Collins took another bite of cabbage, this one with not quite so much enthusiasm as before, then he nodded ruefully.

'Quite a lot of people, probably. People like it when balloons get pricked, don't they? We're no' a country that celebrates success. We glory in failure. We love it when people are brought back down to size. Who the fuck am I living here, when I should be back in the scheme, right?'

Buchan made the point that Collins was ignoring with a steady look across the table.

Eventually, 'Oh wait, you mean... right, OK, right. Someone wants me to fail so much they'd murder folk so that the show cratered?'

'Yes.'

'Fuck me, man.'

Collins stared at an indistinct point on the table. Cheeks puffed, small head shake, exasperated breath.

'I'm going to need more food,' he said, and he pressed a small button beneath the table. 'That feels like a stretch, man,' he continued, looking back at Buchan. For the first time, Buchan thought he didn't sound entirely convincing. 'I mean, double murder, man, that's pretty fucking serious, by the way.'

'Sir,' said Larry the butler, appearing silently in the room.

'Can I have some bacon, please? And more toast. Plain loaf if you've got it.'

'Of course, sir. Sir?' he asked Buchan.

'I'm good,' said Buchan.

The butler turned and left as quietly as he'd arrived.

'Bacon, eh?' said Collins.

'Who wants you to fail more than anyone else?' asked Buchan.

Collins held his gaze for a moment, then bit into another piece of sourdough.

23

Buchan nodded at the duty officer, then walked into Roth's apartment, closing the front door behind him.

Into the open-plan, and he stood in silence. His familiar routine, with familiar intent. There would be nothing new to learn here. The SOCOs had been all over the apartment, Sgt Meyers doing the job with as few officers as possible. This was a fellow officer, who would hopefully be back in the fold soon enough. They didn't need too many people going through the detail of Roth's life. Meyers and two others had done the job, any secrets that had been revealed of Roth and her private life that were obviously unrelated to her disappearance had been ignored, excluded from information passed onto the investigation team.

There was something about the quiet of a strange apartment. The haunting beauty of it, enhanced by the fact that the only time Buchan ever did this was after a crime had been committed.

He thought of the moment the abduction had taken place, then glanced over his shoulder at where the Bluetooth device had been left, playing the music as Roth had entered her apartment. It was gone now, of course, bagged and taken back to SCU.

Roth had come home, she'd checked to see if anyone was waiting for her, she had relaxed, she had called Buchan. She hadn't sounded particularly on edge, confident the place was clear. And by the time the police arrived, she was gone. That there was no sign of a struggle, suggested she'd been attacked unexpectedly from behind.

They'd checked the previous evening, of course. Anywhere someone might have hidden had been examined, samples of dust, fragments of fibre removed. He just couldn't imagine Roth doing a sloppy job, however. Which would leave the possibility that someone arrived not long after she'd called it in, and that someone had attacked her. But how would they have known when to come? The window between the call being made and the police arriving would have been very tight. To get in, knock her out – or kill her, but he didn't want to think about that – and then remove the body without being seen, would easily have taken not much less time than it would have taken the police to get here.

'They would've had to have had access to our calls then,' said Buchan to the room, disinterestedly staring at the Glastonbury poster, reading the names of bands and artists almost none of whom he'd heard of.

He shook his head. The obvious thought, that it had been an inside job, just didn't feel right.

He walked to the window, and looked down on the street. A weak sun shining now, a cold day. There was a guy walking by in T-shirt and shorts, pulling along a reluctant cat on a lead, the cat with a blue puffer coat wrapped around it.

He watched them for a moment, then turned back to the apartment.

'Someone sets the place up, then leaves the apartment,' said Buchan, as though he was discussing this with Kane, or Roth herself. 'Agnes comes home, she discovers the music. She calls it in. The perpetrator bides his time. He knows Agnes will call it in. Maybe he stands at the door listening. Maybe he's bugged her apartment. He knows when she's called. He gives it a minute, he knocks.'

Buchan let the words vanish into the silence of the room, his eyes now falling on the chess set. He wondered if the moves had been made before Agnes came home. She hadn't mentioned them, but it would have been secondary to the music and, for all that she'd sounded relaxed about it, to the possibility that the killer was in her home.

Even then, Roth would have had to be caught unawares. There was no doubt she could take care of herself.

He shook his head, as once more he considered the notion that it could be an inside job. It made sense, in equal measure with it just not making sense.

'Agnes would like the sound of it, though,' he said to the room, this time his voice a low mutter. 'Just the kind of crap you'd find in one of those books.'

His phone rang, and though the volume was low and it was

in his coat pocket, it still rudely shattered the silence.

'Sam,' he said, pulling the phone out and, as usual when not in public, putting it on speaker rather than to his ear.

'Another one, sir,' said Kane. Her tone said it all. Fear and loathing and exasperation and desperation and hopelessness.

'Dammit,' said Buchan, his voice low, and then the question emerged as 'Where?' rather than who, which might have said something about his state of mind.

'Largs,' she said. And as she added, 'Louise Hathaway,' Buchan said the name along with her, already picturing the woman in her home, the Clyde and the island before her, looking glorious on a beautiful, chill winter's day.

'Dammit,' he repeated. A moment, and then he said, 'I'm at Agnes's place. No point in us going down separately. I'll swing by and grab you. But all the other stuff we've got going on,' he continued, as he walked out of the house, slammed the door behind him and nodded grimly at the officer, 'we can't let that go. Revisiting people Agnes has spoken to, and looking for similarities in works of fiction or film. Make sure Danny and Ian, and whoever else they need, stay on that.'

'Sir. I'll see they're on point, then be waiting for you downstairs.'

They hung up, Buchan bounded down the stairs, two at a time.

24

'Oh, Jesus,' said Buchan.

He took a few seconds looking at the corpse, soaked in the scene, and then turned quickly away.

The local police had locked the place down, but had left the scene as it was, waiting for the big leagues to arrive. The apartment door to the right of Louise Hathaway's was open, and from inside, as they had passed briefly down the corridor, they could hear the sound of someone sobbing.

Buchan and Kane had arrived marginally before Meyers' SOCO team, and they'd left them in the carpark while they got their equipment together.

The local officer who'd stayed in the apartment was standing resolutely by the front door, staring out to sea. It would be unavoidable, as she looked across the large, open sitting room, for her to miss the massive, naked corpse slumped backwards over the table, the great slit down her chest and abdomen.

The music was playing, now familiar, the harbinger of death. Perhaps they'd become desensitised to it, so that it no longer added to the atmosphere. Now it was little more than a calling card, the Pink Panther leaving a white glove lying around. Maybe a calling card was all it had ever been.

Kane stood beside the body, forcing herself to look at it. Thinking through how this position would have been arrived at. The body on the table, and naked. Her clothes off to the side, strewn on the floor.

'No blood on the clothes,' said Kane to the room, 'which means she was naked before she was murdered. And unless we're thinking of arresting like Dwayne Johnson or someone here, it's hard to imagine her killer was able to lift her up onto the table.' A gap, and then she added, 'Big girl.'

Buchan glanced over. He was looking out of the window,

looking to see if this spot would've been overlooked at any point. And while someone down on the promenade might have been able to look up at the window, very unlikely they would actually have seen anything during the hours of daylight. Only at night, with the curtains open, and the room backlit, would the sitting room have been in full view. Just from the colour of Hathaway's skin, it was apparent she'd been murdered earlier that afternoon.

'It would also have been a hell of a messy business to move her,' said Buchan. He swallowed. Could feel the vomit fomenting in his stomach. 'There would have been a lot more blood strewn around, and the killer would've been covered in it. You're right. You do that to someone that size, you leave them where they lie.'

'Which means she was lying back on the table, naked.'

Kane looked over at Buchan, he turned and shared the gaze, and then looked quickly away. Neither of them stated the obvious.

Buchan felt the rising frustration, the curse stalling in his throat.

'Turn the bloody music off, will you, Sam,' he said, irritated, annoyed at himself even for asking Kane to do it, rather than just doing it himself.

A last look out at the late afternoon sun glinting off the blue-grey flat calm of the Clyde, the music stopped, then he turned away from the window to speak to the officer on duty.

'Constable?'

'Folk,' she said.

Mid-thirties, blonde hair tied back. Her face was deadpan, having shut herself off from the horror in order to get through the rest of the day. She already knew this moment would stay with her. There was far less horrific than this burned into her brain.

Buchan asked the question with a look, and she said, 'Amanda... Mandy.'

'The woman who's crying in the next apartment called it in?'

The ping of the lift, and then the bustle of movement along the corridor, and then Donoghue was walking into the apartment ahead of Meyers and two of her staff.

They all stopped as soon as they saw what awaited them.

'Jesus,' said Meyers.

Donoghue grimaced, but quickly found the required grim humour to see her through the next half hour.

'At least someone took the trouble to do part of my job for me,' she said, and then she put whatever emotion needed to be tucked away into the relevant compartment, and approached the corpse.

Buchan watched her for a moment, and then turned back to Constable Folk.

'Yes, sir,' said Folk. 'She noticed the door was slightly ajar. That was around three p.m. She didn't think anything particular of it, but thought to check half an hour later just to make sure Ms Hathaway hadn't left it open unintentionally. It was still open, obviously, so she rang the bell, knocked, and when there was no answer...' A pause, and then she added, 'Her 999 call sounds like it might have been a little hysterical.'

Buchan nodded ruefully at Folk's understated delivery, said, 'Thanks, Mandy. You're OK to be here for a little longer, or do you need to –'

'I'm fine, sir. Get this kind of thing in Largs all the time these days.'

Buchan nodded, again acknowledging her dry delivery, then he hesitated for a moment. They were in a hallway, a few yards down the corridor, and however far into the neighbouring apartment away from the crying woman, and the sound was still clear.

'I'll try to speak to her,' said Buchan, half over his shoulder to Kane. 'You talk to the doc, see if she has any different first impressions from us.'

'Boss,' said Kane.

Buchan nodded again at Folk, then he was out into the corridor, as another two SOCOs emerged from the lift, then he entered the next apartment. He took a moment before going into the sitting room, then he was through into another bright room, windows on two sides, the aspect different. Cumbrae across the water, and then the view to the right of that, the stretch of the firth back west, and the town of Largs directly before them, from the windows in the end wall of the building.

There was a uniformed officer holding the hand of the woman who was crying loudly. Great sobs through deep breaths. Tissues strewn around the floor. In front of her, on the low coffee table, a glass of water, a cup of tea, a tumbler of whisky, none of which appeared to have done any good.

Buchan flashed his ID at the constable, and then, knowing how he was going to have to handle this, he made a small gesture to tell the constable he could leave. The constable looked a little unsure, and Buchan said, 'It's OK. Just wait outside, please,' and then the constable slowly prised the woman's fingers from his, patted her on the back of the hand, and eased himself out of the seat.

The woman watched him go, the tears temporarily stalling. She swallowed, she stared with some horror at Buchan's arrival, and then she lifted a tissue from the box and loudly blew her nose, finishing with another gasped sob at the far end.

'What's your name?' asked Buchan.

His voice was cold, bordering on the harsh. She swallowed again. Recognising she was in the presence of authority, it was as though she realised she suddenly had to be a better standard of witness. More was expected of her.

'Margaret.'

'Margaret?'

'Hughes.'

'How long have you lived next door to Louise?'

Another swallow, and then, 'Ten years. No, wait, eleven. I've been saying ten for so long, but it's more like eleven.'

Her voice was uneven, but the stern approach was working so far. Indeed, Buchan was hopeful he wasn't going to have to go as far as he'd feared he might. And while he'd been intending to stop some way short of a Bogartesque slap across the face, the constable who'd just departed was obviously trained in the modern arts of the compassionate witness interview, and would have little time for Buchan's uncaring brusqueness.

'Do you see her often? She told us previously she doesn't go out much.'

'Much?' She swallowed again. 'I thought she never went out. Well, I met her in the lift once. That was a while ago.' Another pause, she leant forward, blew her nose again. 'I was a bit worried getting in the lift with her, to be honest, but I thought it would be rude to say I'd wait.'

With every word, conversational normality became more of a reality. Still, any sign of sympathy, he thought, and she would lapse.

'Did you hear anything from her apartment today?'

She held his gaze for a moment, and he couldn't tell if this was her giving the answer serious thought, or whether she was surprised to have been asked.

'I never hear anything from the apartment.'

'In eleven years?'

'Never. The walls are great. Soundproofing. This...,' and she indicated the room and her apartment and the building with a quick sweep of her eyes, 'it's a good build. Only twenty years old, but they don't do them like this anymore.'

'You and Louise never had coffee, lunch, anything like that?'

She shook her head.

'When was the last time you spoke to her?'

'Actually spoke?'

'Actually spoke,' said Buchan, nodding. He wasn't sure what not actually speaking to your neighbour would involve.

'Six months maybe. We didn't talk much.' A pause, then, 'Got on fine, just didn't talk.'

'You know if many people came and went? Do you hear the lift when you're in the kitchen?'

'Well, I always say, though you can't hear it, you kind of feel it, you know. Like you instinctively know it's happening.'

'So, you know if anyone ever visited Louise?'

'There's Tom and Alice at the end there, so maybe them. They're away at the moment, though. South of France.'

'Were you aware of the lift coming up here this afternoon?'

She looked steadily at him across the coffee table. Thinking. Buchan hadn't sat down, hadn't made any effort to try to get close to her, or to comfort her. This was being conducted like a business meeting, serious matters to be discussed, and he had managed to bend her to his will.

'It came up once, I think. Went back down straight away, didn't come back.'

'Did you hear anyone in or out of Louise's apartment?'

She shook her head.

'So, whoever came to see Louise either arrived, or left using the stairs?'

'I suppose.'

She swallowed again, and this time her eyes widened.

'They're not still there?' she asked.

'No one's still there.'

Now she pushed herself back against the sofa, her eyes darting around the room.

'Maybe they got in here.'

135

The horror and self-pity of her discovery which Buchan had managed to counteract, was now to be replaced by fear. It hadn't occurred to her that the killer might still be on the loose. Or, if it had at first, the arrival of the police on the scene had relaxed her. Now, the spectre of the killer lying somewhere in wait came barrelling into her brain.

'Don't worry,' said Buchan, who was liable to be even more contemptuous of someone who felt imaginary fear for themselves. 'No one's lying in wait. And we'll have a huge number of officers in the building shortly. We'll be knocking on every door, looking in every room. We'll check your apartment, top to bottom.'

'You'll what?'

She looked at her bedroom door.

Jesus, thought Buchan. He could not have wanted to know less what secrets she kept behind there.

25

Two hours later, the corpse back at the mortuary, the day shooting by into evening, Buchan and Kane having left the scene and stopping off with Donoghue on their way back to the office.

They were in traditional position, around the body of Louise Hathaway. Although Hathaway's corpse was not so differently posed as she had been on the table in her apartment, there was nothing unnatural about this setting. This was where post-mortems took place. Anyone whose cause of death might be a mystery found themselves here. The majority of them wouldn't have been murdered. So now Louise Hathaway looked as she was supposed to look, lying in a position in which she was supposed to lie.

'This is a nice job,' said Donoghue, indicating the cut.

As usual, the Beatles were playing. *Here, There and Everywhere*. Buchan had always hated the song. Being here, now, looking at this dead woman, the massive slit down her chest and abdomen, only emphasised the syrupy cheesiness of the song.

It would pass.

'You think it was done by a professional?' asked Kane. 'I mean, you're not going to have to make another insertion to get at her stomach and whatever, right?'

'I had work to do to get to her stomach,' said Donoghue. 'And there's nothing to indicate it was done by a professional, just someone with a good eye. They had their victim where they wanted her, and they had their chosen method of murder.' A pause, and then, 'I, like you I suppose, would have no idea why they chose this specifically, but here we are. The victim was naked and prostrate, and distracted, I might add, and then the killer produced a serrated blade from somewhere and did this. Started at the throat, and bang. Two-handed job, I think, to drag the knife down the chest like this. Some amount of strength, but not, you know, not a gargantuan act of vigour.'

'Louise was having sex?'

'She was being orally pleasured. There's no sign of penetration, but her genitals were cleaned with very strong antiseptic. We've taken samples from inside. We'll have to see, maybe some saliva got in there. The killer did not attempt to clean out her vaginal canal, exactly. They did not go deep.'

'Had she orgasmed?' asked Kane.

'I believe so. And then, well I would suggest that perhaps her killer asked her to close her eyes. Or maybe Ms Hathaway naturally kept her eyes closed. She does not appear to have put up anything of a fight. Now, she was hardly in a position to really fight, a large lady like this prone on a table, that was going to take some effort to get up and defend herself, but there's nothing on the hands or arms. Nothing to suggest flailing or any attempt whatsoever to fend off her attacker. A clean cut, out of nowhere. She couldn't have seen it coming.'

'Do we know if she had any relationships?' asked Kane, without taking her eyes off the giant scar down the middle of the body.

'I didn't get that impression,' said Buchan, 'but then, I never specifically asked. Her rarely going out, suggests not, but I guess there could have been someone who visited.' A beat, he shook his head, he could feel his growing sense of frustration and disappointment. This was getting worse, and he felt no nearer even beginning to establish a clear line of inquiry. 'So she wasn't drugged, anything like that?' he asked, to make sure he'd covered the bases.

'No. Alcohol last night. Today, looks like she'd had eggs, toast, and a green vegetable. Some sort of cabbage, I presume. I'll get the exact type of cabbage soon enough, if that's going to make any difference.'

Buchan thought of Benjamin Collins and his cabbage for breakfast.

That person up the stairs at his house, the one they'd claimed was a cleaner? Could that have been Louise Hathaway? If it had been, she would have had to have dashed back down the road to Largs pretty quickly.

He didn't like the sound of it. Yet, it was the kind of detail he should have imparted to Kane, and which he would certainly have expected her to share with him, but the words stayed in his head. It really didn't matter. Sometimes there was just no need to talk.

Silence threatened to engulf them, as they all stood in silent horror around the corpse. The music stopped. That particular silence would not last, and then another tune started up, one Buchan did not recognise. Guitars, drums, bass, no vocals, he had no idea what was playing, and neither did he care.

'This is getting a little out of hand, Inspector,' said Donoghue.

Buchan didn't answer. Kane threw him a quick glance to see what the comment had done to his face.

Nothing. It was hardly something he'd needed pointing out to him.

'Time of death around one-ish?' asked Buchan, moving the conversation along. It wasn't that he didn't want the scrutiny. They needed to get on. He wasn't even going to employ his familiar conversational distraction from the scene of grotesquery before them by asking what they were listening to.

'Yes,' said Donoghue. Business as usual, she wasn't going to question that Buchan had ignored her comment. It had been out of place for her in any case.

'We'll need to speak to Ruth,' said Kane, 'establish if there's kitchen detritus to indicate whether there were two people eating.'

'Might be hard to tell,' said Donoghue caustically, indicating the corpse, and Kane couldn't help the smile.

'Hard to imagine the killer stayed over from the night before,' said Buchan, 'not if they went with the intention of committing murder. They'd have left far too much evidence of themselves around the apartment.'

'So he turns up,' said Kane, talking herself through it, 'they eat together, or not. Things take a romantic turn,' and she got an eyebrow from Donoghue, 'and the fact that it took place on the table rather than the bed, suggests either a quick escalation, or the killer made sure to keep it at the table, as the fewer places in the apartment he had to remove evidence from the better.'

'The bed is going to require a complete change of sheets,' said Buchan, the words feeling pointless as he said them.

'Yes. So the killer maybe seduces her, they have sex on the spot, and bam.'

Kane grimaced slightly at her own use of the final word, but there was no comment from either of the others. Buchan nodded. That was about the size of it.

'And, obviously,' continued Kane, 'Louise had absolutely no idea that this person was the killer.'

'Unless she had an ill-merited sense of bravado,' said Donoghue. 'A belief she could take care of herself if and when it got out of hand.'

'I like that,' said Buchan. 'Maybe she was suspicious, particularly if she wasn't used to this guy turning up at her house on a Saturday. But she's also curious. She runs with it. If it's someone she knows well, she's not going to really believe they've committed these murders.'

'People don't,' chipped in Kane.

'Maybe she gets thrown by the sex. Maybe she's used to having sex with him.'

He paused, he finished with a shrug that never quite made it all the way to his shoulders.

'It feels a plausible, workable scenario, except one thing,' he said, and then he left it there, and neither of the others bothered filling the gap.

They simply had no idea who it was.

*

Buchan rambled through gritted teeth, accelerating along a short stretch of road, a brief burst of speed that would meet a red light in less than a hundred yards.

'It's driving me nuts that none of the main players, *none of them*, are taking this seriously. This thing, it's happening to someone else, other people, nothing to do with them. Even though they could clearly be next. Unless they know more than we do. And that's one of the things here. The most important people in the structure of a show appear to be the producers at the top, who are the managers, and then the director, who's in charge of the creative side. So, if someone is targeting the show, why wouldn't you start there? Why wouldn't you go after the people running the ship? The writer and the camera guy, their parts in the show are long since done. Same with Zelinger, if he's a victim, rather than the perpetrator.'

'And if we're right about Louise, it seems unlikely that was Zelinger who had her on the table. The guy's missing, having disappeared from the crime scene. Unless they were in league up until that point, she's hardly going to have invited him in for sex.'

'So, if Zelinger tips over into the victim column, then the same applies to him as the others. He was a bit-part player, his death means nothing to the show now.' A pause, and then the other potential victim, the one whose disappearance troubled him more than any of the others. 'And Agnes... again, unrelated to the show.'

He slowed the car, the lights determinedly did not change, he came to a halt behind a green 307.

'You think maybe there's something else going on with Albright and Collins?' asked Kane. 'Goddard, maybe. Something we can't see. There's all this crap, but the show's not actually getting hurt. In fact, of course, when it does make it to release, there's going to be a hell of a lot more interest in it.'

'There's that. It seems extreme, all the same. One murder would probably have done it.'

'Hmm. You're right. As Agnes was saying about motive...'

Buchan's gaze drifted away, he put the palms of his hands to his eyes and rubbed them. Roth. She was out there somewhere, hopefully still alive. Held captive. They had no idea of the conditions she was being held in or how she'd be getting treated. Given the way the killer had dealt with his other victims so far, the chances were not good.

'I want to bring them all in,' said Buchan. 'I want to lock them up until one of them actually tells us something useful.'

Hopeless words, pointing to his feelings of desperation. They had nothing on them, and consequently very little with which they could apply any pressure. He would have thought the situation itself would have applied the pressure, but it wasn't happening.

Silence fell across the car. The lights changed. Buchan went through the motions.

26

'Ms Carr, good to get hold of you at last,' said Buchan, and the writer smiled and nodded.

'Sorry it's proved so difficult. I've been travelling.'

Miriam Carr, the writer of the novel on which *Beware The Watcher* was based, was sitting in a booth in a café. The large coffee cup on the table said Starbucks. There was a closed MacBook on the table beside it. She had earphones in, and the speaker in her left hand, something to fiddle with while she spoke.

'Where are you now?'

'Oh, I'm back home in Vancouver. Corner of Powell and Cordova.' She smiled like that reference would mean something to Buchan.

'You don't work in the house?'

'God, it is *so* soul-destroying. I mean, like, *are you kidding me*? I don't know how people do it. Like, you know, like writers and whoever. I *do not* know how they sit at home all day, surrounded by silence. Those Covid lockdown months, everyone working from home. Like, *oh my God*. It drove me *nuts*. I just need to get out, you know. I sit in cafés *all day*. And the bonus is, like, you don't end up talking to yourself, or wandering around the house doing other shit. You know, like housework, or fitting a piece or two into a jigsaw, or whatever. I never get anything done, like, *anything* written when I'm at home. So I sit here, or in Horton's, or wherever, you know, and it's great. I can concentrate, I can work. Some days, right here, right in this booth, I'm writing five, six thousand words. At home, lucky if I can do a *tenth* of that.'

'Tell me about *Beware The Watcher*,' said Buchan, cutting in as soon as there was a gap in Carr's narrative of the self.

'What d'you want to know?'

She took a drink of coffee.

'You've heard about the murders?'

'The music guy and the cinematographer? Oh my God, yes. That is just... that's *horrific*. You have any idea who did it?'

Well, thought Buchan, that sounded fake.

'Our inquiries are continuing,' he said. 'Did you work with the writer of the screenplay?'

'Louise?'

Buchan nodded. Sitting in the ops room, the door slightly ajar so that anyone passing would see he was interviewing and would only come in if they had something that needed to be said.

'I did not. I mean, we all said it up front, I wouldn't have anything to do with this show. I know nothing about making shows, and I'm not bothered about starting to learn. You know, some people, they are all about getting into TV and movies and whatever, they would *eat your liver* to get one of their books on Netflix. I could care less. I was happy to take the money. And, as it turned out, that Scottish kid was happy to give it to me.'

She laughed, then took another drink.

'Louise is dead,' said Buchan bluntly.

Carr choked on her coffee. Some of it splurted from her lips, and she wiped her wrist across her mouth.

'Like, *murdered* dead?'

'Yes.'

'Holy cow.'

'This is all getting a little out of hand,' said Buchan, parroting Donoghue's line, which was still in his head. Carr smiled and nodded, like they were discussing some minor irony. 'We're throwing a pretty wide net, talking to everyone. I'd like to hear about your part in the process, everyone at the production you've dealt with, a precis, start to finish.'

She smiled again, this time with a familiar accompanying head shake.

'That net you're talking about, you're going to have to throw it wider than me, my friend.'

'Just answer the question, please.'

He hadn't been optimistic about this conversation, just making a call he knew he should make. However, her breezy attitude to multiple murder was darkening his mood even further.

'I wrote the book. There was nothing... you know, from what I've heard about these murders, I don't know what this

---

143

killer's thinking 'n all, but it's not like we've been inspired by the same thing. I was just inspired by the kind of nutjob that stalks the shit out of strangers. No biggie. Nothing original about it, to be honest, but I guess I did a decent job, painted some good characters. The stalker, the villain…'

'Corran?'

'There we go. Corran's an interesting guy, you know? People love Corran, even though he's this, like, total psychopath. But other than some generic, timeless, psycho kind of a thing, there's nothing specific going on there. It all came out of here.' She tapped the side of her head. 'I'm not going to bang on about the heart of darkness that all writers possess, that shit gets old quick.'

'So, you wrote the book, you published the book…?'

'Sure, I did all that myself. I kind of half-heartedly gave it to my agent, and she kind of half-heartedly went out with it, but I was always ready to pull the trigger and do it myself. Worked a treat. By two months in, I was pulling in a hundred K a month. Dollars, not sales, but that's decent money. Word got around, I got an audiobook offer, then I said to Cal, go for it, see if you can get a screen deal. Tonne of interest straight off the bat, we're closing in on, like, we're actually closing in on a deal with Prime, and then *boom*! Here comes the Scottish kid outta left field. Holy shit. No one saw him coming. Tonne of money up front, then he and Prime get into this stupid bitch-fight, and before you know, he's paying me an *absurd* amount. He says straight off the bat he doesn't want me involved in the show, and I do not care. I can't tell you how much I do not care.'

'You met him?'

'Nope. Cal didn't even meet him. Cal spoke to him a lot, like they Zoomed, you know, but Cal's never even been to England, and far as I know, the kid never came to New York. Me? I had nothing to do with it.'

'Did you get any updates on the process as it was taking place? Any…,' and he let the question go at the shake of her head. He had asked it with virtually no expectation in any case. The course of the conversation had already been established, and there was nowhere for it to go.

'Like I say, I've got nothing to tell you. They didn't tell me anything, but I didn't care. I got money up front, I got more money when they went into production. Sales of the book get a boost every time the show gets mentioned, and then, God knows

---

where or when, but at some point it's going to air, and *boom*, guess what? More sales. More money. And, hey, look, I'm not like celebrating it or anything, but sales have picked up the last couple of days too, you know, particularly in England. It's sad 'n all, but I ain't complaining.'

She lifted the Starbucks coffee cup. Buchan looked into her eyes over the bottom edge of the giant container.

*

The day wound towards its end, Buchan restless and annoyed, aggravated about their lack of progress. It was a desperate stretch, and he hadn't voiced the opinion to anyone else, but the death of Louise Hathaway had made him a little more hopeful about Roth. The killer was up to something with her, and while it did not take much imagination to think it would be unspeakably awful, perhaps at least he had not killed her. He was keeping her alive for a reason, and they just needed to find her before it was too late.

Just needed to find her. That was all.

He stood outside the Winter Moon, looking in. Saturday evening, getting late, not many people, the usual suspects in position.

He didn't want to go in. Not tonight. He'd come here, almost as though his feet had directed him, his brain having no part in the decision. Yet, now that he was here, he had no desire to enter. Didn't want to speak to Duncan, didn't even want to see Janey.

Two nights' previously had been the third time they'd slept together since the break-up. As with those first two occasions, it had happened because Janey had wanted it to. She was always drawn to him, and three times now she had given in to it. Buchan, the cipher, had happily gone along with it each time. And each time she backed further away, and each time Buchan had been hurt.

Not today, he thought. He wasn't going to be hurt. He could love Janey unconditionally, he could think about her too often, he could place himself right in front of her every damned night, but it hurt, it always did. If he wanted it not to – and today he just couldn't handle it on top of everything else – then he had to back away completely.

Anyway, tonight he didn't want company. Too troubled,

thoughts too plagued by this horror of a case, thoughts too plagued by his missing constable who he'd let down, and he turned away from the door, and began walking back through town towards the river.

There was drink at home, and there was Edelman, and should he want it, there was food. That was all.

Every few hundred yards, every couple of minutes, he would take his phone out of his pocket to see if he'd missed any messages. The phone remained resolutely silent.

27

Sunday morning. Cherry had found a connection between the murders and a small crime novel that had been published a few years previously, and Buchan and Kane had come to speak to the writer.

Buchan parked the Facel on the road outside a large detached Victorian house. A quiet, affluent street in Shawlands, huge gardens, houses with large bay windows, this one dominated by an enormous monkey puzzle tree planted in the middle of the front lawn.

Buchan and Kane got out of the car and stood for a moment looking up at the tree. Buchan found himself impressed by it, but couldn't think of anything to say.

'My dad planted one of those in the back garden when I was wee,' said Kane. 'Wonder how it's doing.'

'This one looks as old as the house,' said Buchan, mundanely.

'Nope,' said Kane, and Buchan asked the question with an understated sideways glance.

'When you see monkey puzzle trees with all the lower branches missing, you think they've been pruned for aesthetics' sake. But when they get to around a hundred-years-old, all the lower branches fall off. So, when you see one like this, branches intact all the way down, you know it's still young.'

'Huh,' said Buchan, nodding, impressed, as he always was, by anyone with a piece of arcane knowledge. 'Why does the tree do that?'

A pause, then Kane, long since having reached the limit of her knowledge on monkey puzzle trees, said, 'Science.'

Buchan smiled, opened the gate, and then, switching back to work mode after the brief respite, walked quickly up the garden path, the monkey puzzle tree to his left now forgotten, and rang the doorbell.

'You write seven novels a year?' said Kane.

Ronald Naismith had reluctantly invited them into the house, showing them to the room he described as the study. He had then taken his place at an imposing desk, the wall behind him lined with rows of books, albeit it looked like the kind of library one would find in a National Trust property, with hundreds of Victorian, dark red, leather-bound volumes, most of which had likely never been read.

'Yes.'

'Seems a lot,' said Buchan.

'I suppose,' said Naismith. He was in his early sixties, wearing a soft-collared tweed shirt, and was sitting with his arms folded.

The house was completely silent. It was unclear whether there was anyone else at home.

'You publish these yourself?' asked Kane.

'I did at first, but I got picked up by Bow Street Digital. They run a nice operation. Lucky to have them.'

'Where do the ideas come from for seven crime novels a year?' asked Buchan, and Naismith gave him a wary look.

'How many times have I been asked that?' he said.

'You'll have an answer for us then,' said Kane.

He left it a beat, another, then finally seemed to settle on the reply, opening his hands to indicate the library around him. Or, perhaps, the world around him, it wasn't entirely clear which.

'I read, I watch the news, I think. Mainly, I think.' He tapped the side of his head. 'We all have a darkness inside us, you must know that. All people, when put under the right conditions, when they are tested, when needs must, they have a heart of darkness. I am no different, except I rarely go anywhere, or do anything. This is my life, and I live it within the confines of this house. And within the confines of this.' He tapped the side of his head again. 'Ideas come to me all the time. I make notes. A notebook of ideas. When the time comes, I peruse my notebook, I pick something, then I write. The first draft will come in a few weeks. I let it sit for a month, while I work on something else. I read it over, make any changes. Call that another week, then I send it to my editor. She's very light touch.

She returns the manuscript, I have a final look, and then we're ready for copy and proof. A last read-through, and we're done. Start to finish, call it three months, but then there are other books in the works the whole time, three or four in various stages of progress, all that resulting in around seven new titles a year.'

'You have a big following?'

He shook his head.

'Not especially. It keeps me busy, that's the main thing. Since Janice died… that's been eight years now. I drank heavily for the first two or three years. Got a warning shot or two. Heart trouble. More than one doctor told me I had to slow down. I didn't care. Then Anita had the twins, and… well, family, we all know what it's like. Anita said I had to find something else to do with my life other than drink three bottles of wine a day or she was going to stop bringing the kids over. And here we are.'

Momentarily their eyes were drawn to a photograph on the desk of two young girls in shades of pink.

'So, tell us about *The Devil In The Shadows*,' said Kane.

'What about it?'

'Where did that particular idea come from?'

He stared blankly across the desk. You can see the leftover of the drinking, thought Buchan. In the eyes, the veins in the cheeks. He used to drink and he doesn't anymore. It wasn't something he'd had to say.

'So, let me see,' he began. 'That was the sixth book in the DI Gronkowski series. That was a tough one. Got a little out of hand, I thought.'

'How'd you mean?'

'Well, it's all about… Well, you see, crime writing, as with everything, should be about simplicity. You may, if you wish, give the impression of convolution, perhaps you care to bamboozle the reader, but at its heart, your story must be simple. And believable, that's important. But that one got out of hand. I ran out of ideas. I wasn't sure what to do or where it should be going, and so I ended up doing that thing I hate. Killing off characters as a substitute for plot. You see it so often. The writer doesn't know what to do, so they keep the reader or the viewer engaged with another bloody murder. Such a tiresome trope of the genre, and that was one of mine. As I say, it all got quite out of hand.'

'Where did the story come from?' asked Buchan. 'The genesis of the idea?'

'That one...?' he said, looking off to the side as though imagining himself to be at his creative peak, interviewed by Melvin Bragg for the South Bank Show. 'I believe it started with those sorry tales of Russian oligarchs supposedly killing themselves. I mean, it's an epidemic now, of course. You know, since Ukraine. Really, how many oligarchs are there left? But it's been going on for years. And that started me off on a story of a killer murdering in a way that the victim may well have committed suicide. Of course, within a couple of chapters, within one murder, I'd got away from that, but that's the creative process for you. You have to let it run free. Try to constrain it, and then you're not being true to the story.'

'Have you been following the murders that have been in the news in town the last few days?' asked Kane, knowing that Buchan would be as dismissive of his author-speak as she herself.

'I, em... no, sorry, haven't see anything about that.'

'You just said you read the news,' said Buchan sharply.

'Not while I'm, you know,' and he indicated the closed laptop. 'You know, when I'm actually writing, the first draft, it's like, full on. One hundred per cent, full on. Five, six, sometimes seven thousand words a day. I try to get the first draft done in three weeks, give myself the fourth week as overflow. Rarely look at the news while I'm going through the process.' He made a gesture encircling his head. 'Messes with the, you know, the carefully crafted creative juices.' A beat, and then, 'There've been murders?'

'Are you aware of the television production, *Beware The Watcher*?' asked Buchan.

'Nope. Don't really watch a lot of TV. Football, if I do.'

'It's based on a book by a Canadian author. Bestseller on Amazon. You might have noticed it.'

Naismith stared blankly across the desk for a moment, and then finally shrugged.

'Nope. I mean, that's not avoidance on my part, it's just indicative of how little attention I pay to my fellow writers and their work. I'm not interested in the competition. There are no rivalries for me. Simply put, it's me against the system, and this is me, with my seven crime novels a year, trying to crack it. The system.' Another beat, and then, 'Hasn't happened yet,' accompanied by a small, self-conscious laugh.

'There have been a series of murders around this TV

production,' said Kane, and Naismith watched her warily, his lips slightly parted. 'And we've noticed there's a correlation between the real-life murders, and the murders that take place in your book, *The Devil In The Shadows*.'

'Really?'

'Yes, really. Would you have any idea why that might be?'

'Well, that's extraordinary, and I'm not sure there really is a practical explanation for extraordinary.'

Working silently in tandem as they so often did, Buchan and Kane stopped asking questions, and stared harshly across the desk. Naismith, however, was not to be cowed by the looks of a couple of stern police officers.

'I'm not sure what you're looking for,' he said, nevertheless, feeling the need to fill the silence.

'The story came from your imagination?' asked Buchan.

'Yes! I mean, I said, you know, the thing about oligarchs. But that aside…'

'So, then, whoever's committing these murders must be someone who's read your book.'

Another long silent stare across the desk.

'Or else, you're the killer,' added Buchan.

'Now look, that's not on. That's just…'

'Do you know who's read the book?' asked Kane.

'How would I know that?'

'Amazon don't have a record of who buys what?'

'They don't tell me! They don't tell Bow Street. So, yes, Amazon will know. Good luck finding someone there to help you.'

Buchan gave Kane the *make sure we chase that up* glance, then turned back to Naismith.

'How many copies have been sold?'

'Of *The Devil in The Shadows*?'

'Obviously!'

'Oh, I'd need to check. One of my less successful series, that one. I dropped it eventually. If you were looking for a ballpark figure, then perhaps around twelve hundred, thirteen hundred maybe. Oh wait, that one I also had a Bookbub deal on, so that's going to add on several hundred. Let's say two thousand tops. But Bow Street send these very convoluted statements on Excel spreadsheets, nothing collated. Quite tiresome for an old dog like me. I'm mainly interested in the ballpark. You know, how much money are they paying me.'

It may have been a start, but on the off-chance they ever got the names from Amazon, and Buchan was pretty sure that wouldn't happen, that was an awful lot of people. And, of course, there'd be nothing to say that someone couldn't have read a book on someone else's Amazon account, or had been told the details by another reader, and had used those details accordingly.

'You know a Benjamin Collins?' asked Kane, and Naismith answered with a vague stare, which led into a shaking head and a, 'Nope. He's on the TV show, or what?'

'Daniel Harptree?' tossed in Buchan.

'Nope. On the show?'

'Sara Albright?'

This time there was a noticeable difference in his face, and they picked up on it instantly. The shadow that crossed his eyes.

'There we go,' said Kane. 'Tell us about Sara Albright.'

'I mean,' said Naismith, widening his hands a little, 'you're asking all these questions, but obviously you've got some idea about *Devil In The Shadows*. Obviously you know it got optioned for film, which is pretty rare for me, by the way. But it's definitely the way forward. I mean, it's the easiest money a writer can make.'

'Tell us about Sara Albright,' said Buchan.

'Well, yes,' said Naismith, 'the little there is to tell. That one, I'm not sure why, that one sparked a bit of interest. I mean, Bow Street never try to sell screen options, but we got this thing based entirely on the book's brief stay in the top one hundred chart after the ad. Astonishing, really. It showed in that chart for less than a day, and suddenly I get this e-mail. Just shows you the close tabs these people keep on things. Everyone's desperate for new content. Sadly it never happened, but the production company that Sara Albright's with, Searchcraft, they took the rights for a year. The year came and went, never heard anything, nothing happened, they never renewed. She seemed keen for a while, right up to the point where, surprise, surprise, she wasn't anymore.' He shrugged, managing to affect a look of self-effacement.

'What was Albright's part in it?' asked Kane.

'She read the book. I'm not sure if she has people, you know readers, but she'd definitely read it, and she was all over it. She loved it.'

'How much progress did they make?'

'Like I say, I don't know. I'm assuming none, but I wouldn't know.'

'The company took the rights, and you were no longer in the loop,' said Buchan, unsurprised the conversation was going down the same route as the one he'd had with the Canadian author. Patterns repeated in all aspects of life.

'That's correct.'

'When was the last time you had contact with Sara Albright?' asked Kane.

'Oh, that was... three years ago. At the start of the process. My understanding is that these people are all the same. They love the creator of the original work until they've got control, and once they've done that, they no longer care. Basically, once she had the rights, I never heard from her again. Towards the end of the year I got Bow Street to contact them to see if anything was happening, and we never got anywhere near her. We spoke to someone there, but I don't know who. The receptionist maybe. Maybe it was the cleaner. They didn't know much, but they knew enough to tell us not to get too excited. Not to expect an extension of the option period.' A pause, and then, 'And that was that.'

'There was a police officer kidnapped in your book,' said Buchan.

'In *Devil In The Shadows*, yes. I don't know what I was thinking. I thought it might work, but really, it trapped me for a while. So I just had her killed.' A pause, and then the shrug. 'Very weak plotting. Sometimes it's not my strong point.'

'How long was she held hostage?' asked Buchan.

He already knew that the fictional kidnapped police officer had been killed, Cherry having given Kane the outline of the plot. Nevertheless, talking about it with the creator of the story was making him anxious, making the hand around his guts squeeze a little harder.

'Oh, three days, I think. She was killed after three days. Not particularly proud of that one, I must admit. I would say I'm astonished a film company bought it up, but then, should anyone be? Look at the state of it, the state of television. So much dross.'

'I thought you didn't watch television,' said Kane.

'Is there any wonder why?'

28

Buchan was sitting at his desk, flicking quickly through the novel that had sparked the latest move in the investigation. His mind was unavoidably on Roth. Roth and her pink hair, and her funny little tattoo on her hip, and her nose ring. Roth, who read several crime novels a week, and who made intermittent attempts to get him reading, as though it was something everyone ought to do. Roth, with her enthusiasm and her determination and her insight, and her smile, which Kane thought flirtatious, and which Buchan didn't really understand, and which he could never decide if he wanted to be flirtatious or not. Roth, who under other circumstances he would have tasked with quickly reading this book and writing a report, and in whom he would have had complete confidence in nothing being missed.

So why hadn't he asked one of the others to do the same in her absence?

Because he felt he owed her this. He was taking her disappearance personally, just as he absolutely would take her death personally if it happened. If he couldn't save her, it would be the last thing he failed to do as a police officer. How could he possibly justify being here, if he couldn't even save one of his own staff?

If the timing and content of the novel were anything to go by, they had around three days to find her. And in those three days, Roth was going to be sexually assaulted.

With every word he read, the grip on his stomach tightened.

Movement at the door to the open-plan, and he turned instinctively. Kane, who'd been dispatched with Cherry to bring Sara Albright to the station, had stopped at the door, half in, half out.

'She's downstairs, boss. You ready now?'

'Yep,' said Buchan.

He turned off the iPad and pushed it across the desk. A last slurp of a cooling cup of coffee, jacket on, and then he was leaving the open-plan, the office quiet on a Sunday afternoon, drifting towards early darkness.

*

'I mean, really?' said Albright, kicking off the conversation as soon as Buchan had sat down opposite her. Kane was next to him, Albright was unaccompanied. 'What's the charge? I cannot believe this. I mean, I haven't called my lawyer, because you know what these people are like. And I have good lawyers, but with quality comes,' and she made the money gesture with her right hand. 'Just them answering the phone sets you back about five grand. Ha! But guess who'll be paying for it once this all comes out in the wash. So, really, what's the charge?'

'You haven't been charged with anything,' said Buchan.

'Why the fuck am I here?'

She looked around, as though there was an audience. She concentrated on the large mirror, assuming there were people behind it. There was, in fact, no one.

'The potential charges range from obstruction to aiding and abetting to, well, murder and abduction of an officer, so let's see how it goes.'

Albright barked out a laugh.

'It's going to be a bumpy ride,' she said, smiling. 'Bring it on, Inspector, what have you got?'

Buchan stared blankly across the desk. Looking to slow things down before they got into the questioning. They would be getting straight to it, after all, but she was a little wired with the thrill of being brought to a police station on a Sunday afternoon.

'Tell us about *Devil In The Shadows*,' he said, having left it long enough for her to begin to look bored with having to wait.

She stared blankly across the desk. Her lips started to move, but not to enable speech. It was more about expressing doubt and confusion. Finally, with a movement of her shoulders and a curious smile, she said, 'Sorry? Devil in the what now?'

'*Devil In The Shadows*,' said Buchan, his tone flatlining, as it usually did when faced with an interviewee and their incredulity.

This time Albright made a more expansive gesture of puzzlement, looking between Buchan and Kane, and said, 'I genuinely have no idea what you're talking about. Like, none.'

'It's a crime novel you optioned for screen a few years ago,' said Kane.

Albright looked at Kane, squinting eyes accompanying more lip movement.

'It's a crime novel I optioned a few years ago?'

'Yes.'

'For Searchcraft?'

Neither Buchan nor Kane answered. If Albright was feigning her confusion, she was sticking with it. Once she'd started, it made sense to see it through, thought Buchan. At some point, however, they were going to have to find a way to prick the bubble.

'I'd need to check,' she said.

'The novel's writer said you were enthusiastic,' said Kane, and Albright laughed.

'The *writer* said that? That's funny.'

Buchan indicated *go on* with his hands, the disappointment beginning to grow inside him. For all her dismissive contempt, he believed her.

'I mean, it's in my job description. You know how many books, scripts, ideas jotted down on the back of a lottery ticket we option every year? I mean, the option is buttons. In movie money terms, the option is, like, sweetie money. We buy forty projects a year. In a good year, we make one of them, palm a couple off to other producers, a few others get put into some sort of development. Most of that stuff though, it never happens, but the person whose work gets optioned, particularly the newbies, they still get excited. So, Project A, whatever it is, likely means everything to them, and means next to didley-squat for us. The poor bastards have no idea, of course, but them's the breaks. *Devil In The Shadows*? Remind me?'

'Forty projects?' said Kane. 'How much per project? Doesn't that add up?'

'If we pick up a book that some newbie published herself, the newbie doesn't have an agent, and no one else has come calling? Two grand, if we're being generous. Might stretch that to five, but I'd say the average is two, two and a half. So forty projects, maybe a hundred grand a year.'

'Didn't Benjamin pay at least a million up front for *Beware The Watcher*?' said Buchan. He was irritated, but mainly because he could see them not getting anywhere when he'd thought they'd been making progress.

She smiled knowingly. She, at least, seemed to be enjoying her Sunday afternoon trip to the police station, like it was a trip to the movies or the local park.

'Look, to give him the benefit of the doubt here, there was a lot of interest in it. That changes the figures. The kind of things we buy up front, when it's our money, we're playing in the minors. Bennie stumbled into the major leagues. Bennie would have been better off playing pick-up ball in the park, but instead he ended up trying to outbid the Yankees for the World Series MVP.'

'*Devil In The Shadows*,' said Buchan, leaning into the question, 'begins with a hanging. One that is intended to look like suicide, but which, it becomes apparent, is obviously murder. There quickly follows a murder which mirrors *exactly* the killing of Blake Philips. At the same time, an associate of the victim disappears, later to turn up dead.'

Her expression was changing as he spoke, though it was not obvious whether she was remembering the book in question, or whether she was starting to realise the discomfort of her position. Maybe this wasn't a walk in the park after all.

'So someone read this book,' she said.

'Looks like it,' said Buchan.

'You think it might have been me?'

'You have alibis for the murders,' said Buchan, 'so not necessarily. But that book went through the system at Searchcraft, and you were not presumably the only one to have read it.'

'If it's on general sale, then any member of the public could have read it.'

'Nevertheless, we have a clear triangulation,' said Buchan. 'The murders are connected to the book, the book's connected to Searchcraft, Searchcraft's connected to the murders. At the moment, we are nowhere near looking at the general public, not when we have Searchcraft staring us in the face.'

'And the writer of the book, surely,' said Albright, straight away. 'Have you considered he's pissed at us for not taking on his book, and he takes it out on something we chose to do instead?'

'We're speaking to the writer,' said Buchan. 'You can leave that to us. Now we're speaking to you. So, we're going to need to know everyone at Searchcraft involved in the evaluation process, everyone who's liable to have read the book, or even read the synopsis of the book, if that's how you work.'

'And this was three years ago?' she said, the scepticism starting to re-enter her voice.

Buchan stared harshly across the desk.

29

'You let her go?' asked Chief Inspector Liddell

Buchan nodded, making a slightly hopeless gesture. There had been, unfortunately, no reason to keep her. They'd got names of anyone who might have come across the manuscript, her readiness to hand them over either through aforethought or genuine belief that Searchcraft had nothing to worry about, and his team were already into checking them out, and making calls. It may have been early Sunday evening, but Roth was still gone, and if she was being held to the same timescale as the police victim in *Devil In The Shadows*, the clock would be running down in the next twenty-four hours.

'What about this writer?' she asked.

'We've got him watched for the moment,' said Buchan. 'We'll make sure he doesn't go anywhere. I don't want to rely too heavily on gut instinct, but there's just nothing about this guy.'

'So too early to barge in there, full pelt, and upend his house looking for a place where he keeps hostages.'

'I think so.'

'And how many people from Searchcraft are you having to speak to?'

'Six in all, although three of them are no longer there. And of the six, Albright said, four are likely a stretch. Don't be surprised if they don't remember anything.'

Liddell let out a long breath, nodding as she did so. She looked annoyed, tense, and Buchan shared her discomfort.

'I'm sorry,' he said. Hands briefly run through his hair, a gesture he felt affected as soon as he'd done it, and he shook his head.

'Don't be. We're doing everything we –'

'Naismith said it perfectly. He was writing his book, and he lost control of the plot. Started killing people just for the hell of it, because he couldn't think of what else to do. And that's what we have here, perfectly replicated. Murder for the sake of it, murder because someone wants to mimic a series of out of control murders. And they're executing it perfectly. Goddammit…'

His head twitched in annoyance. Liddell watched him for a moment, standing out there on the ledge with him, sharing his feeling of failure. Roth was just as much one of her members of staff.

'OK,' she said, 'we can allow ourselves a few moments, but we can't wallow in self-pity. And you're better than that, inspector. So, this is us, right now, hating ourselves. But you know what? It's over. We've done that, we've looked in the mirror and decided we don't like what we see. Now we have to get back to work. You know what else needs to be done tonight, who else needs to be spoken to?'

Buchan nodded, not looking at her, eyes still drifting over the carpet.

'Yes, we're on it. We're doing everything we can.'

'Then no one's asking for anything else. *Everything* is all you can do. So, get back downstairs, and get stuck back into –'

A knock at the door, and then it opened and Cherry entered at a clip.

'Boss,' he said, also acknowledging Liddell. 'I hope this is OK…'

'Go ahead, constable,' said Liddell.

'I've been looking into Ronald Naismith, the writer of *Devil In The…*,' and he cut himself off in the face of Buchan nodding, 'and it's pretty interesting. Sarge said in her report that he claims he gets, like, the spark of an idea from reading the news or whatever, but then his imagination takes over, and the bulk of what he writes comes from the depths of his psyche. Some bullshit like that.' He winced slightly at the term, but Buchan was nodding, so he talked on. 'There's a lot of talk about the guy, however. Online. Doesn't seem to matter that he doesn't sell a great deal. I guess social media for writers is the same as everything else. An online nest of vipers. There was muttering about the guy cribbing ideas from elsewhere, then someone did a hit job on him, looked at all his books, and drew comparisons with a variety of other novels that he might have stolen from. The guy has thirty-four novels out there, and twenty-seven of them are, according to this hit piece, cribbed from other novels.' He paused, but didn't wait for either Liddell or Buchan to ask the obvious question. 'Sadly, not this one. But it doesn't mean he didn't crib *Devil In The Shadows* from another book, but the writer of the hit job – who claimed an encyclopaedic knowledge of crime writing – couldn't identify it. I'd say we need to speak to him again. Because he knows people are saying these things about him, he's on these forums defending himself, but why anyone would go to the trouble to malign a guy like that, when he barely sells, I'm not sure. Other than that he's an idea-thief, and no one likes a thief. If he has an elaborate plot in one of his novels, there's a fair chance he didn't think of it himself.'

That was all Buchan had needed to hear. He looked at Liddell, she waved in the direction of the door, then he was past Cherry, clapping him on the shoulder as he went by, with a, 'Good work, Dan, thanks,' then he was down the stairs and on his way.

*

They had an officer posted outside Naismith's house, and they knew Naismith hadn't gone anywhere. Neither did they suspect he was about to make a dash for freedom, so there was no need to arrive all guns blazing. Nevertheless, Buchan liked the tactic, and so he had the siren on, and when he pulled up abruptly outside the house they'd visited only a few hours previously, he left the blue light swirling in the cold, January sky, and instructed the officer in the other car to do the same. All for effect.

Up the garden path, Buchan and Kane, noticing the twitch of the curtain in the front room, then they arrived at the front door and banged loudly.

'Mr Naismith,' shouted Buchan.

Kane couldn't stop herself, leant forward, banged on the door, shouted the same.

The door opened.

Naismith looked no different from earlier, except now the concern was written across his face, and 'What?' blurted from his lips, followed by, 'Really?'

'We're coming in,' said Buchan, and he and Kane walked forward, Naismith stepping aside, powerless to stop them.

He shut the door, though not before glancing around,

perhaps expecting to see another team to augment the sudden arrival, then he turned to Buchan and Kane, arms spread in confusion.

Buchan wanted to step forward, grab him by the collar, press him up against the door. Stopped himself, but his energy and urgency were still evident.

'You lied to us earlier,' he snapped.

'I didn't! What? I mean –'

'All that baloney about ideas coming from the darkness inside you, or from the news, or whatever. It was bullshit. You steal.'

'I do not!'

'You steal your ideas, Mr Naismith, it's well documented on the Internet,' said Buchan harshly, taking Cherry's update and stretching it to the required shape.

'That's an outrage,' said Naismith, but there was no exclamation in his tone. He was in the process of being busted – indeed, he'd obviously already been busted online – and while he may have been able to happily hide behind his keyboard and deny everything, it wasn't going to be so easy in the face of two angry police officers.

'You know Dorothy Squire?' said Kane, referencing the woman who had written the detailed online report on Naismith's thievery.

'Oh, you're listening to her, are you?' he said, attempting bravado, but not really carrying it off.

'One of our officers is missing,' said Buchan. 'People are getting murdered. Yesterday afternoon, someone had her abdomen sliced open, right down the middle.' Naismith visibly winced. 'And it happened because you wrote it. You put it in a damned book. Where did you get the idea?'

Naismith had backed up against the front door. A pair of boots on a mat next to him; to his right, coats on pegs; on the wall on his left, Eilean Donan castle in snow and black and white.

'You just can't... you can't make that kind of correlation,' said Naismith. 'No one would ever do anything creative if, you know...,' and the words drifted off as he tried, and failed, to think of some other example of evil inspiration.

'Like Manson invoking *Helter Skelter*?' said Kane, doing his job for him.

'Exactly!'

'Yeah, that's it. A bit two-faced of you to be appalled by the action when you make your living out of it.'

'Well, I hardly make a living. It's something I do…'

'Jesus!' snapped Buchan. 'Which book did you steal the idea from? Tell us now, and we'll be out your hair. There are plenty people more important than you to talk to.'

'I don't steal!'

'Borrow, be inspired by, I don't care!' said Buchan, his voice hissing fury, the words squeezed out through gritted teeth.

Naismith was pressing himself so hard back against the front door he was threatening to become part of the wood. A loud swallow in the sudden silence of the hallway. No music playing, no TV, no voices. Anger raged in Buchan's head and he didn't hear the silence. Just the delay.

'It wasn't a book,' came finally, quietly, reluctantly from the writer's lips.

Buchan and Kane asked the question with the same gesture, all shoulders and arms and expression.

'There was a story I read in a book.'

'You just said it wasn't a book!' barked Kane.

'Yes, yes, all right. It was non-fiction. A collection of, like, true crime horror from around the world. You know, obscure murder stories that wouldn't have got much coverage in the UK. We're too busy talking about the Royal Family and whatever, and you get these fascinating tales that are happening all over. Grotesque stories. I suppose there'd be no reason for –'

'So, tell us about this one,' said Buchan, his voice losing none of its anger. 'Where did the idea for *Devil In The Shadows* come from?'

Another pause, and then, shoulders slightly raised as though it was of no significance, he said, 'Canada.'

'The fuck?' blurted Kane.

'Yes, Canada, I'm pretty sure.'

'British Colombia?'

'I don't think so. Somewhere in the middle.'

'What was the name of the book?' said Kane.

'You have the book in the house?' said Buchan, his words swiping across Kane's.

Naismith held his look for a moment, and then his eyes drifted towards the door into the library.

'Come on,' said Buchan, pushing the library door open, 'we need that book right now.'

163

30

They drove hurriedly back through Glasgow, Buchan at the wheel, driving angrily and sloppily, the blue light on to get people out of his way, even though there wasn't much traffic. While he drove, Kane read the chapter on the murders in Regina, Saskatchewan. A series of deaths and disappearances which were being perfectly mirrored by their current crime spree.

As she read, she realised that events here in the city were even more closely related to the real murders than how they'd been reinterpreted by Naismith for *Devil In The Shadows*.

'Shit,' she said, having been reading in silence for a few minutes, after making her initial observation.

'What?' said Buchan, his voice still tipping over into urgency and annoyance.

'This thing where Naismith took the source material and amended it for his own plotline, it's not doing us any favours.'

'Lead detectives about to get murdered, are they?'

'Worse. The police officer who got kidnapped was killed sometime on the third night.'

Buchan unavoidably looked at the clock. Three minutes to six, a Sunday in January.

'How long have we got?'

'Hard to say from this. The officer was killed in the middle of the night, her body dumped in a river. She wasn't found for a couple of days, so at first she was missing, fate unknown for a lot longer than she was actually still alive.'

She read on quickly, Buchan accelerated, even though there wasn't much scope for it. The hand tightening around his stomach was brutal, bile lingered at the back of his throat.

'Shit,' said Kane again. This time Buchan waited, unsure what was worse than the news that Roth was liable to be killed this evening. 'She really was brutally sexually abused.'

Nothing from Buchan. There wasn't an expletive vile

enough.

Down off the motorway, quickly around the back streets towards the office, Kane onto the phone.

'Danny, we need to find the original writer,' said Kane.

'Which one?' Danny couldn't stop himself saying, as Kane put the phone on speaker so that Buchan was included.

'The Canadian. Miriam Carr.'

'I thought she was in Canada?'

'She said she was when I spoke to her,' said Buchan, 'but she could've been anywhere.'

'The storyline Naismith used for his novel was based on a true-life crime in Canada.'

'Shit,' from Cherry, down the phone.

'Sure, Canada's enormous, Canada's the size of Europe, but that's way too much of a coincidence. Get on it, Danny, will you? We'll be back in two minutes.'

'Boss.'

They hung up. Buchan grimaced, taking a corner too quickly, stabbed the brake, forcing himself to slow as they approached the entrance to the Serious Crime Unit car park.

*

Standing at the window of the open-plan, his familiar position. The anger and the urgency had not dissipated, but now they were impotent. There was nothing to be done with them, nowhere to go. He had delegated it all, the team was working hard, everyone was reading the facts of the case and the book, or on the phone to borders, checking credit cards, doing their best to identify Miriam Carr's movements.

They had quickly come to the fact that she was in the UK, and had been for the previous month, arriving not long before Christmas. She had travelled, that much they had so far, but they did not yet have her current whereabouts. If they learned she'd been in London for the past few weeks, it would do nothing for them, but Buchan was sure that wasn't going to happen. She was in Scotland, there was no doubt in his mind. That line, where she'd conflated England and the UK when talking about increased book sales, that had been playing to a stereotype, all part of the lie. Now they needed to find her as quickly as possible. That evening. In the next hour, before anything else happened to Roth. And who knew what horrors had already been

---

165

inflicted upon her.

Was it a stretch? Coincidences happened. But it wasn't just that these murders were following the path of a true Canadian crime, when there was a Canadian at the heart of the drama. She'd been lying about her whereabouts. When lies met coincidence it couldn't be ignored.

'Funny,' he said, even though there was no one close enough to pay any attention, 'we started off thinking this was about music and musicians, and it turns out, again, to be about writers.'

Words at a mumble, while he replayed over and over his conversation with her, reconstructing her surroundings. There'd been the Starbucks mug on the table, but that didn't mean anything, didn't mean she'd actually been in a Starbucks. Since her whole thing had been about deception, that had likely just been another part of it.

There was a tap on the desk from just down the office – the place buzzing with life, phone calls and conversation and agitation – as Houston hit on something, and he caught Buchan's eye as he looked round.

'Getting there, sir,' he said. 'Carr's Canadian debit card was used at a cash point on West Nile Street three days ago.'

'Dammit,' said Buchan.

With the confirmation that she was in town, Buchan had the familiar feeling of self-doubt, the thought that he really ought to have realised she wasn't where she'd claimed when they'd spoken online.

'How are we getting on with the phone network?' asked Buchan, looking over at Kane.

'On hold. We've got people higher up making other calls. I'm optimistic. I think it's a matter of if, not when.'

Buchan waited to see if there was anything else, but Kane was done. He nodded, he turned away, stood with his hands on his hips staring out at the river. Wasn't this where the moments of genius were supposed to happen?

Jesus. Once, maybe, fifteen years earlier. Now, moments of genius were far outweighed by moments of competence, and that was really all he could hope for.

He returned to his desk, brought up the file they'd been putting together on Miriam Carr, and began reading it again.

*

Fifty-seven minutes later, the urgency and frustration refusing to go anywhere, the breakthrough came, not with a car chase or with the bursting down of a door, but after a series of phone calls, pressure brought to bear, quiet words spoken between the right people on a Sunday evening.

'She's four blocks away, sir,' said Kane, hanging up the phone, piece of paper in hand, making a gesture to the room that it was time to mobilise. They'd been closing in as the minutes ticked by, and now they had her. 'The Watts apartment building on the corner of South and Govan. Seventh floor.'

'That's the penthouse, right?'

Kane nodded.

Buchan grabbed his car keys, already had it thought through, waiting for the tip. If Carr was playing this out with the mimicry she'd shown up to this point, Roth would still be alive. Impossible to know what had been done to her – the true crime murders, and their accompanying sexual assaults had been carried out by a man – but it wasn't as though Carr would've had much trouble mimicking those as well.

'Sam, you're with me. Ian, you and Danny take the Polo. Better have two cars, just in case.'

'Right,' said Houston.

'No blue lights, no sirens, no anything until we're at the front door. We take our time, we assemble on the landing, or whatever there's going to be there, then we take the door out and enter.'

'We should be armed,' said Houston.

Buchan was about to object, when Kane nodded.

'I've done the paperwork, boss. Malcolm's in the armoury, we're sorted to pick the weapons up on the way out.'

'Nope,' said Buchan, head shaking. 'Look at the murders so far, the murders in the story she's copycatting. This is a knife fight. We are not taking guns to a knife fight.'

'What if she's armed?' said Kane. 'What if she just hasn't used a gun, this time, because that's not required by the script? Doesn't mean she won't have one as back-up.'

'Boss,' said Houston, nodding.

Buchan knew they were right, but he'd got this far in his career without ever being armed on a raid, and he wasn't about to start. Guns were an escalation, whoever had them, and he intended that it was never going to be him. If it turned out to be a mistake, he would be out in front, the first to take a bullet, and hopefully the others would have the chance to take evasive action.

It sounded weak even as he thought it – it wasn't as though shooters only ever hit one person – but it was something he intended to live the rest of his career by.

'No guns,' he said. He didn't bother with the rest of the thought. *Bad things happen when there are guns. We're not America.*

Along the corridor, the lift summoned, now they stood and waited.

Tension settled upon them, with its accompanying silence.

31

Six minutes later, same grouping, same silence, the tension multiplied a hundred-fold.

Standing in the hallway on the seventh floor of the apartment block. The nicest looking foyer of a building Buchan had ever seen. Two comfortable sofas, rugs, lamps, Rosetti prints on the walls. It looked like the entrance hallway to one of the apartments, but there were two separate residences up here. This was a shared area. A window at one end, looking out over the river and the city. For all its fine finishing, Buchan couldn't imagine why anyone would actually sit out here.

Cherry had the enforcer for putting in the door. Houston looked nervous, Kane face set hard. Buchan had always found it difficult to read Kane, except that he knew to trust her.

'Does this feel right?' said Kane, her voice low.

They'd been standing for no more than twenty seconds, yet it already felt like hesitation.

'You want a seedy hovel out in the woods somewhere?' asked Buchan.

A moment, then Kane nodded. 'I think I do.'

'We're not knocking,' said Buchan. 'Everyone ready?'

He looked around at the others, receiving a universal nod in response.

'Danny,' he said.

Cherry stepped forward, set himself, and then firmly, and expertly applied the enforcer to the door by the lock. A loud crack, and then Houston moved, his anxiety leading to an intervention, and he put his foot to the door, it burst open, and he led the way in.

'Every room,' shouted Buchan, and immediately Kane and Cherry were opening doors.

Lights from one open door up head, and then that door was flung back, and Carr appeared, surprise and horror on her face, an ornament in her hand. She saw Buchan, she didn't immediately recognise him, she looked around the others, 'What the fuck?' gasped out into the night.

'Every room,' said Buchan, repeating his instruction, as the others hesitated. 'Now!'

And they were quickly searching the apartment, every door opened, ever light turned on. Soon enough, to a soundtrack of loud footfalls and doors being flung asunder, Buchan and Carr were alone in the hallway.

'Jesus,' said Carr, recognition finally arriving. 'The police? You're the police guy?'

Buchan was on edge, waiting for the shout, not put off by Carr's shock, not trusting anything.

'Put that down, please,' he said, indicating the glass vase in her hand.

'What the fuck are you doing?'

Cherry was first back, and he shook his head at Buchan, and then crossed between them and checked out a room that had already been gone through.

'What are you doing in Glasgow?' said Buchan.

Carr stared at him, at last her situation seeming to dawn on her. Her mouth dropped open, the vase was lowered to her side, she couldn't look away from Buchan.

'You're doing this because you found out I'm not in Vancouver?'

'You lied. Why are you here?'

Houston passed through with a head shake, and then found himself bumping into Cherry as he went to check the room he was emerging from. They split up and went in different directions. It was a big apartment, six doors off the central hallway.

'I'm here for my own damn business,' said Carr, 'and I lied to you for the fun of it.'

'What?' shouted Buchan, unable to control the anger.

Where had his certainty come from in the first place? A lie multiplied by a coincidence and he'd taken it as proof.

He shook his head, partly at his own anger, partly to dismiss the doubt. Just because Roth wasn't being kept in this apartment, didn't mean she wasn't being kept elsewhere.

'What does that mean?' Buchan snapped, the hot-headed anger dispatched, replaced by cold fury. 'This is a triple murder. There are two people missing, including one of my officers, and you lied *for the fun of it?*'

He'd taken another step towards her. Any flippancy she'd had in her words vanished, she looked around the hallway at the assembled officers, who'd returned with head shakes and grim expressions.

'Nothing,' said Kane.

'Why are you here?' asked Buchan again.

'If you think I'm holding these people here…,' said Carr. 'I mean, is that what this is about? You think because I lied to you, that makes me a triple murderer? Oh my good God. Well, I guess you must be desperate.' She shook her head, looking at one or two of the others. No one spoke. They were all deferring to Buchan. None of them felt the weight of the mistake, the guilt at making an unwarranted intrusion into someone's apartment. 'I do not want to tell you why I'm here, Inspector, because it really is none of your business, and I will stick by that for as long as I can. This is not, I don't think, a police state. As for lying to you, well, yes, that was unthinking. I apologise. I was playing a game, as these murders… they mean nothing to me. They're happening to people I don't know in a country I don't live in. That makes me heartless, perhaps, but it does not make me a killer.'

Buchan shared a look with Kane, anger and disappointment, and then he walked through to the main sitting area, open-plan to the kitchen.

The television was playing – a black and white movie he didn't recognise – the lights were low, the curtains open to the view across the river. Floor to ceiling windows, an apartment that Buchan would have loved.

He walked to the window, hands in his pockets, and stared out across the view.

In the reflection in the window, he saw them all follow him into the room behind. Kane and Houston and Cherry, all waiting for what was next. In front of them, Miriam Carr, the ornament still in her hand.

*

'But this has nothing to do with *Beware The Watcher*, though, right?' said Carr. 'There's literally nothing linking those murders and anything I've done, other than, wait for it, the Saskatchewan murders were in Canada, and, oh, big-ass coincidence, I'm from Canada. You know that Canada's, wait for it *again*, absolutely *fucking gigantic*, right?'

They'd brought her into the station anyway. They had nothing else, and the hours were running down. Roth's life on the line. Buchan couldn't think straight. Cursing the tension of it, wishing he could compartmentalise. He felt he was choking the investigation as badly as a golfer with a two-shot lead hitting his tee-shot out of bounds on the eighteenth.

'You're far more likely to have known about those murders than anyone else in the UK,' said Buchan, and the words and their tone felt stupid as soon as they were out of his mouth.

'Sure, because there's no one else who's ever been to Canada, or read the Canadian news, currently in the UK.'

'No one else that we've spoken to in the course of this investigation,' said Buchan sharply.

'You're clutching, Inspector,' she said.

Carr glanced at Kane, who had been sitting silently beside Buchan for the last twenty minutes.

'You can see it, right?' said Carr to Kane. 'You guys know you've got nothing. Fact is, I didn't know about those murders in Regina. Must've missed it. Big deal. You mentioned some book that used that true narrative as a plotline, well there you are. If the guy who wrote that is Scottish, far more likely your killer here took the idea from the book, than the true crime in Regina.'

She had been addressing Kane throughout, Kane responding with a cold look across the table. She had nothing, really, other than agreement, and she wasn't going to undermine Buchan while they sat there. She felt it, though, sharing in his feeling of hopelessness.

'You still haven't told us why you're here, and why you lied to me,' said Buchan. 'Until we get an answer to that, we're sitting here. We may not have a direct link between you and these murders, as you pointed out, but we already know you're lying, and we're going to stay here until we get the truth.'

Carr kind of smiled, and then couldn't stop the gentle eye roll.

'I guess there ain't no mystery anymore, is there?'

'It's a triple murder investigation!' shouted Buchan, then took a deep breath, cursed himself, cursed the fact that he was losing control.

'I'm screwing Bennie,' said Carr, suddenly blurting out the

172

words. 'There? Happy? Me and Bennie. It's no big deal, it's not like either of us is married or anything, but you know, sometimes a girl likes a bit of privacy.'

'Jesus,' said Kane, unable to stop herself.

'What?'

'That's it? You're having sex and you didn't want anyone to know about it?'

'There we go.'

'Are you fifteen? I mean...'

'Don't give me any shit,' said Carr. 'I do not want your shit. That whole production, everything about it, has been a complete *shitshow*. I kind of felt sorry for Bennie all along, mainly because of the amount of money the poor bastard ended up giving me. I guess I wanted to give him something back.' She paused, the flippancy was returning to her voice. 'It kind of felt a bit like guilt-whoring myself, so you know, I didn't want to talk about it.'

'Sex?' said Buchan. 'That's all you've got?'

'Oldest reason in the book.'

She smiled.

'Oldest lie in the book, as well,' said Kane.

'An easy enough one to check up on though, isn't it?'

She glanced to her right at the two-way mirror.

'Go ahead,' she said. 'Give Bennie a call. He won't mind. He was keeping it secret just 'cause I asked him to. He won't mind telling people about me. That girl he's got staying with him is just for show, anyways. She won't care.'

'When was the last time you slept with him?'

'Yesterday morning.'

She smiled.

'You were there when I arrived?' said Buchan.

'I was. Sorry about that, thought I'd keep out of sight. You're right, triple murder investigation, and all that. Should've shown my face.'

'And the woman at the pool?'

'Russian. She's all show. I guess her previous overlord fell out of a window, and she looked around for some other poor fool with money to attach herself to. Bennie could have sex with the breakfast fruit and she wouldn't give a shit. And he just likes looking at her. However, just like his money, it won't last.'

Buchan turned to the mirror and nodded. *Make the call.* Then he looked back at Carr. Carr recognised that he had given up. Kane, sitting next to Buchan, felt it in the energy in the room.

This part of the investigation, the hope they had invested in finding Miriam Carr, was over. However, Roth was still out there, and there wasn't much time left.

Kane, unexpectedly, brought her hand swiftly down on the top of the table.

'Boss,' she said, 'come on, we've got work to do.'

She rose quickly, she didn't look at Carr, she walked to the door. Buchan got to his feet, pushing his chair back, staring at the writer the whole time.

32

Thirty-three minutes after midnight. A hush over the open-plan. Only three of them left, the numbers dropping one by one. Buchan knew he had to go home to let the others go home. No one wanted to, but they were getting nowhere. They'd left Miriam Carr in a cell for the night, leaving the problem of her and her lawyer to the morning. What was the reasoning though? Little more than chance, little more than clutching at the most random hope. That despite her explanations, despite Collins backing up her story, despite the obviousness of it all, the complete lack of evidence or even gut instinct on the part of the police that she might be guilty, they had the hope, if hope it was, that she was holding Roth and Zelinger somewhere, anywhere, and that her being in custody would be a stay of execution until they'd managed to unearth some other piece of impossible evidence.

They'd all been working for over fifteen hours. Every so often for the previous two hours Buchan had exhorted his staff to go home and get some sleep. Come back in, refreshed, at seven the next morning. In ones and twos they'd finally left. Now, there was just Buchan and Kane and Houston. Cherry had been agitated, had not wanted to go. Had admitted to Buchan, with more personal detail than Buchan cared to hear, that his girlfriend was jealous of his friendship with Roth, and that he was starting to get a hard time working so late, when Roth's life was on the line. Buchan had stopped himself telling Cherry he needed to get a new girlfriend. None of his business.

Somewhere, in the dark, negative compartment that plagues everyone's head, Buchan acknowledged to himself that he had not realised Cherry and Roth were particularly friendly, and that the thought of it, that Cherry was far more suited to be Roth's friend than he ever would be, made him a little jealous. The thought came and it went, easily dismissed, perhaps because it had so many other negative thoughts with which to compete.

He wanted Kane and Houston to leave, he wanted to sit here himself. To pace up and down, to stand at the window, to go through the panoply of annoyance and frustration without the judgement of others, but they were never leaving while he was still here. The three of them, bound in desperation and responsibility, staring at computers, reading details, checking up on people, reading stories both fact and fiction.

They tried to get in touch with Canada, but had been unable to speak to the right person. Late Sunday afternoon in Saskatchewan now, it would likely be the following afternoon Glasgow time before he got to speak to anyone.

'We need to go home,' he said suddenly to the room. He knew the words themselves would have no effect, so he ostentatiously turned off his computer, then pushed the seat back and got to his feet. No dramatic stretch, no further show for the crowd. 'Come on. Close it up, go home and get a few hours, back in here for seven. I doubt anyone's doing anything useful by now.'

He'd been expecting objections from the two of them, but they were as deflated as he was, and all he received in response were a couple of nods, reluctant last looks at their computer screens, and then the screens were shut down.

'Fuck it,' said Kane, with the last stab at the keyboard. Then she shook her head, and made a small gesture, as though she had to apologise for the profanity.

Houston got up, hands in pockets, and walked to the window. Buchan's usual spot. Below, the city at night, Clyde Street quiet, no one abroad, the river calm and silent.

Buchan and Kane unavoidably found themselves drawn to the same spot, and the three of them stood in a line, looking out on the night, all of them weighed down.

Perhaps they each had the words in their mouths, the regret, the sense of failure, the feeling of having let Roth down, but none of those words made their way into the world. A minute passed, depression and guilt sat heavily upon them, and then they turned away from the window and walked together to the lift.

*

Buchan had not missed the Winter Moon this evening. He didn't want to sit in front of Janey. He wasn't sure he even wanted to see Janey. The case was dominating his thoughts, completely consuming him, so that his night with Janey, only three days ago, now seemed from another lifetime. There were always cases which occupied him, but rarely was Janey pushed so far into the distance. Now, Roth was taking over. He didn't like it, but he thought it would be cured by finding her alive. That was all. No big deal. Just solve the crime in the next couple of hours, and everything would be all right.

He had a MacBook at home which he rarely looked at. It was just something he had. Nine years old now. Now, however, he sat on it, reading through the details of the murders in Saskatchewan, just as he had been doing most of the evening, since walking out on Miriam Carr.

This was where it had begun. Those murders were the root of this drama – if not the drama that the TV show had been about – and the root of something was always a good place to start looking. If the answer was to be found there, it might explain why they hadn't been getting anywhere in the first few days of the investigation. They hadn't known where to look.

There was much to study. There had been a lot of murder, there had been the two disappearances, where both victims had ended up dead, and then there had been another murder and an attempted murder before the perpetrator had been caught. There were a lot of names, a lot of different families involved, the killer had thrown a wide net around the community.

In this, at least, it differed from this series of murders they were investigating. While these crimes were focussed around the TV show, a very specific thing, the original murders had been entirely random, the killer picking off victims whenever he had the chance.

It had, of course, been a huge story locally, even if it had never had the kind of international news appeal of a mass shooting or hostage situation. There were myriad articles stretching back to the first murder, which had taken place more than two months before the killer was apprehended. There were numerous true crime podcast episodes to listen to, there were news reports and features. Another world of crime, much like their own, and he felt for the much-maligned officers as he read the unfolding story. They had not, as far as he could see, particularly put a foot wrong. The answer had just not been there for them to discover. Nevertheless, they took the blame for every subsequent death after the first.

Ultimately, the killer's discovery had been entirely down to chance, so nothing there to really let the police off the hook, or to give Buchan a steer.

It was two-seventeen in the morning. Buchan wouldn't be sleeping this night. Sitting at the kitchen table, the MacBook open. To his right, the second glass of gin. He wanted to drink the entire bottle, but somewhere in the dark recesses of his head, in amongst the depression and the self-loathing and the feelings of inadequacy and ineptitude, there was still hope. Something would present itself. Something would leap out, and suddenly, in the middle of the night, he would know where to go and what to do. And he wouldn't be able to do that on the back of half a bottle of gin. Heavy drinking, the wallowing self-hate of it, would be for when this was all over, regardless of the outcome.

The music was playing. *Corran's Theme*, the two versions on rotation. He needed it. It set the scene, it played to his guilt. He deserved to be haunted by it.

For the last hour, Edelman had been sitting in one of the other seats at the table. Back straight, staring at Buchan. It was as though he knew he was needed. Buchan was alone and in despair, Buchan needed someone to talk to. This was why Edelman was here. This was why Edelman had turned up in Buchan's apartment in the first place. For moments such as this. Not being able to reply didn't matter. What Buchan needed was someone to bounce things off, and whatever came from that would come from within himself in any case. That was what usually happened, regardless of whether he was talking to a human, a cat, or just someone who wasn't actually in the room at the time.

A moment's silence as the track ended, and then, for the twenty-ninth time since he'd sat down, it started up again.

'Why would someone, anyone, from back then, want to take their revenge on a TV show *now*?' he said. 'And this TV show, which is completely unrelated to those murders. But if not that, then someone completely unrelated to those murders back then in Canada, is using that m.o. to commit murder now.' He looked up at Edelman, who stared back with the practiced silence of the would-be sage. *He who knows does not speak, he who speaks does not know*. 'Which seems more likely?'

He'd already made up his mind on that question, which was why he'd spent so long looking through the background, just as

Kane and Cherry had been doing. There had been no bolt of lightning.

Beside him on the table there was an A4 notebook. Notes scribbled over seventeen pages, three of those pages attempts to condense everything of use into a single page. Currently looking at the list of everyone they'd spoken to, cross-referenced with the ones Roth had spoken to, as they were clinging to the notion the killer was someone with whom she'd had contact.

On the MacBook he was making a file of all the photographs from the original Canadian case. Anyone involved, anyone who'd spoken about it or written about it, from any of the affected families.

The studio engineer, Daryll Henderson, the fat American, stood out to him. Buchan had already run the background, had got as much of the man's life history as he could find on the Internet. He had a Wikipedia page, which mostly related to his career, and the more famous artists he'd worked with. Born in upstate New York. Saratoga Springs. Not so far from Canada, but still a long way from Saskatchewan, and with nothing to suggest that he'd ever lived there or had ever even visited.

Miriam Carr aside, he was the only one with a north American accent. That was it. Perhaps he was worth speaking to again the following day, but Buchan could hardly turn up at his house at three a.m. The memory of the busted bust on Miriam Carr still burned. The stupidity of the drama, the breaking down of the door, the tension and hope he'd allowed to build.

He trawled through the families of the Canadian victims. They were the ones who'd want to take revenge. The families. The ones who didn't think they'd got justice. The ones who'd thought the police should have done more, who believed their loved one should never have been allowed to fall into the killer's crosshairs.

'But why here and now? Why take it out on this show?'

He looked at Edelman, mind working, as clear and focussed as if it was ten a.m. after a decent night's sleep, and received the familiar silent, wise counsel in return.

'Who wants revenge on a TV show, furball?' said Buchan, and he lifted the glass and took another small sip. He let the liquid sit in his mouth for a few seconds, swallowed. The thrill of it was gone for the evening. He'd been drinking too slowly for too long, and now it was just a mechanical aide, something to do with his hands while his brain worked.

'Well, that makes sense,' he said. 'Let's say you've been involved in a true crime case. A horror crime. You lost someone you care about to such a crime. What then do you think of this... this fetish people have for fake crime? For fiction? I suppose...' and his mind wandered and his thoughts gathered and he looked away from Edelman, his gaze drifting to the window, to the lights of the tower across the river. 'I don't understand the true crime addicts, but at least there's some honesty in it. There's truth. It's in the title. But imagine you've been a victim, or someone you care about has been a victim.' *Don't think about Agnes, not in that way.* 'Then you put on your TV, and there's a show. A show, with people acting, and maybe there's a comedy sidekick, or maybe there's just some shittily written piece of drama, or maybe it's all perfect, beautifully written, perfectly performed, and that might be even worse. Your husband or your wife or your father or child or whoever has been brutally murdered, and here are people making entertainment from it.'

He looked at Edelman. 'So, what do you do then? You infiltrate a production and take your revenge?'

He looked at the cat, and then back at the list of names. And so what if he was right? So what if he'd just nailed the motive? It didn't narrow it down *at all*.

'Stop it,' he said to the room. To himself. No one anywhere on earth did their best work, head down in a funk.

He dragged another photograph into the file, took another drink, ran the large file back to the top. He had at least seventy photographs now, long past the stage where he was still studying them in as much detail as he ought to have been doing.

He was looking for the fat guy. The fat guy was the kind of man who could easily have looked different five or six years previously. If he'd been clean shaven, wearing glasses, twenty kilos lighter, he could be anyone, particularly if it was in a group photo. A guy at the back, a random member of a random family.

And that applied to more than just the fat guy.

He went back to the first picture on the list. The first victim. A twenty-two-year-old woman, found hanging. A couple of days later, a woman in her thirties, related to the first victim neither by family nor circumstance, stabbed in the face, her body pulled along a floor, knives buried in her chest. At the same time, her husband had vanished. The husband had become a suspect. And then another woman, another victim, a knife dragged through her guts. By then a policewoman had gone missing, and was found several days later, her body dumped in a river, sexually abused, strangled. Another few weeks, and the body of the second victim's husband, who'd still been considered the likely perpetrator, was found dead in the remote woods. The body had been there all along, and only then did the police realise that the killer had never intended for the man to be a red herring. Another victim a month later – a man, severed neck, head almost decapitated, left hanging by little more than skin – then another week, and finally the killer had bitten off more than he could chew. Either that or he'd been careless, the police couldn't decide which. Regardless, he'd picked another victim, then came off worse in the fight, ending up in the hands of the police.

The killer was currently four and a half years into spending the rest of his life in prison.

'I know what you're thinking,' he said to Edelman. He took another drink, forcing himself to look at the photographs more slowly, a forensic study of each face. 'You're thinking this is speculative, right? Clutching at straws.' On to the next picture. 'If we knew for sure there was a direct connection between those murders and our murders, then sure, this makes sense. But why should there be? Our killer could have read about them, or listened to one of these podcasts. He could've read *Devil In The Shadows* by that idiot.'

He looked over another photograph, the first victim and her family – mum, dad, aunt, three brothers, a younger sister – and then glanced back at Edelman. 'But you'd be wrong. This is how it's done. Yes, sometimes we know where to look. We can go right to the thing. But more often than not we end up doing this. The speculative search. If you do one of them, then you really are clutching. But we don't. We do fifty. We do a hundred. We do…'

He looked back at the photograph. He grimaced. The curse came to his lips, it stalled, finally he said, 'Dammit,' then he lifted the glass and finished off the drink.

He closed his eyes, tried to picture the woman he'd spoken to however many days ago it had been. He'd lost count. And, it hadn't just been him who'd spoken to her, it had also been Roth.

He opened his eyes, looked again at the list of people Roth had been in contact with. She wasn't there. Because this woman had had nothing to do with the TV production, he hadn't given her any thought. She was a random player, an accidental bit-part, stumbling into the narrative. Up until now she'd meant nothing.

He looked back at the picture. The younger sister. Maybe she still meant nothing. The girl in this picture would have been twenty maybe, so now twenty-five. Was it the same person?

He shook his head as he looked. It was impossible to tell. The hair was completely different, her face in the picture much heavier.

What was her name again? He opened his phone, flicked back through the notes he'd made, brought the girl's name up. Looked online, found her on Facebook, brought up a couple of photographs – short hair, thin face – then started to compare the two pictures.

'Dammit,' he said again. 'What d'you think, furball?'

Edelman neither answered nor bothered moving round to look at the photographs. Buchan leant forward, elbows on the table, hands clasped, lips pressed against his fingers. He scrolled down the woman's Facebook page, and in amongst the useless garbage of the times, something, another killer clue, suddenly leapt out at him. Right there, staring him in the face.

She was a chess player. That was all.

'Here we go,' he said.

He clicked on the reference she'd made to playing in a tournament, but that was never going to add anything to it. Giving himself time to think.

'Do we turn up at her place tonight, or do we…,' and he let the sentence go. He glanced at Edelman. The chess seemed like another perfect piece of evidence, but then it was once more circumstantial.

There was more to do. He could run the facial recognition software, and he could run a check on where she lived, and who exactly she was. But not from his kitchen table.

He looked at the time. Two-forty-seven. Already knew what his decision was. There never had been going to be any sleep tonight.

He sent himself a couple of Internet links, then closed the laptop, slipped the phone into his pocket, turned off the music, stared grudgingly at the Bluetooth speaker as though it had been its fault it had been playing *Corran's Theme* this entire time, and then he walked quickly to the hallway, grabbed his coat, and was off out the door.

33

Less than an hour later. The dead of night. Buchan sitting in the outside lane of the M74 at one hundred and fifteen miles per hour, heading to the coast. Blue light spinning through the night, no need for the siren. A few other cars around, but the road not busy.

He had not called this in to the local police, he had not called any of his team and brought them back to work. He had been so convinced that Miriam Carr was the one they were looking for, so confident in bursting through her front door, and yet, not for the first time in his career, he'd been left feeling stupid and inadequate. None of the team would have blamed him, none of them would have been thinking the boss had blundered. They would have shared his shame.

It didn't matter. Here he was again, possibly about to make another massive error, and this one in the middle of the night. This was on him, and he had no plan. He could hardly knock on the woman's door and ask to come in. Easy enough for her to affect curiosity or anger or any of the multitude of reactions that anyone might have at four a.m., and then not let him in, or have him standing in the kitchen while she looked exasperated. Was he going to casually ask if he could search every room in her house?

He'd returned to the office. Had wondered as he entered the building if the others would have come back, just as he was doing, having only reluctantly departed in the first instance on his instruction.

'Any of my lot here?' he'd asked Sgt Atholl on the night desk.

'Not tonight, sir,' he'd said, and Buchan hadn't stopped to ask exactly what he'd meant by that. He'd speak to him about it later.

He'd got into the office, hadn't done any of his usual

morning procedures. No look out of the window, no coffee, no staring at the whiteboards in the ops room. Straight on to the computer to check up on Mary Kaepernick, the younger sister of the first victim of the Canadian killer.

What had become of her after the murders?

It hadn't taken long to establish she'd come to Scotland, and it hadn't taken long to trace her movements, and to see how she would have come to know about the TV production, *Beware The Watcher*. Why she'd chosen to then take this kind of revenge on it, if indeed it would turn out to be her, he could only guess, but it potentially would tie in with his earlier speculation, directed to no one bar Edelman the cat.

Off the motorway, and down the dark roads of Ayrshire, past Howwood and Lochwinnoch, quickly through Kilbirnie, then heading along the long, straight roads towards Largs. Blue light long since gone, now speeding through the night, the car lifting occasionally on the bumps of the back roads.

Down the hill towards the coast, the firth of Clyde, Cumbrae in the middle, bathed in an unexpected moonlight, then he was driving through Largs, and heading back out on the coastal road towards Wemyss Bay, the beating of his heart picking up the closer he got to his destination.

Despite his doubts, he wasn't going to hesitate when he got there. He needed to see the lay of the land first before making a decision, but once he'd arrived, there'd be no point in coming all this way and prevaricating.

Soon enough, back out of town, away from the coast, driving on narrow country roads. A passing place a hundred yards short of the house, and he pulled into it, dimmed the lights, and turned off the engine.

In the darkness he could see the top of the house over the bare branches of hedgerows. He got out of the car and started walking quickly along the lane. Beginning to feel the nerves now. This felt instinctively much more like it, much more plausible than Carr's ridiculously expensive penthouse apartment overlooking the river.

An old cottage, standing alone, a mile out of town. He hadn't passed another house since he'd hit this road.

He arrived at an open driveway, the house set back twenty yards. Before it, a front garden of lawn and scrawny rose bushes that suffered in the cold darkness.

Buchan stood by the gatepost, studying the house. Just a

house, a bungalow, nothing exciting or notable about it. Front door, a window on either side. On this end, another door, the wall stretching behind. A small window on the same side near the back.

Carefully placing his feet, he began to walk round the house. Shallow breaths, tension across his shoulders, down his back, wrapping him up inside.

'Get a grip, Buchan,' he muttered.

Round the back of the house. No door here, but two large windows. Curtains drawn on both. To the far side. Another side door, another window, this one with no curtain drawn. Buchan eyed it warily before stepping across, and then he was round the side of the house and back to the front.

Decision time, and there was no point in coming down here at any time of the day, never mind four a.m., to stand outside the door. Either he was walking into the home of a triple murderer, whose work was not yet done; or else he was about to break into the house of someone with no part whatsoever to play in this drama, someone who had run away from trauma in her own country.

He turned back the way he'd come, hesitated by the window with the curtains undrawn, then peered round the side into the room. Pitch darkness, nothing to be seen. He stood still, letting his eyes adjust to it. Slowly shapes came into view. A back bedroom, a single bed, a cabinet, something, a coat perhaps, draped across the bed.

He looked in the corners, though they remained in shadow, then he walked quickly back across the line of vision and came to the door.

In the darkness he took the small pick from his pocket and got to work on the Yale lock. If there was a bolt thrown inside, he would have two other doors to try. If they were all bolted, then he would return to the side bedroom, and would put in the window. A last resort.

The lock turned, and he slowly pushed the door open. A half-hearted protest from the hinge, the sound lost in the night, and then he was inside the house and closing the door quickly behind him.

Another pause, taking the temperature of the hallway and the house. Steadying his breathing, trying to still the rapid beating of his heart. Too early to use the flashlight on his phone.

Six doors off, three of them open, including the door to the bedroom on his right. He tried to align the doors with the windows he'd walked past. Should Mary Kaepernick be sleeping, which room was she likely to be in?

He took a couple of steps along the hall, careful footfalls once more, the floorboards silent, and then stood by each of the closed doors. Silence.

At the end of the short hallway, the door to the large kitchen/diner/sitting room, another to a small bathroom; at the far end, another closed door which he surmised would lead to a porch and the other side door. He did not bother trying to open it. He turned back. Two doors remained. One now on his right, at the rear of the house, one on the left, in between the side bedroom and the door to the large open-plan. That was the one he couldn't line up with a window. The other would be the main bedroom.

He mouthed an expletive, the word lost in the night. Deep breath. Back along the corridor, slowly opened the door on his left, aware now that he was opposite the bedroom door, his back turned on it.

A short flight of stairs leading down to a shallow basement. Darkness, but there didn't seem to be a door at the bottom.

He ran his fingers along the edge of the door, and found what he hadn't wanted to. The bolt high up. It hadn't been thrown, which perhaps meant he wasn't about to find down here what he thought he might, yet it would also mean he could be bolted in. He briefly considered disabling the bolt by some means, but he couldn't think how he would do that without shining a light and making noise. He was going to have to take his chances.

A glance over his shoulder, the door across the hallway remained closed. Careful steps on the wooden stairs, but this time, unavoidably more noise. A step, pause, listen for any movement, another step.

Five steps down, the basement began to open out into complete darkness. Impossible to see the depth of the room. Now walking into nothingness. Slow footfalls, and then a shallower step and he was on the floor. He took a moment. Reached out all around, touched a wall to his left. Cobwebs. A look over his shoulder, back up the steps. The vague outline of the doorway at the top. No figure etched in the shadows.·

A movement somewhere in the depths. A quiet sound, the drag of a foot. He turned quickly, stopped, strained to hear.

Nothing.

He took another step, lifted his foot. Stickiness. Becoming aware of the smell. *What in God's name is that?* Hairs standing on the back of his neck, fear gripping his stomach.

He took the phone from his pocket, the screen lit dully, then he clicked on the torch, the light aimed at his feet.

Dark, glutinous, sticky. Blood, not so fresh, but not yet dried in.

'Dammit,' he muttered. He was in the right place, that was all that mattered.

He lifted the light, following the trail of blood.

A body slumped against the wall. A corpse. Zelinger. Hands bound. Naked, throat slit, blood down over his chest. Hirsute, thought Buchan. Killed elsewhere, then dragged across the floor and dumped against the wall. Awful colour, dead a couple of days.

He swung the light to the left. Nothing. A low shelf, two tins of paint. Back past the corpse to the right.

An expletive loudly from his lips.

Roth, dumped in a similar position to Zelinger. Naked, hands and feet roughly tied, the thin rope from her hands bound around a pipe on the wall. Her body cold and bruised, scratched and cut. Blood had run.

'Agnes.'

Careful not to shine the light in her eyes. His cold fingers to her colder neck. Still alive, the merest pulse.

'Agnes!' he said, voice straining, lips close to her ear.

Her head moved a little, eyes flickered but didn't manage to open. A sound from her lips, indistinguishable.

He took his coat off, and threw it around her, and then opened his phone. No coverage down here.

'Dammit,' he muttered.

'Would you like the Wi-Fi code?'

Buchan spun quickly, heart leaping, back against the wall.

34

Even though he'd been waiting for it, the voice caught him off guard, and he staggered to the side, the curse on his lips, then he straightened up and shot the phone around the room.

A figure at the bottom of the stairs. Mary Kaepernick, who had briefly passed through their story as Chloe Harmon, Daniel Harptree's short-haired hairdresser. The obviousness of it, Buchan had thought, when he'd realised. She hadn't just happened to come to Harptree's house that afternoon. And that day she'd met Roth, only present because Buchan had asked her to join him on a whim, and yet Buchan had not thought to include Harmon on the list of those who Roth had interviewed as part of the investigation. Then having had nothing to do with the TV show, she'd been on the periphery. An outlier who he had allowed himself to forget about. And this was why he was now standing here beside his dying officer, in a basement, looking at a killer in the night.

The gun in her hand threw a shadow on the wall.

Silence.

There had been no guns up to this point. Buchan had been sure there would not be any. That was what he'd said to Houston. This wasn't a gunfight.

Maybe it was for show. Not loaded, or a replica.

'Yes,' he said eventually.

'Yes?'

'Yes, I'll take the Wi-Fi code. You're under arrest for the murders of Adam Zelinger, Daniel Harptree, Blake Philips and Louise Hathaway. Put down the gun, give me the code. I need to call an ambulance.'

'Ballsy, I suppose.'

Now she turned on a small flashlight in her other hand, and shone it towards him.

His face twisted. Now that it was here, the danger out in the open, all he had was contempt for this woman. And for himself, for having been so unsure as to come down here on his own.

'Put down the gun,' he said, and he started to walk towards her.

She fired a shot at his feet, the bullet skidding off the floor, embedding in the wall.

'Back off, boss,' she said. 'Another step, you get it in the kneecap, then your constable here dies. Then you die.'

'Isn't that what's going to happen anyway?'

Kaepernick smiled.

'I guess.'

'Give it up,' said Buchan. 'Let me get the constable to hospital.'

'So that the judge goes more easily on me?' she said, and she laughed.

'It's a start.'

'Just don't…'

'You're done, your game is up.'

'I'm the one with the gun, genius. You came alone. I have zero idea why you did that, but here you are, walking into the lion's den, all on your lonesome.'

She shrugged, then she looked at Buchan as though disappointed, head shaking.

'Now I have to decide what to do with you.'

'I don't meet your criteria,' he said. 'The lead officer investigating your sister's murder never got killed.'

'You worked it out then, genius. I guess you must've or you wouldn't be here.'

Another silence, both of them trying to work out what to do next. This wasn't a movie, and Buchan wasn't about to go leaping across the room, rolling in the dirt, avoiding the spray of bullets to take her down with a punch to the knee.

'How were you going to get Zelinger's body up the stairs?'

She glanced in Zelinger's direction, his legs caught by the edge of a beam of light.

'You're doing that thing where you distract me with conversation,' she said, as though disappointed in him.

'Sure,' he said. 'You need it too. You have no idea what you'll do with me if you have to kill me down here. You didn't mean to have a corpse in the basement, as you can't lift him up the stairs. The amount of blood on the floor suggests you've tried, and you ended up dragging him back there, and just

---

189

dumping him.' He paused, and she didn't contradict him. 'So, you don't want a second corpse. That one's already beginning to smell, and no one wants to sleep with three dead bodies in the basement. No one normal, that is. And you were normal up until this time last week.'

She blurted out a laugh.

'You'd know about normal, detective.'

'I know about everything,' said Buchan. Dead pan. No boast, no exaggeration, just a statement of how it was. Twenty-five years in the police was more than enough for the full panoply of human life.

'Well, you'd know there's no normal after your sister's been murdered. There's no forgetting it happened. There's no getting on with life, thinking anything will ever be the same. Thinking you'll ever trust anyone ever again. No matter how far you run.'

'Put the gun down. Killing me, killing Constable Roth, and whoever else you've got in your sights, it won't mean anything. Won't save anyone. Won't bring anyone back.' He paused, and then added, 'It won't bring Julia back.'

She grimaced at the mention of the name but cut off the rebuke.

'Enough,' she said, finally. 'And bully for you, you nailed it. I'm standing here hesitating because I won't be able to lift you up the stairs. So here's what we're going to do. You're going to lift this guy and put him in the back of my car. Then you're going to come back down here and do the same with your friend. And then all three of you will be upstairs, and … what?'

'I'm not doing it.'

'I have plenty of bullets,' she said. 'Don't do it, and I'll shoot the constable.'

'Isn't the point of me taking her upstairs, so that you can kill her and dump her in the car? Why would this threat make me do *anything* you ask?'

'Because that's who you are. You're a cop. You need to play for time. You need to stall and delay. You'll take anything that elongates the end game, while you frantically think things through, hoping to come up with a solution. So, to save everyone the drama, you play your part, and you never know what may come of it. But it starts with you, right now, taking the corpse up the stairs.'

Buchan didn't move.

'Shall we be boring and shall I count to five?'

'You won't shoot,' said Buchan.

'You say that, but at some point, if you do nothing, I have a decision to make. And if the decision is kill you, let her die, then go out tomorrow and find some other poor schmuck to come here to lift the bodies, someone who'll be pliable and might actually believe I'll let them go when it's done, then that's what I'll do. So... you have five seconds. Make your call. One... two...'

'I understand why you're here,' said Buchan. 'I get –'

'You have no idea why I'm here.'

'Your sister was murdered, your family splintered, you decided you'd leave home. Go far away to escape. You came to Scotland. You set up as a hairdresser. Perhaps you did more than that, if you were telling the truth, because you needed the money, but either way, you had a new life. Changed your name, and you even lost your accent. Maybe things were going well, but you just couldn't forget your sister. And reminders of that would be all around. Turn on the TV, there'd be a crime drama. A serial killer drama. Go into a bookshop, there's an entire section on crime fiction. All these people making up stories, profiting from the horror, which is only believable because occasionally it does happen in real life. And then along came Daniel's latest project. A serial killer drama. He told you all about it. He let you hear the music. In fact, he gave you his own copy of the piece of music. And Daniel was enthusiastic about it. Too enthusiastic. Talked a little too much, about the story and about the personalities. And these were people doing what you've come to hate. Making money out of fictionalising real-life horror. Fine for most people, not so fine for you who'd lost someone to that real life horror. Who knew what it was like to discover your sister's body hanging in the woods. Who still remembers the guilt of thinking you could have done more to save her. To stop her killing herself. And then the horror of being told she'd been murdered. And that was a horror that wouldn't let up. Weeks and months in the news, and always Julia's picture in the paper.'

Enough, he thought. She'll be turning the gun on herself.

She looked blankly at him. The gun had begun to dip. Too early to take for granted that this was over.

'Like a book,' she said.

All Buchan had left to say to her was to put the gun down,

191

but he was hoping she would do it without further persuasion.

'If you're such a mind-reading genius, why'd it take you so long to find me?'

He had a straightforward answer to that, and he would not shy away from it.

'I screwed up,' he said.

He lowered his eyes, he finally allowed himself to look away from her, turning the torch back on Roth. She hadn't moved, eyes still closed.

He turned back round to Kaepernick. She hadn't moved either, she hadn't taken the time of his distraction to run. A quick dash up the stairs, then throwing the bolt across the door, remained on the cards.

'I need to get an ambulance out here,' he said. 'You need to put down the gun, then I'm going upstairs, calling this in, then I'm coming back down here to untie Constable Roth, and make her as comfortable as I can until help arrives. And you're going to sit somewhere and do nothing.'

She stared silently across the wasteland of the bloody basement floor, then finally shook her head.

'No.'

'Mary, you don't need any more death on your hands.'

'Doesn't matter. The fact that you're here alone means only one thing. You worked it out, you couldn't wait, you didn't alert any of your colleagues. I kill you, I leave her, she'll die at some point anyway, and I disappear. I can get on a plane easily enough, leave the country, by the time anyone works it out, if they ever work it out, who knows where I'll be...? That's not closure and it's not redemption, and I don't for a second imagine I'm going to feel any better than I do now. But I'll have moved on, and... well, whatever's next, it won't be a prison in Scotland.'

Noise from somewhere. Out on the road, and then getting closer. Suddenly a rush of sound, distant car doors, pounding feet, people calling.

'Put the gun down,' said Buchan. 'No one will be armed, but you'll be overwhelmed, and if you start firing that thing you're going to hurt a lot of people before you're taken down. So, please, just lay it down.'

Kaepernick laughed, a peculiar sound he hadn't heard from her before.

'That was dumb,' she said.

'What?'

'I have the gun, and you're telling me they don't have guns?'

The shouting was inside the house now, footsteps overhead. Houston and Kane, another voice Buchan didn't pick up in the tumult.

Kaepernick backed up a little so she had a view of the door. The gun shifted away from Buchan, and was now held somewhere between the two, waiting to see where it would be needed first.

'You stay where you are,' she said to him, her eyes distracted.

'Put the gun down,' said Buchan, and he took a step towards her.

'Stay where you are!'

'Gun! Gun!' came the cry from the top of the stairs.

Kaepernick whirled to face the voice, gun raised. Shots fired from above, one, two, a third, and Kaepernick fell backwards, her gun flying off to the side.

Houston thumped down the stairs, appearing in Buchan's vision, handgun at the ready.

'Ian!' shouted Buchan. 'Stand down! Stand down!'

He turned immediately back to Roth, as the flashlight beams swirled around the basement.

'Ambulance!' shouted Buchan. 'Make the call! Make the call!'

The sound of Kaepernick's gun being kicked across the floor then lifted; cries of 'fuck's sake'; Kane shouting, 'We need an ambulance!'; 'She's dead,' and another, 'Aw, fuck it'; more footfalls on the stairs, sound all around; and Buchan knelt next to Roth, placing his hand in hers, the other lightly touching her face.

'We're here, Agnes,' he said softly. 'It's going to be OK,' and he was untying the ropes that bound her.

35

'Honestly, Inspector, what on earth were you thinking?'

Eight-seventeen a.m., Buchan in with Chief Inspector Liddell. He hadn't slept. He hadn't eaten anything. He'd got home at six-forty-nine. Cleaned his teeth, taken a shower, had sat at the kitchen table staring at nothing, drinking a glass of water and a cup of coffee.

The two most important things had been putting an end to the murders, and finding Roth before it was too late. They'd succeeded. The killer was dead, Roth was in hospital, alive, would not take long to make a full recovery. Physically at least.

However, on virtually every other measure he had failed. Zelinger was dead. The culprit had been shot by one of his own staff. God knows what mental and physical torture Roth had been put through. And on top of all that, the perpetrator was literally the first person Buchan had interviewed in the investigation. That she had seemed such a casual bystander was no excuse. Despite the end result, Buchan, in his own estimation, had failed in virtually every conceivable way. Beyond the first murder, every bad turn had been down to him.

'We looked ridiculous moving in on Miriam Carr so heavy-handedly,' he said. 'I didn't want to do that again. My suspicions about Kaepernick were, ultimately, founded on ground that was barely more solid than those about Carr. I couldn't wait, but I didn't want to drag the others in on it.'

'You have two very capable sergeants,' said Liddell. Her tone was terse. She really was pissed off at him, though it meant little to Buchan. She was unlikely to be as annoyed as he was at himself, and he'd have thought it completely undeserved if she was going to say anything in his favour.

After Buchan had left the building in the middle of the night, Sgt Atholl on the front desk had called Kane to alert her to the fact that her boss was on the move. She and Buchan had phone trackers set up on each other's devices. It wasn't something Kane had ever used before, or that she had ever given any thought to. But as soon as she'd taken the call, she'd remembered she had the ability to see where he was going.

She didn't understand it, she hadn't known who he was looking for, but she'd known her boss. She'd known he wasn't going home to sleep, she'd known there was no way it was a private matter. He'd worked something out, and because of the imminent danger to Roth he had been unwilling to wait. Typically he hadn't wanted to involve any of his staff. Everything in his actions was from a familiar playbook.

Houston, who lived close to the HQ, had stopped off to sign out a weapon. Kane had known Buchan would be unhappy about it, but did not try to stop him. Houston, at least, had brought his gun to a gunfight. Buchan could believe that Kaepernick would never have fired her weapon at an actual person, but that was attributing a little too much of an ethical code to someone who was randomly committing serial murder.

Buchan stared across the desk. He had no more justification. Liddell wanted to talk about it, but he had nothing to say. She knew what he'd been thinking, and more than likely he would make the same decision again. However, standing here in this office this morning, he wasn't sure he was ever likely to be in this position again.

Liddell was mad, but unlikely to ask for his resignation. Nevertheless, he thought it was due. He was just going to have to write it himself.

'Ultimately you could have got Agnes killed,' said Liddell. 'Make these decisions for yourself if you like. I would not have liked it anymore, but nevertheless, we all make calls about ourselves. But this was a fellow officer whose life you put at risk, because… why? You didn't want to wake your sergeants up in the middle of the night? Newsflash, as I'm sure you already know, they weren't sleeping either. You didn't want to embarrass them with another pointless raid? If you actually thought it might be pointless, you shouldn't have been making it in the first place. You make the raid, you take back-up, I don't care what the time of day is. And they would have been completely behind you, just as they were when you raided Miriam Carr.'

She was not wrong, and Buchan had no argument. Perhaps an apology was warranted, but he wasn't going to make one, and neither would Liddell demand it. She was saying what had to be said, asking the necessary questions, but ultimately she expected in return what she was getting. Nothing.

She took the composed breath of the manager stepping away from her annoyance. They had barely broken the stare across the desk.

'You have work to do,' she said. 'And do not, under any circumstances, attempt to take the responsibility for Sgt Houston's use of a firearm.'

That was something Buchan had not yet considered. He would have done, at some point, however. And she was right. Again.

Liddell nodded in the direction of the door.

'Get to work. And you look terrible, so I don't want you working past five this evening. None of your team should. Go home, get some sleep. And when you've got this thing wrapped up, we need to talk about you taking a holiday.'

Buchan stood still for a moment. Suddenly aware that he didn't really want this meeting to come to an end. Now that it was over, it was back downstairs to the open-plan. The on-going work of the investigation. The paperwork. The explanations. Talking to Kane and Houston, writing reports. Speaking to Sara Albright and Benjamin Collins and Adrian Goddard, letting them know how this thing had played out.

It was all sorts of things that he didn't want to do, because at the heart of it all was the one inescapable truth. They'd interviewed the killer on day one, and then he'd given her no more consideration.

*

When he entered the room, Roth was lying in bed beneath dishevelled sheets, eyes open, staring at the ceiling. She registered his arrival without turning her head or making any sound.

Buchan hesitated just inside the door, and then approached the bed. Now she looked at him, though her face remained expressionless. She looked pale and thin and small. A reduced version of herself. Her cheek was bruised, her lips cut and bruised. There was a long scratch on her forehead. Her hair, flat and unwashed.

He hadn't known what he was going to say, but the first

word that came out was instinctive and obvious.

'Sorry.'

She stared blankly back.

A bright day, though the sun was still low to the east. Outside, the M8 and traffic and life continuing, as it does.

'Why?'

'I should have known. I was looking at everyone you'd spoken to in the course of the investigation, and completely forgot about her. Interviewing the killer on the first day, and then not thinking about her again while she commits three more murders... demands an apology to the person who was nearly the fifth victim.'

'We had no idea,' she said. Her voice sounded dull. Almost disinterested. They'd told Buchan she'd been sedated in the night, and that she would not yet have slept it off.

'It's my job to have the idea,' said Buchan.

A smile threatened her lips, but stopped somewhere along the way and then never appeared.

'Mine too,' she said.

Silence returned. He had plenty of questions for her, but had not come expecting to be able to ask them, and had decided as soon as he entered that he wasn't going to. What else, then, did he have to say?

He made a small gesture towards the white plastic chair on the other side of the bed.

'You mind if I sit awhile?'

A moment, and then she did kind of smile, accompanying it with a small shake of the head.

Buchan walked around the bed, pulled the chair a little closer to her, then sat down. He stared down the length of the bed, to the white wall opposite. He had nothing to say.

When he glanced at her, her eyes were closed.

*

They found Goddard and Albright at Lost World Studios, in the engineering room with the large engineer, Darryl Henderson, listening to another piece of music that was readily identifiable as being by Daniel Harptree. A variation on *Corran's Theme*. They were watching a scene from the show as the music played. Buchan and Kane paid the monitor no attention as they waited. For their part, neither Goddard nor the engineer made any effort to end the clip early because they had visitors.

The music faded, the scene segued neatly into another, finally Goddard pressed the pause button, the screen freezing on a still of a cold autumn morning in Glasgow. And now the three of them turned to the door.

'I read the news,' said Albright, unavoidably smiling at the detectives' arrival.

'Today, oh boy,' added the engineer, his smile even broader.

Albright looked a little curious, Goddard laughed. Buchan and Kane were not for laughing about anything.

'So, then, you know that Adam Zelinger is dead,' said Kane, her tone harsh.

'Well,' said Goddard, taking on the responsibility of defending the apparent good humour of the group, 'I don't think Adam's career was really going anywhere in any case. Stuck in the perennial loop of the AD. Once the bridesmaid and all that.'

'So, because he was never going to be a great director, *like you*,' said Buchan, 'it's OK that he's dead?'

'I didn't say that.'

'You've heard that we identified Mary Kaepernick, who'd been working as a hairdresser under the name Chloe Harmon, as the killer of Daniel Harptree and the others?' asked Buchan. Now that he was here and in this room, he just wanted to get on with it.

'Like I say,' said Albright, 'we read the news. I take it you'll be leaving us alone now?'

'That's all you're interested in?' said Kane.

'We have a show to deliver,' said Albright, 'so frankly, yes.'

'Did any of you have any contact with Chloe Harmon? Do you know if anyone else involved in the production had any contact with her?'

Albright and Goddard gave Buchan the same look. The engineer seemed to be finding the whole thing pretty funny, the smile never leaving his face. The engineer clearly did not care at all about the victims or, quite possibly, about the show. All studio engineers have stories to tell, and this would be another one to add to the list. The sound engineer and his part in the quadruple murder enquiry.

'Really?' said Goddard. 'Why on earth would anyone in the production have had anything to do with this woman? She was literally Daniel's private hairdresser, wasn't she?'

'Presumably you have hair and make-up on the show,' said Kane, when Buchan didn't immediately dive in.

'We have a production crew. Jesus, we're not some two-bit independent, scrabbling around, borrowing people and getting, like, complete randoms in off the street to do a job. We have hair and make-up, because of course we have hair and make-up. We have people. Daniel getting his hair cut is just a guy getting his hair cut. He wasn't part of the production, he was just a guy doing a job over here, on the sidelines.'

'Had Daniel ever mentioned Chloe Harmon to any of you?' asked Buchan, having had enough of Goddard's tone, the fake outrage, the deliberate gaslighting, marginally stopping short of saying, *how stupid a question is that?*

'I'm not sure why that would have happened,' said Albright, to the accompaniment of Goddard snorting, the engineer laughing.

'Sounds like Daniel was sleeping with his barber,' said Buchan. They only had her word for that, based on their initial interview with her a million light years ago. 'Maybe he mentioned that to someone. How are things, Daniel? Pretty good, Daniel might have said. Seeing my barber at the moment. Or, given the possibility that the barber was, in fact, prostituting herself, perhaps Daniel shared her details with others. Shared *her* with others.'

'What d'you call that guy,' said Albright, looking at the engineer, 'you know, the leader of the Fantastic Four? Captain Stretch or something like that. The Amazing Stretch Man?'

'Mister Fantastic,' said the engineer through a big belly laugh, 'but yeah, I know what you mean. Can stretch himself out real long.'

'Mister Fantastic,' said Albright, turning back to Buchan. 'There we are. That's who you are, Inspector. Mister Fantastic, stretching your narrative more than that guy would need to stretch his arms to paint over the ceiling of the Sistine Chapel.'

Another laugh from the engineer, while Goddard had started looking bored with the discussion.

'None of you seem terribly concerned there have been four murders,' said Kane. 'These were people you know. People you'd worked with.'

'I'd never met any of them,' chipped in the engineer, ''cept Daniel, and as we discussed, there ain't many people missing

Daniel. Maybe his wine supplier.'

Albright and Goddard stared at them, nothing to say, impossible to read.

Buchan suddenly felt as though they were still continuing an active investigation. Where was that coming from? They had their killer, caught in the act. While they had spared Roth the in-depth interview for now, she had at least confirmed there was no one else involved. She had been caught unawares by Kaepernick in her apartment, taken prisoner, held, abused. She hadn't wanted to talk about the abuse. But that was the story, no one else contributing as far as she knew.

And yet it felt as though there was something going on in the room. Someone was lying.

Buchan turned his gaze on Goddard, who was happy to return the stare.

'What?' he said, after a while, though it appeared to be out of curiosity rather than discomfort.

'You don't care that your assistant on this show was killed? Your cinematographer, your composer, your writer? That's a lot of close collaborators, your time with them must have added up to a lot of working hours.'

'If it helps, I'm autistic,' he said, his voice deadpan.

'Jesus,' muttered Kane.

Buchan held the look for a moment, then turned to Albright.

'And you? You're also autistic? Or some other condition?'

'I'm afraid young Bennie was right about me all along,' said Albright. 'I'm just a cunt.' She laughed, though not as loudly as the engineer. 'For me, it's all about the show. That's all that matters. We make the show, we deliver the show, people notice the show, and then my next show gets to be bigger and better, and the next after that bigger and better again. That's how this works.'

'Well, you're not wrong about one thing,' said Kane, drily, and again the engineer laughed.

*

Sitting in the Facel on the way back to the office. Silence for a long time, Kane as unhappy with the way the whole thing had worked out as Buchan. Perhaps there was added resentment at Buchan that he had gone off and done something on his own in the middle of the night, but it was not something she would ever voice.

'What d'you make of that?' asked Buchan after a while.

'Cannot believe them. *I'm autistic* for god's sake. And that woman…'

'And the damned fat guy and his laugh.'

His lips curled at the use of the word fat, though Kane wouldn't care.

'I wanted to throttle him,' said Kane, head shaking.

'And you know, there's something else that's just passed us by' said Buchan. 'The guitar. Remember the guitar? There was no sign of Daniel Harptree's guitar at Kaepernick's cottage. So what happened to that guitar? And that guy in there, the fat guy, well, he knew all about the guitar.'

'Does it matter though? I mean, we're not assuming, or even wondering really, about Kaepernick having an accomplice. If the engineer has the guitar, maybe he bought it off Daniel a few weeks ago. Or just borrowed it.'

'Presumably he'd have said.'

'Maybe Kaepernick just sold it somewhere, or knew someone else she could give it to. We have no idea who she knew, what kind of life she had. We're only just starting to piece that together, and so far, unsurprisingly, there's nothing to suggest she knew Darryl Henderson.'

Buchan drove on in silence, slowing behind a red Nissan Note, then coming to a halt at a red light.

'I've got a feeling about that guitar,' said Buchan.

She glanced at him, a small smile coming to her face. Buchan, of course, was in no mood for joking.

'You've got a feeling? Like you had a feeling about Miriam Carr and Chloe Harmon?'

'No. I was going off something with those two. This is entirely a feeling. And yet…'

'You want to check out Henderson's house, see if he has the guitar?'

The lights changed, the Nissan Note stalled. Buchan sat, one hand on the steering wheel, one hand on the gear lever, waiting.

'Let's make another home raid,' he said. 'Best two out of three.'

Kane laughed and, for the first time that day, Buchan allowed a smile to come to his face.

Epilogue

A week had gone by. Work had continued on wrapping up the case, just as somewhere, in sound studios and editing suites and meeting rooms, executives and creatives were working on wrapping up the final edit of *Beware The Watcher*, and selling *Beware The Watcher*, the latter job becoming so much easier given the publicity afforded it by the murder spree of Mary Kaepernick.

A Tuesday evening, Buchan standing at the window of his apartment. Seven minutes after eight, the rest of the evening stretching before him. He hadn't been to the Winter Moon in ten days. He didn't want to speak to anyone. He couldn't face Janey. The thought of her, the thought of how it would play out, the two of them together again at the bar, was too confusing.

He was happy to lie to himself and think it was because he didn't want to discuss the rotten end to the lousy case, one that had plagued him throughout, and which would now plague him for years to come. He didn't want Janey's concern, because he didn't deserve it. He didn't want to sit in front of her, even more sullen than before.

He felt like the Winter Moon had been lost, and he didn't understand why. But it hadn't gone anywhere, it wasn't going to have changed, so it wasn't about the Winter Moon.

Three more days and he was going on holiday. Forcing himself to get away. The first time he'd done anything other than work in more years than he could remember. Taking the Facel and heading south, aiming to drive through the Alps in winter. He'd stop for a while in Switzerland, though he had no idea what he was going to do when he got there.

He'd spoken to his neighbour, who had reluctantly agreed to feed Edelman. He suspected Edelman would have moved in with her by the time he got back.

They had won their best of three home raids. Having struck

out with Miriam Carr, and struck grim gold with Mary Kaepernick, they had what amounted to a pyrrhic victory at the home of the engineer. They'd found the guitar. The fat man had not been present when they'd arrived, although his girlfriend, a twenty-year-old named Cindy, had been strangely delighted to let them in. The guitar had been resting on a stand in an upstairs room, in amongst five others.

Henderson had not tried to deny it was Daniel Harptree's. More than anything, he'd seemed annoyed at having to explain himself. He said he'd won it off Harptree on a stupid bet that he hadn't wanted to talk about. The stupid bet turned out to involve being drunk and urinating high up a wall. Given that half million pound guitars had been at stake, it had been, right enough, unbelievably stupid.

That was all. It didn't matter whether they believed him or not, they had spent the week since investigating the idea that it wasn't true and that he'd in some way been in league with the killer, and had found zero evidence. There was barely a minute of any day when he did not have an alibi, and he even had photographic evidence of the guitar being in his house for several weeks.

That was all the guitar had been. A red herring, something to occupy Buchan's time when he'd already had more than enough to do.

And so the time had gone by, and he had been unable to shake the feeling of self-loathing and all-consuming depression. It seemed too often that he had messed up, too often people had died when he should have been able to find killers before they had been able to continue their work.

The glass of Monkey 47 was at his lips when there was a knock at the door, the sound quiet in the room, blending with the low music. *Night Train*, again. The extended version. *C Jam Blues*.

He passed Edelman sitting on the sofa as he walked to the door.

'If this is Mrs Sutherland, shall I just hand you over now, furball?' he said, and Edelman yawned in response.

He didn't look through the peephole, he opened the door.

Roth. A couple of marks still on her face, but more colour about her than the last time he'd seen her. Hair restored to its familiar pink lustre, nose ring in place, a short leather jacket and dark jeans, a bottle of white wine in her hand.

Despite the improvement in her well-being, she looked diminished.

'Agnes.'

He didn't automatically step back to usher her in.

'I wanted to say thank you.'

He didn't move.

'You could've done that at work.'

'The chief ordered me not to come in until Monday, and you'll be away by then.' A pause, and she smiled reluctantly. Neither of them really felt like smiling. 'You saved my life. I don't know if a ten-pound bottle of Viognier really covers the debt, but it was all I could think of.'

He hesitated. There was really only one thing he could do, presented with this situation. He had to ask her in. But he didn't want to.

A beat became two. The silence threatened to become awkward, but Roth, while perhaps not the same woman she'd been two weeks previously, was not one to stand an uncomfortable silence.

She held the bottle of wine forward.

'Decision time, boss,' she said. 'I can leave the wine and go. I'll see you when you get back.'

Buchan took the bottle, but at the same time, stepped back and opened the door fully.

'Come in,' he said.

Edelman watched Roth into the open-plan, his head raised, and then he decided she was worth speaking to, and jumped down off the sofa.

Buchan placed the wine on the kitchen counter, as Roth bent to scratch Edelman's ears.

'Hello, boy, what's your name then?' she said.

She glanced over her shoulder at Buchan who said, 'Edelman,' and she kind of smiled and said, 'After Julian?' and Buchan said, 'My wife named him.'

Two wine glasses from the cupboard, corkscrew from the drawer, he opened the wine and poured. Roth took off her jacket, so she was now just wearing a familiar Foo Fighters T-shirt. She looked thin.

Buchan held the glass towards her, she took it, they did not clink the glasses.

'I don't have any snacks,' said Buchan.

'That's OK, it's good to drink on its own. It says so on the bottle, anyway.'

They each took a drink, setting their glasses back down.

'What are we listening to?'

'Oscar Peterson.'

She leant her head to the side for a moment, then nodded.

'It's great.'

Another silence. They stood by the kitchen table. If they were to move it would be to stand by the window. Buchan wasn't about to suggest the sofa.

'How are you feeling?' he asked.

She took another drink. He saw the shadow cross her eyes.

The doctor had not shared with his team the precise details of what had been done to her, but Buchan knew, nevertheless. Mary Kaepernick was carrying out copycat crimes, and had been, up to that point, entirely meticulous. The original police victim had been horrifically treated while alive, sexually abused and debased. Kaepernick had mimicked the abuse the best she could, given the obvious natural deficiencies. In all likelihood, the replacement methods might well have been even more brutal than the original.

'I'm good,' she said eventually.

'You can give me a little more than that,' said Buchan.

A pause, and then she said, 'I'm not good.'

Another gap, and then, with a small head shake, she added, 'I don't want to talk about it. I'm OK. I'll get over it. Just not yet.' And then, quickly, 'Sarge said you handed in your resignation.'

'Did she?'

He looked unimpressed. Didn't like the staff talking about him, though it was inevitable. The people in charge got talked about in every organisation on earth.

Roth reached out, squeezed his hand, held her fingers there through his automatic flinch, and then withdrew her hand as he looked at her.

'Sir, please, relax. I'm not going to jump you. It will be a long, long time before I jump anyone. I just wanted to say thanks, that's all. We'll have a couple of glasses of wine, then I'll leave you to your evening.'

She held his gaze for a moment, and then looked around the apartment. No television, no sign that Buchan had actually been doing anything at all, there was just a cat, and a nearly empty glass of gin placed on a table by the window.

'Whatever that actually was,' she said with a smile, and Buchan finally couldn't help smiling with her.

'Thank you,' he said, and he lifted the glass, and took another drink, finally beginning to relax. *I'm not going to jump you...* 'And yes, I handed in my notice, but the chief wouldn't accept it. Told me to take two weeks off. Ordered me to leave the city, to go and do something. We'll talk when I get back.'

'You going anywhere nice?'

'Switzerland. I'll take the Facel for a drive.'

She looked wide-eyed, the most amount of life she'd shown since arriving. 'Wow, that sounds like a trip. The Alps in winter.'

'Should be good,' said Buchan mundanely.

'You'll have to put snow chains on.'

'I have a guy at a garage in Rutherglen. He's fitting winter tyres on the car tomorrow.'

'I love Switzerland.' She took a drink, smiling at herself. 'Not that I've ever been. I think I like the idea of Switzerland.' A pause, and then she couldn't help herself. 'You'll have room for a passenger.'

She said it with such an infectious smile, he couldn't stop himself laughing.

'I'm afraid they're going to need you at the office, given my absence. I'll send you a postcard.'

'What are you going to do there?'

'No idea. Same as I do here, I expect, but with mountains in the background rather than the Science Centre.'

'You'll need to get out and about, walking at least, if you don't ski.'

'I don't ski.'

She'd looked so distant since she'd arrived, like she'd been starting to fade away. Now she was showing some life.

I did that, thought Buchan. Or, at least, being in my presence allowed her to do that for herself. There was no need to hate himself for absolutely everything in life.

The music ended, a short hiatus, then *Easy Does It* started up, behind Peterson's light touch piano.

Silence had returned to them, but this one was easier, more relaxed. A comfortable silence of the kind with which Buchan was familiar.

They each took a drink. It hadn't taken long, but they were both glad she'd come.

BUCHAN

(DI Buchan Book 1)

A mystery written in blood.

The head of a literary publishing house is murdered, and Detective Inspector Buchan and his team enter a world of writers and editors, of passion, jealousy and hate. Suspects are not in short supply, but before the investigation can really get going, there's a second murder, this one throwing up the existence of an unknown manuscript.

Now clues and motives and suspects abound, and the hunt is on for *Ladybird*, a book that no one knows anything about. There's a game being played, and Buchan needs to find out what it is before anyone else dies. For that is the only certainty: sooner or later, as rain sweeps across the rundown city, and the players drift in and out of suspicion, the killer will strike again.

BUCHAN is the first title in a major new Scottish detective series, featuring DI Buchan and his team from Glasgow's Serious Crime Unit.

PAINTED IN BLOOD

(DI Buchan Book 2)

Where every murder is a masterpiece.

A double murder, a public spectacle, a killer toying with the police. And then, from nowhere, a mysterious woman with a story to tell, a suspect handed to **DI Buchan** on a plate.

It's been a bad few months for Buchan and his team, little going right. They need a win. What they don't need is a murder victim, the naked corpse of the young woman posed on a park bench, erotically summoning viewers to the scene of her death. Then a week later, a second victim.

Out of nowhere, a woman finds Buchan in the Winter Moon, claiming the posing of the corpses was based on two paintings by a little known Spanish artist. And she brings ill news; there's a third painting in the series, and she herself will be the victim.

It is so unexpected, and so alien to everything they've investigated so far, suddenly it seems Buchan is carrying out an entirely new line of inquiry. However, as he gets closer to the heart of darkness, it becomes evident the two strands of the investigation are linked, the threat is imminent, and that the re-enactment of the third painting is close to being realised…

A LONG DAY'S JOURNEY INTO DEATH

(DI Buchan Book 4)

A regular day at the Serious Crime Unit quickly spirals out of control, when DI Buchan and his team are asked to investigate the case of a missing film director.

The story of Claire Avercamp has been in the news, but her life has been a tale of a wasted career, failed relationships, drugs, alcohol and bad decisions. She's been missing for over a week, presumed drunk, comatose or dead, but she's burned so many bridges, no one seems particularly concerned.

However, an old colleague of the chief inspector is personally involved, and brings new information. Avercamp had been working on a film about the theft of antique manuscripts. Despite all the evidence to the contrary, he thinks her disappearance is not an act of self-sabotage.

At first reluctant to get involved, Buchan quickly realises this is a high stakes game, and there are more players than anyone realised. Money is at play, lives are on the line, and deadly intrigue lurks around every twist and turn of a day that will stretch deep into the darkness of night…

Printed in Great Britain
by Amazon

20424837R00124